KT-520-584

AD 02999341

PAST LOVE

Bart Sadler had always been the black sheep of the Dorset town of Wenham. Held responsible for the death of Laurence Yetman and the ruin of Sophi's reputation, there can be little joy now at his unexpected return. When he attempts to manoeuvre his way back into Wenham society, the people of the town unite in disapproval. All except Deborah, Sopie's daughter. Disgraced and an outcast like himself, Bart senses a kindred spirit - but can she trust his claim to be reformed, or will he be her downfall, just as he was for her mother?

PAST LOVE

by

Nicola Thorne
writing as
Rosemary Ellerbeck

Magna Large Print Books
Long Preston, North Yorkshire,
BD23 4ND. England.

British Library Cataloguing in Publication Data.

Thorne, Nicola *writing as* Ellerbeck, Rosemary
    Past love

    A catalogue record of this book is
    available from the British Library

    ISBN   0-7505-1461-2

First published in Great Britain by Severn House Publishers Ltd., 1998

Copyright © 1998 by Nicola Thorne

Cover illustration © Len Thurston by arrangement with P.W.A. International Ltd.

The moral right of the author has been asserted

Published in Large Print 2000 by arrangement with Severn House Publishers Ltd.

All rights reserved. No part of this publication may be reproduced, stored in a retrieval system, or transmitted in any form or by any means, electronic, mechanical, photocopying, recording or otherwise without the prior permission of the copyright owner.

All situations in this publication are fictitious and any resemblance to living persons is purely coincidental.

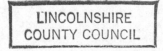

LINCOLNSHIRE
COUNTY COUNCIL

Magna Large Print is an imprint of Library Magna Books Ltd.

Printed and bound in Great Britain by
T.J. (International) Ltd., Cornwall, PL28 8RW

Family Tree of the Yetman Family 1800–1928

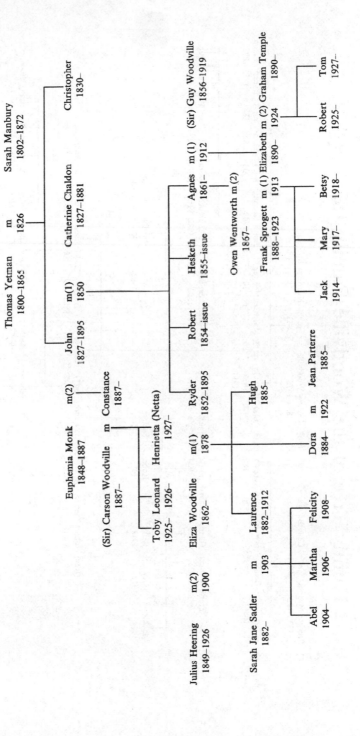

Family Tree of the Woodville Family 1820–1928

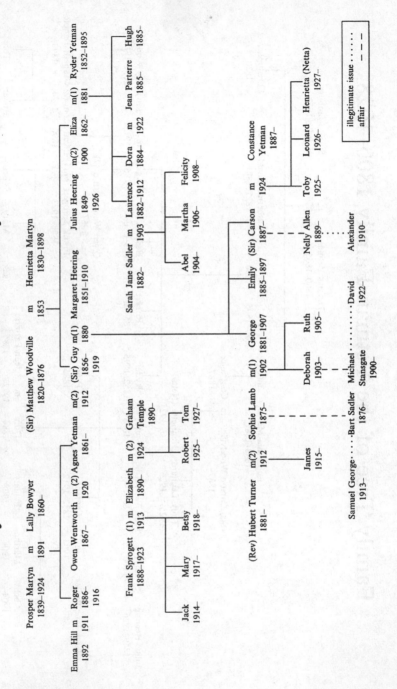

'The People of this Parish' series

The story so far:

In 1880 young Sir Guy Woodville brings his Dutch bride Margaret to his ancient Dorset family home, Pelham's Oak. With Margaret comes a much needed dowry to restore the fortunes of the impoverished but noble Woodville family. The marriage is one of convenience for Guy, if not for the rather plain bride who is very much in love with her handsome husband.

Guy has a rebellious and high-spirited younger sister, Eliza, who spurns her family's attempts to marry her well. She elopes with Ryder Yetman, the son of a local builder, thus causing great scandal in the sleepy market town of Wenham, over which the Woodvilles have presided for centuries as lords of the manor. Volume One, *The People of this Parish* (1880–1898), follows the fortunes of the Woodvilles and the Yetmans as they intermarry and breed, their joys and sorrows, triumphs and disasters.

Margaret and Guy have three children. Pious George falls in love with the rector's daughter, Sophie Lamb, and elopes with her

7

to Papua New Guinea, where he quickly dies of fever. The only daughter, Emily, dies young, and the heir is Carson, a charming rebel with an eye for the ladies or, preferably, the buxom country girls, who would rather be a farmer than a baronet with a large estate.

Eliza, meanwhile, has been ecstatically married to Ryder, who becomes a prosperous builder, and they too have three children. When Ryder is killed in an accident, Eliza marries Julius, the brother of Margaret, her sister-in-law. A cold, mean-minded man, he refuses to help his stepson Laurence when he is facing bankruptcy. This leads Laurence to commit suicide, leaving an embittered widow and a young family.

Volume Two, *The Rector's Daughter* (1907–1913), follows the fortunes of Sophie Woodville when she returns as a widow to her birthplace, accompanied by her two young children. She is not welcomed by George's parents, who feel she is responsible for his untimely death; her own parents, too, disapproved of the marriage. Sophie endures many vicissitudes before being happily married to her father's curate, even though when he proposes he knows she is pregnant with another man's child.

Also in this book, Carson, after his mother's death, is prevailed upon to propose to a wealthy but plain and withdrawn young girl, Connie, in order to save Pelham's Oak and the Woodvilles from financial ruin. But he does not love her and when his father remarries, to a supposedly rich woman, Agnes, Connie leaves Wenham to travel the world with her wealthy guardian. Volume Two ends on the eve of the First World War.

In This Quiet Earth (1919–1921), the third volume, takes up the story of war hero Carson who, having inherited the title from his late father, returns at the end of hostilities to find the Woodville estate once more in financial difficulties, due largely to the excesses of Agnes, his stepmother.

Soon after Carson's return the rejected Connie, transformed from a duckling into a swan, once more enters his life, now a very wealthy woman. Carson, who proves adept at running the family estates and has no need of her money, sets out to woo her back.

His stepmother continues to plague him, especially after her marriage to fortune hunter Owen Wentworth, who has assumed a spurious title and marries Agnes for her money only to find that she has none either. He makes off with what jewellery she possesses and she is left destitute, dependent on Carson and Connie, who rally to her support.

This book also concerns the fortunes of Agnes's daughter by Sir Guy, Elizabeth, who lives in penury with her war-wounded husband and three children, only to discover that she is a Woodville by birth. She is determined to exact revenge on the family who have disowned her, but kind-hearted Carson tries to make amends.

Prologue

May 1928

'I baptise thee Henrietta Euphemia in the name of the Father and of the Son and of the Holy Ghost.'

The Rector of Wenham held the baby in his arms tenderly as he pronounced the words of baptism, pouring the water over her head. Perhaps because she was conscious of her patrimony Henrietta was as good as gold and smiled round at everyone, a natural scene-stealer. She was already six months old so had some practice in capturing hearts.

Carson adored her; the longed-for girl. Now the family was complete. He looked lovingly across at his wife who returned his glance, as if she understood. Yes, thankfully, there would be no more. Connie had found childbearing irksome despite its rewards and, a late baby, they had nearly lost Henrietta and the mother as well, which was why the christening was so long delayed.

Henrietta's small brothers Toby and Leonard, their hands tightly clasping those of their nurse, looked on in some awe as the baby was carefully restored to the arms of her godmother, her aunt Elizabeth, Carson's half-sister.

The church, of course, was full. All the inhabitants of Wenham had pressed in for the occasion. It was Sunday, but even if it had been a weekday every shop in the town would have been shut, only the pubs would have stayed open for the hoped for influx of revellers. The Woodvilles and Wenham were synonymous. So many events concerning the family had been enacted here over the years, solemn as well as happy, that many of the people of the parish, some of whom were now very old, could still recall.

The marriage in 1880 of Carson's father and mother, Guy and Henrietta. The christenings of their three children, George, Emily and Carson. The marriage of his sister, Eliza Woodville, and Ryder Yetman whose elopement had scandalised the town. The marriage of Laurence Yetman, Carson's cousin, to Sarah-Jane Sadler and the subsequent christenings of their children. The sad, sad funeral of little Emily, still a child and, later, of her uncle Ryder and cousin Laurence, both tragic deaths. The marriage of Sophie Woodville to Henry Lamb, now Rector of Wenham, and the christenings of their two sons. The funerals of Sir Guy and Lady Woodville, almost state occasions when everyone had worn mourning and shops and buildings were hung with black ribbons.

More recent was Carson's grand wedding to Constance Yetman, a woman he had once proposed to only to change his mind and then, years later, change it back again. And now, happily, the christening of his third child, the much wanted daughter.

The Woodvilles and the little town of Wenham were inextricably linked. Woodvilles had been Lords of the Manor of Wenham since the sixteenth century when a prosperous burgher, Pelham Woodville, had built a great house on top of a hill three miles or so out of the small town which was visible from its grounds. His heir, Charles, who had been a soldier, was later ennobled by Charles II for services rendered to that monarch when he had served him in exile.

Over the years, like other noble families, the Woodvilles had known good times and bad. Some had been clever businessmen and managers of money, and the estate had prospered. Others were hopeless and it went into a decline. Unfortunately, two recent holders of the title, Carson's father, Guy, and his grandfather, Matthew, had been among the less astute and had to be bailed out by marrying rich women.

But Carson had stemmed the tide. Inheriting a bankrupt property on his father's death just after he had returned from the war, he had restored the house and turned the many farms, wood mills and small businesses on the estate into flourishing concerns. He had also married a woman of considerable wealth, but for love, and her money remained hers for the benefit, perhaps, of their children in the fullness of time.

The baptism over, prayers were said, the blessing given and the congregation piled out of doors into the spring sunshine. Everyone gathered around the family who, as all families do, posed for a long time for photographs. There were photos of the parents alone with the baby; they were then joined by the two small sons, then by close members of the family. The numbers swelled to more distant ones, to family retainers and hangers-on and, finally, as many townsfolk who could get a look in, pushing and jostling good-humouredly for a coveted place in the picture.

And after the family had departed, as so often in the past, a procession set on its way to follow them, a giant caterpillar of vehicles of all kinds – carts, traps, automobiles, even bicycles – which wound along the narrow lanes towards the Woodville family seat where Carson, fourteenth baronet, waited to greet them.

PART ONE

The Black Sheep of the Family

One

It was a glorious spring day, the country-side of North Dorset at its best.

The swifts, returning to their breeding sites, were whirling high in the sky looking for nest holes. Sometimes when they found them, often occupied by other birds, they became quarrelsome and their indignant shrieks pierced the air as territorial battles raged.

A few bluebells remained in the hedge-rows but their hour was almost done and the fragrant cow parsley, ox-eye daisies, red campion and purple mallow flowers were now jostling for room with a scattering of dog roses, their thick buds turning into floppy pink petals. In the fields on either side of the narrow road, the grass was already high, ready for the first cutting.

Carson's cousin, Dora Parterre, drove in her open tourer, her husband beside her. In the back seat was her mother, Eliza, and brother, Hugh. Dora flung her head back, her spirits high.

'It's so *glorious* to be back,' she cried glancing behind her at her mother who sat holding firmly on to her hat.

17

'I hope you're going to stay a few weeks,' Eliza Heering said.

Dora looked at her husband, Jean, always nervous when he was beside her in the car because she drove at such speed. For some odd reason, though he was a builder and a man of action, he had never learned to drive.

He was a strange, rather taciturn man and he sat ramrod straight, staring in front of him.

'Jean?' Dora looked quizzically at him.

'Well, at least you can stay, my dear, as long as you like.' He gave her a pleasant smile and then fastened his eyes again on the road as if he were driving and a moment's diversion would cause an accident. Dora was used to this and took no notice, putting her foot on the pedal as hard as circumstances allowed.

'I thought Connie looked tired,' Eliza said after a few moments' silence. 'I don't think she should have had that last baby.'

'They so wanted a girl,' Hugh, who was unmarried, said, trying unsuccessfully to light a cigarette in the wind.

'Well, there won't be any more,' Eliza said firmly, 'that's for sure. Poor Connie had a horrible time ... and dear little Henrietta...' She faltered, too upset by the memory of those anxious days to continue.

'But you couldn't have a healthier baby

now.' As Dora once again looked back at her mother Eliza couldn't help wondering if her daughter, married now for four years, had any regrets about her own childlessness. It was a subject about which, up to now, they had not spoken.

They turned into the gates and joined the queue of assorted vehicles slowly making their way along the drive towards the house which had once been Eliza's home. She was born there and always thought of it as the place where she really belonged.

Despite her two marriages she was a true Woodville at heart, happy and content among the Woodvilles, in the place that so many centuries before Pelham had built.

This, standing at the top of the incline up which they now drove, was a stately Palladian mansion faced with Chilmark stone, with a large portico and a broad balustrade staircase running down to the gravel drive. On the lawn beyond it, facing the town of Wenham, stood a majestic oak which tradition said Pelham had planted over three hundred years before, and which gave the house its name: Pelham's Oak.

As they edged at a snail's pace towards the house some people passed them on foot and hailed Eliza and Dora, who most of them knew, with a cheery greeting. Jean was not so well known, a man of some mystery who had arrived at Pelham's Oak soon after the

19

war to renew his friendship with his comrade-in-arms, Carson, and had stayed on to marry his cousin Dora.

Eventually they arrived at the house where Carson was busy shaking hands. In the old days, when Eliza was young, only the gentry were invited into the house, while the ordinary people – local farmers, tenants, servants, shopkeepers and their families – celebrated under cover of a marquee on the lawn, and instead of drinking fine champagne and eating smoked salmon and quails' eggs were offered beer, of which there was plenty, and robust country fare.

Now the situation was very different. The war had changed attitudes and the local people, if not considered the peers of the Woodvilles, in everything else were treated as equals. All sorts of people from all walks of life were there, but they had one thing in common: they were all dressed in their best as they slowly ascended the steps leading to the stately porch to shake Sir Carson's hand.

Helping to greet the guests was Carson's half-sister, Elizabeth, and his brother-in-law, Graham Temple, Elizabeth's second husband. In the background various youthful Yetman and Woodville cousins milled around, helping to escort the guests into the grand first floor drawing room with its splendid view of the town on the hill.

Elizabeth Temple was a handsome woman: tall, fair and blue-eyed. She had a sense of style and dressed well. Her besotted husband, who had been a bachelor until he married in his thirties, could deny her nothing. The consequence of this was that, like her mother before her, whom she very much resembled in looks as well as character, Elizabeth got through a vast amount of money. Her mother, Agnes Woodville, was not there that day. For many years the two women had not spoken to each other and Elizabeth now circulated round the vast white and gold drawing room, cultivating the quality and ignoring the peasantry, giving the cold shoulder to many who had known her for years as she was growing up in their midst.

Arriving some time later Connie, having fed her baby and put her to rest and had a little rest herself, stood for a while unnoticed at the door watching the throng, some two hundred or so people, though there were really too many to count. It was difficult not to notice Elizabeth and her progress through the room, Carson in respectful attendance as if it was she and not Connie who was the mistress of Pelham's Oak.

But Connie knew better than to criticise her sister-in-law, towards whom Carson felt a sense of guilt, and she slowly made her way into the room stopping to greet people, to receive congratulations, to respond to enquiries about the baby and her own health which at the moment was not too robust. Her mother had died in childbirth and, subconsciously, this was something Connie had always dreaded especially as, like her mother, hers was a late marriage and she was a little old for childbearing.

Carson put out his arm as he saw her and gently drew her towards him.

'All right, darling?'

She nodded.

'Did you manage a little rest?'

'I rested while I fed baby. She is asleep now.'

She put out a hand to steady Toby who was racing round the room in the company of several local boys. He shook her off and continued his run, cannoning into the rector, Hubert Turner.

'Here steady on,' Hubert cried good-naturedly and he looked over to his son, James, who caught up with young Toby and appeared to be giving him a lecture.

'Where's Debbie?' Connie asked looking around. 'She was at the church.'

Hubert's expression grew solemn.

'She said she had a headache. I imagine she...' He paused awkwardly, 'Well, you know she dislikes crowds. She thinks people are talking about her.'

'Surely not after all this time?' Connie looked surprised.

'She says people have long memories and perhaps she's right. I'm afraid my dear step-daughter will never get over her unfortunate experience.'

Deborah's sister, Ruth, meanwhile was chatting to Mr Greatheart, the bank manager, Mr Sweeney the grocer and Miss Harvey who kept the haberdashery store that had once belonged to Connie's guardian, Victoria Fairchild, from whom she had inherited her fortune. Eliza hovered in the background greeting old friends while Dora introduced her French husband to the many people who didn't know him. Across the room another cousin, Laurence's son Abel Yetman, a handsome young man of twenty-four who shouldered the family building business, was deep in conversation with one of his contractors, but out of the corner of his eye he was watching Ruth, whom he hoped some day to make his wife. Ruth's eyes occasionally caught his and she smiled. They lived very near each other; they had grown up together and the realisation that cousinly affection and friendship had burgeoned into something more profound had made them both shy.

Carson loved these family occasions and, hand in hand with Connie, he strolled through the room greeting all and sundry and receiving their congratulations, while servants moved around with trays on which there were glasses of champagne or plates of *canapes, fois gras,* smoked salmon and asparagus which cook and her assistants in the kitchen had spent most of the night preparing.

However, the rector's wife, Sophie Turner, was not particularly enjoying the party. She loved family occasions less than the others because her first husband had been George Woodville, Carson's elder brother and, but for his untimely death, he would now be standing where Carson stood, and herself and their two daughters beside him. It was not that she coveted Pelham's Oak – Heaven knew it had been a burden to her father-in-law and his father before him – but things might have been very different if George had lived.

George might now be the Rector of Wenham – he had been in Holy Orders when he died – and her elder daughter might not be the mother of a child born out of wedlock to a workman who had deserted her, and thus consigned her to a life of shame.

For, whatever people said, it was still shameful to be an unwed mother and Deborah experienced that sense of shame keenly, and seldom went out. People could be so cruel, even in Wenham. Hubert

24

Turner, to whom Sophie and her daughters owed so much, was now engaged in an apparently engrossing conversation with several of the pious ladies of the parish who looked after the church, did the flowers and embroidered hassocks to ease the arthritic pains of the older members of the congregation while attending divine service at the church of St Mark.

Naturally the ladies, many of them unmarried due to the terrible toll of young eligible males taken in the war, doted on the rector. Some people laughed at them behind their backs, talking cruelly about repression and spinsterhood but, for the most part, they were admirable women: self-sufficient, independent, generous-hearted, who had made the best of the circumstances that denied them the some-times questionable delights of marriage and children. Most of them not only led useful and happy lives, fulfilling themselves in good works and subtle acts of piety, but were mostly well off too with their own houses and money in the bank. They were the worthy descendants of Victoria Fairchild and Connie's own mother, Euphemia Monk, to whom married bliss had only come late in a life which she had forfeited on Connie's birth.

Connie, looking round, smiling and waving, anxious not to exclude anyone, was the first to see a stranger hovering on the edge of the crowd, a dark-haired, good-looking man with a weather-beaten face, aged about fifty. He wore a well-cut dark grey suit, a white shirt and a discreet blue tie. His black hair, plastered back, was grey at the sides and sparse on the top of his head. There was something about him that was familiar, but she couldn't place him and she tugged at her husband's arm.

'Carson, who's that? The face is familiar but I can't think why.'

Carson followed her gaze whereupon he was seen by the stranger who, hailing him, made his way through the crowd, hand outstretched in recognition.

Carson searched the recesses of his memory, but was unable to come up with a name. Nevertheless, with a broad smile on his face, he clasped the hand of the man, who said:

'I can see by the look on your face your don't remember me, Carson.'

'Forgive me,' Carson said, feeling embarrassed. 'Was it in the war?'

The man shook his head.

'*Bart!*' cried a voice behind him. '*Whatever* are you doing here?' Sarah-Jane Yetman was staring at the man with an expression of astonishment, almost outrage on her face.

'I realise I'm the uninvited guest–' the visitor began.

'Bart Sadler. Of course!' Carson pumped his hand warmly. 'Everyone is welcome here. There were no invitations. Connie, you remember Bart Sadler, Sarah-Jane's brother?'

'Bart Sadler ... Bart Sadler...' The whisper echoed round the room as everyone turned to stare.

Bart Sadler, their looks seemed to say, *back from the dead.*

'And where did *you* spring from?' his sister demanded, her tone far from welcoming. 'After all these years and not a word.'

'Sarah-Jane, I think we can discuss these matters in private.' Bart tried to lower his voice. 'I have only just arrived in the town, and heard there was a christening...'

'And what made you think *you* would be welcome?' Sarah-Jane said shrilly as Abel appeared at his mother's side and quietly took her arm, whispering something in her ear.

'Bart, you are very welcome,' Carson said hastily. 'But I hardly recognised you.'

'Sixteen years is a long time, Carson. You've changed too.'

'I don't remember Mr Sadler at all.' Connie shook her head.

'But I remember *you*, madam.' Bart looked knowingly at her. *'Lady Woodville, I* should say. I recall what a shy little thing you were. But my, how you've come on.'

'When did you leave Wenham?' Carson took his guest's arm and led him over to a table on which there was a plentiful assortment of food, bottles of wine and champagne. Filling a glass he held it out to him at the same time handing him a plate. 'Eat all you wish, you must be hungry.'

Bart was. He took the plate and moved along the table from dish to dish taking his fill of home-cured ham, local beef, farm chickens, salads of all kinds, minted hot potatoes from the kitchen gardens.

'Well before the war, Carson, 1912 or thereabouts. Seeing there was little future in my living as a stonemason I went abroad to South America. There I discovered tin and copper...'

'And were you able to make a living from that?' Carson looked at him with polite interest.

'A fortune. I am glad to say that, although I am just over fifty, I have made enough money to retire, and live in comfort for the rest of my life. I thought I would return to my roots, to my native land which I have always loved. I intend to settle, to find or build a home and, maybe, seek a bride, for I have never married.'

His eyes, which had been restlessly roving the room, seemed finally to alight on the person he was seeking. She, for her part, stood at the far side of the room gazing at him, as if mesmerised, rather as a rabbit watches a stoat who is about to seize it by the neck and, with one deft movement, kill it.

As Bart and Sophie Turner gazed at each other across the room, memories for each came flooding back. Pleasant, obviously, for one; terrifying for the other.

Too late, Sophie tried to avert her eyes and, as Bart walked towards her, she looked around as if for some means of escape, but the crowd hemmed her in. Then he stood in front of her and she found his presence, his nearness, almost as overwhelming as it had been sixteen years before when she, the rector's daughter and widow of a man in holy orders, had lain in his arms savouring the delights of illicit love.

'Sixteen years is a long time, Sophie,' Bart said gently as, with a slight bow, he reached for her hand.

'How are you, Mr Sadler?' she replied coldly.

'Very well, thank you, Sophie. But why such formality?' His expression had a hint of mockery, and a feeling of rage welled up inside her, but his proximity almost rendered her speechless. 'I hear you have become the rector's wife. My, how the Church *do* attract you, ma'am, the daughter of a parson and then married to two, one after the other.'

29

At a loss as to how to reply, Sophie turned gratefully as a voice spoke behind her and a hand touched her arm.

'Sophie, my dear, it is almost three and you have the children's Bible class at four.'

'I was just thinking the same thing, Hubert,' she said, turning round swiftly. 'Hubert, I think you remember Mr Sadler, Sarah-Jane's brother?'

'Of course I remember you, Mr Sadler.' The jovial rector warmly shook Bart's hand. 'But you have been gone from here a very long time.'

'Too long, Mr Turner,' Bart said in his deep, mellifluous voice, reminding Sophie agonisingly of those endearments once whispered in her ear. 'Now that I am at home I hope to settle. A little belatedly, I know, but I have to congratulate you on being so fortunate as to have persuaded Mrs Woodville to be your wife.'

The rector beamed.

'Wasn't I fortunate?'

'I was already on the point of making preparations to go abroad, so I missed the wedding.'

'How *fortunate* too that you escaped the war,' Sophie observed with studied irony.

Bart looked at her sharply. 'I wanted to return and serve my King and country, I assure you, Mrs Turner. But I was unable to find a ship. It was no joy to me to be so far

30

away from hostilities in Europe.'

'Good day to you, Mr Sadler,' Sophie said abruptly, taking her husband's arm and turning her back on the last person she wished to see in the world.

'My dear, I don't think that was very polite,' Hubert protested, looking uncomfortable. 'You were very abrupt.'

'I have no liking for Mr Sadler. Don't forget he was partly responsible for Laurence's death.'

'Surely that can't be true?'

'Not *directly* responsible. But he introduced Laurence to the man who *was* responsible, who asked him to build a factory and then defaulted, leaving Laurence with a mountain of debts and bankruptcy.'

'But you can hardly blame Mr Sadler for *that*,' Hubert said reasonably.

'Well, I do. I blame him a lot. He knew what he was doing in vouching for someone Laurence thought he could trust. He also thought, understandably, that he could trust his brother-in-law. He was mistaken and the family has suffered grievously for it ever since. You could see how displeased, even shocked, Sarah-Jane was to see him. I noticed her face as soon as he came into the room. He is an unsavoury character and I am sorry to see he has come back to Wenham. Now we must hurry home, my dear. The day has made me tired and I have my class to prepare for, as you reminded me.'

'Certainly. I'll just gather up the youngsters,' Hubert replied amiably. 'Now where is James...'

Bart Sadler stood for some time watching Sophie and her husband as they walked towards the door, a smile on his thin lips. His attention was then taken by a youth who had gone over to Sophie and Hubert and appeared to be arguing with them. Sophie was becoming very cross as the rector put his hand on the youth's arm as if reprimanding him. The boy jerked his arm away as another, who closely resembled the rector and looked a year or two younger than the first, also came up and joined in the argument.

'Dear dear,' Bart said to a man standing next to him. 'There appears to be some altercation going on. Are those the rector's two sons?'

The man nodded. 'And as unalike as chalk and cheese. Sam, the one you see arguing with his mother now, is a tearaway. He never does as he is told, gives her and his father a lot of pain, whereas young James is the apple of his parents' eyes. As devout and clever as he is a good and obedient son, the image, as you can see, of his father.'

'Do I know you?' Bart looked at the man,

who shook his head.

'I am not a Wenham man, sir, but I have the good fortune to be married to a Wenham lady. You may know her. Elizabeth Yewell?'

'Of course I know Elizabeth Yewell,' Bart said, spinning round. 'Where is she? I would like to make her acquaintance again.'

'Oh, she'll be gossiping with her friends,' the man said, taking a card out of his pocket and handing it to Bart. 'My name is Graham Temple, a solicitor of Blandford. Did I overhear you say you were looking for property in the district? I should be delighted if at any time my firm could be of service to you,' and he put his card into Bart's outstretched hand. Bart stood for a few moments examining it thoughtfully. When eventually he looked up a pair of twinkling blue eyes were gazing merrily at him.

'So you *do* remember me, Bart Sadler?' Elizabeth's smile was mischievous, her manner coquettish. Bart, as if anxious to recover from Sophie's snub, looked at her with delight.

'I am most happy to see you again looking so well and, if I may say so, prosperous. Your husband is a very fortunate man. I think the last time you and I met you were a milkmaid on my brother's farm.'

Elizabeth seemed not altogether pleased at

33

the reference.

'I was *very* young then, Bart Sadler. Since then I have been married and widowed. Mr Temple is my second husband. My first husband was a victim of the war.'

'I'm very sorry to hear that.' Bart produced a cigarette from a silver case, offered it to Elizabeth, who shook her head, offered it to her husband who also declined and then, selecting one, lit it.

'Then you may *also* not have heard, Bart Sadler, that since the time you were here I have learned that my mother and father were not Ted and Beth Yewell, as I had been led to believe, which is why I was brought up as a servant, but none other than Sir Guy and Lady Agnes Woodville. There!' She flashed him a look of triumph. 'What do you think of that?'

'I am very impressed.' Bart blew smoke towards the ceiling. 'That is to say I am amazed. That must have caused a stir in Wenham.'

'Oh, it caused a stir all right.' Elizabeth chuckled maliciously. 'There were a few red faces. The only one who had not known was Carson who had been left in the dark as much as I...'

'And who has behaved impeccably towards my wife ever since,' Mr Temple said with an air of outraged virtue. 'He removed her from the wretched hovel in which she

34

had been incarcerated due to the illness and poverty of her then husband, and gave her a home. Although not a man of means he paid for the late Frank Sprogett's hospital bills from his own pocket. He has been kindness itself to Elizabeth's children by Mr Sprogett, all of whom are here today,' he glanced around, 'and then when I was fortunate enough to have Elizabeth accept my proposal of marriage he gave her away, and he is godfather to our own first-born.'

'*Not* a man of means?' Bart asked somewhat incredulously, looking around the splendid drawing room with its painted ceiling, its intricate cornice resplendent with gold leaf, the family portraits of Woodvilles by revered masters going back hundreds of years. 'I would have thought this room alone was evidence of a man of considerable means.'

'At that time he, er...' Mr Temple paused awkwardly, 'at the time we are speaking of.'

'*Before* he married Constance,' Elizabeth said meaningfully.

Bart Sadler smote his brow theatrically, as if he had suddenly remembered something.

'Ah, now I *do* recall ... yes, yes it all comes flooding back. Carson was due to marry Constance Yetman before, was he not? I couldn't quite place Lady Woodville. Put her in context, so to speak. She has so changed I hardly recognised her from the

35

time when she was the timid little ward of Miss Fairchild. Maybe I made an indiscreet remark, I don't know. I hope I didn't offend her ladyship.' He looked anxiously towards the door where Connie stood surrounded by friends who were on the verge of departure, among them the rector, his wife and two sons, still arguing. 'And then, if I remember right, the reason Carson was marrying a lady so singularly ill-endowed, at that time, so unprepossessing to look at, was that she was an heiress. So he married her after all?'

'*After* he came back from the war without any money.' Elizabeth nodded her head. Despite her affection for him, her innate meanness of spirit made her unable to resist malicious gossip even about those for whom she professed to care.

'But people say he never touched a penny.' Mr Temple was at pains to make up for his wife's unkind innuendo. 'He has done well on his own account, he and Constance married for love and, as a couple, are blissfully happy. Elizabeth spent some time living in this house, a year or two while Mr Sprogett was so ill and before we were married. Isn't that so, my dear?' Mr Temple looked for confirmation to his wife.

Elizabeth's mouth set in a grimace.

'Please don't ask me about Constance Woodville. I would hate to spoil a happy

36

day. The truth is,' she looked again at Bart, 'Constance was jealous of me. She couldn't stand the fact that Carson offered me and my family a home. She nearly called off the wedding. As if the family hasn't done me *enough* harm! No, we didn't get on then and we don't now, but Carson takes no notice of her. He says I am his sister and I deserve respect which I do not get from Constance.' Elizabeth shut her mouth firmly and threw her husband, who was wiping a perspiring brow, a dark look. 'Maybe I speak out of turn, but that is the truth.'

'Dear me,' Bart said with a bemused air. 'Sixteen years away is a long time, I *do* have a lot of catching up to do. And, tell me, what of your mother, the *other* Lady Woodville, Elizabeth? Where is she now?'

'That *too* is a very long story,' Elizabeth said archly, and suddenly clutched his arm. 'You must come and dine with us, Bart. We can tell you a thing or two about what has been going on at Wenham, in the years you have been away, that will make your hair stand on end.'

Two

Constance Woodville sat in her nursing chair clasping her sleeping baby at her breast, her feet comfortably up on the footstool in front of her. She lay back, her own eyes closed, conscious of the same feeling as, she imagined, the baby had: repletion, fulfilment, happiness. Henrietta exuded that lovely, fragrant baby smell of bath oil, soap and talcum powder, and tiny globules of breast milk adhered to the sides of the sweet, contented-looking little mouth.

The child of elderly parents, orphaned at the age of eight, Connie had grown up a lonely and withdrawn child, insecure despite her comfortable circumstances, the prospects for her future unclouded by financial worry. Her own painful shyness and lack of looks worried her far more, even at a tender age. She knew she was gawky, abnormally thin, bespectacled, with mouse-coloured hair. No man would ever look at her and, as she grew older, she retreated more into her shell.

And then Carson came along and, out of the blue, proposed marriage! Her universe expanded. She had never expected to be loved by anyone other than her father, who doted on her or, after his death, the woman who had adopted her. She had been sure from an early age that physical love and marriage would pass her by, and prepared herself for a life of spinsterhood.

But Carson, encouraged by his family and her guardian, only wanted her for her money. Even then she would have married him, but he didn't love her. Afterwards they each saw themselves as victims, but by then the damage was done. Collapse of her world; breakdown. Now a life of spinsterhood was assured, though it would be a well-heeled spinsterhood because by the time Miss Fairchild died Connie had been left several fortunes.

It was this wealth that had enabled her to throw off the bitter memories of the past, together with the encumbrances of the ugly duckling, and emerge as a swan. She was helped in this transformation by a worldly Italian woman whose lawyer husband had looked after Miss Fairchild's interests when they were exiled in Rome during the war.

Naturally gifted musically and interested in the arts, Connie was introduced to a circle of sophisticated, artistic people where style was all important. She learned how to change her appearance with the aid of a good cosmetician and hair colourist. This gave her poise and self-confidence, almost a new identity so that when, after the war, she returned to Wenham to sell her guardian's house and finalise her affairs – to leave, she thought, Wenham for good – she captured the heart of the man she had always loved but who had not loved her.

Constance opened her eyes suddenly, the memory of that first meeting in the churchyard so vivid it could have been yesterday. It was about this time of year and she had been laying flowers on the graves of her parents when she had seen him looking at her. She had worn a white coat over a pretty floral dress, made in Rome, and a broad-brimmed white straw hat. It would have been hard to imagine anyone more remote from the shy, gauche young woman she had been and, at first, Carson didn't recognise her. She had learned her Italian lessons well. But Connie was afraid of having her love spurned yet again and this time the tables were turned. She was not to be an easy catch. He pursued her, but she ran. Finally, like all good fairy stories, it had a happy ending, and on a beautiful autumn day in the year 1924 they had married in Wenham Church and ever since then her life had been a dream.

Well, almost a dream.

She very gently rose and laid the sleeping baby in her crib, tenderly tucking her up and kissing her forehead. Then she went and stood by the window of the baby's nursery looking towards the little town on the hill where she had been born. Its whitewashed cottages gleamed in the spring sunshine and between it and the house where she now lived were acres of lush green countryside interspersed with copses, hedges and streams, with cattle contentedly grazing, well-tended fields, and birds flying frantically about completing their nests for their young. It was a lovely time of the year, a time for renewal and hope, and as she was about to turn and attend to the wants of her two little boys she saw a couple on horseback emerging from the copse at the bottom of the hill close by Crooks' farm. Deep in conversation they paused to let their horses drink from the pond in the farmyard and Connie thought what a fine pair they made: Carson and his cousin Dora.

Carson was over six feet tall, well built with hair that was once ash-blond but was now nearly grey, though he was only forty-one. The war had changed him, aged him, matured him. He had seen sights he would never forget and his former values were stood on their heads. From being a tearaway always in trouble, the despair of his parents, he grew up. In 1918 he was a very different man from the one who went to war.

But his grizzled locks and strong athletic frame gave him an air of distinction which went with his upright, military bearing. He had intense blue eyes, open, honest and frank, capable of compassion but also daunting, and although his expression was often forbidding, his mouth resolute, he had mellowed in the years since their marriage as he had found a degree of happiness he had never before known.

It was easy to see the relationship between Carson and Dora, his first cousin. His father and Eliza had been brother and sister. Dora was three years older than Carson, but she looked much younger. She too was tall, fair with the same blue eyes. They could have been taken for brother and sister. Connie didn't ride and Carson loved riding, so he had missed Dora in the years she had been abroad.

On impulse, Connie threw open the window and hailed them, whereupon they looked up and, seeing her, waved vigorously back. Making sure that the baby was sound asleep Connie tiptoed out of the room and ran along the corridor and down the stairs to fetch the nursemaid who was playing with the small boys on the lawn.

'Gertie, would you go upstairs and keep an eye on baby? She has been fed and is asleep, but may want changing. I didn't want to wake her up.'

'Yes, m.' Gertie jumped up obediently. She was a servant of the old-fashioned school who had grown up on the Woodville estates and had no truck with newfangled notions about equality and one class being as good as the next. She emphatically knew her place, as her parents and their parents before them had known theirs, which was to serve the Woodvilles, and do their bidding without question. This was despite all Connie's efforts to make her into a companion and friend rather than a servant. Gertie bobbed and curtsied, she flattened herself against walls if she passed the quality in a corridor, insisting on self-effacement as though it was a way of life. And for her it was. She venerated her charges, particularly the eldest boy because he would one day succeed to his father's title.

She was only twenty-seven but had worked for Connie and Carson since the birth of Toby. As she was rather plain and men were in short supply on account of the war she expected, indeed she hoped, that she would be with them for a good many years, maybe seeing the youngsters into adulthood and enjoying a peaceful old age in a cottage on the estate. Pessimistic about her future Gertie might have been, but she was a realist. Leaving the lawn she went indoors and Connie went over to the boys who, on seeing her, abandoned their game and rushed into her arms.

Both children were like her, brown-haired, brown-eyed, fair-skinned. They were grave little boys, but that was rather an attractive quality, unusual in children, and they didn't laugh for the sake of it but only if something amused them. They weighed things up, they pondered. In fact they were very like Connie as a child, without the disadvantage of being a woman. They were loved and they were loving. It was a very happy family home and now the gift of a daughter seemed to make it complete. They spent hours gazing into Henrietta's crib, noting her tiny fingers with their shiny nails, the little dimple in her chin, the fair hair, unlike theirs, and blue eyes.

They called her Netta because her name was so difficult for them to get their tongues round, and this diminutive would be the name by which she would be known for the rest of her life.

Connie sank on to a long wicker chair and the boys returned to their game with the ball, the two King Charles' spaniels, Charlie and Louie, which had been a wedding present from Carson to Connie, romping with them. Connie lay back in the chair listening to the sounds around her: of children playing, dogs barking, birds singing in the great oak tree and the surrounding hedgerows. She experienced a moment of utter contentment, and she shaded her eyes from the sun which was creeping across the grass as she raised her head to be sure that the boys were all right. In a field beyond the house one of the maids was hanging out the washing, the white sheets billowing in the breeze, and a gardener trundled across the far end of the lawn with a wheelbarrow and raised his hand in greeting to Connie who responded with a wave. It was indeed idyllic.

Just then a new noise impinged on the others and she sat upright and looked towards the drive as an open tourer came in sight, a woman at the wheel, her hat secured with a scarf tied under her chin. The boys stopped playing and ran towards the car which slowed almost to crawling pace as it approached the house. Then, unfastening her scarf, Eliza got out and hugged each of the boys in turn before walking over to Connie, who rose to greet her.

The two women embraced and lingered for a moment clutched in each other's arms. There was a bond between Connie and Eliza that was more than mere affection. Eliza had received the newly born baby from her dying mother and willed the sickly creature to live. She had always kept an eye on her, sympathised with her, cried with her and corresponded with her all the years she lived abroad. Her joy when she married her nephew had known no bounds.

'What a lovely surprise,' Connie said as one of the menservants ran from the house carrying another chair.

'Bring two more please, John, would you?' Connie asked. 'Sir Carson and Mrs Parterre will be with us any minute. Oh, and coffee, Eliza?'

'That *would* be lovely.' Eliza smiled, appraising her hostess as she flopped into a chair and removed her hat. 'How pretty you look today, Connie. You've been so pale of late, but now you've got some colour.'

'Pretty is not a word I'd use, Aunt Eliza.' Connie ruefully screwed back her hair, embarrassed at the compliment.

'Yes, pretty. Vivacious. Motherhood suits you.'

'Once it's over.' Connie grimaced.

Eliza stretched out a hand.

'It is over, all over, and the children are well and happy. I had three children, so did Laurence and Sarah-Jane, and Carson's parents. Threes seem to run in the family. It's a tradition.' She looked across at Connie and smiled.

'Have you come for Dora?'

'Only if she wants to drive back, if she's tired. She came over on her horse and it is a long ride.'

'They're down by the farm. I think they may have gone in to see the Crooks.'

Generations of the Crook family had been farming on the estate since before the time of Carson's great-grandfather which was about as far back as memories went.

'I'm going to Sherborne and as this was on my way thought I'd pop in to see you. And, yes, if Dora wishes to come I'd be pleased because I want to choose new curtain material for the drawing room and I can never make up my mind.'

Eliza lay back and sighed. 'What a blissful day. It reminds me of my youth. There always seemed to be sunshine, and long lazy days.' She paused to remember her parents, the somewhat tempestuous relationship she had with her mother, the father who had died when she was fourteen, her brilliant, handsome brother, Guy, who had somehow failed to fulfil his promise. 'I'm so glad you decided to call baby after my mother. Guy would have been so pleased.'

'Carson has happy memories of his grandmother. She was very special to him. Besides, it's such a pretty name. Jean did not want to come with you?' Connie looked curiously across at Eliza.

'I thought he would want to go riding with Dora and Carson but he has gone off by himself, walking, I think.' Eliza gave a deep sigh and this time it was not one of such contentment. Connie made no comment. A footman arrived with a table followed by another with a silver tray and a maidservant carrying a large silver coffee pot carefully in both hands. Connie rose to help set out the cups and, as the staff turned back into the house, she began to pour.

'We're so lucky to have servants,' she said, passing Eliza a cup. 'Some people can't get them.'

'That's because the Woodvilles have always treated their servants well,' Eliza replied. 'We treat them as people, not as slaves. But I don't know how much longer it will go on for. I think the next generation will be very different. There is much more money to be made in cities.' She smiled up at the maid who had returned with a jug of orange and two glasses which she poured for the two boys.

'How are you, Mary?'

'Very well, thank you, Mrs Heering.'

'And your mother and father?'

'Father is troubled by his rheumatics. Thank you for asking, Mrs Heering.' Mary flashed her a friendly, but not obsequious smile, and returned to the house while the boys sat on the lawn drinking their beverages.

'Mary's two brothers were killed in the war,' Eliza said solemnly. 'She is the only child left. Her brothers were great carousing pals of Carson's when they were all young. No wonder he changed such a lot. So many of the fine young men from this area never came back.'

'Won't you stay for lunch?' Connie asked. Eliza shook her head.

'You're too kind, but I expect Jean will be back.'

'You could leave a message?'

'Believe me, we shall be choosing curtain material for ages.' Eliza took her coffee and sipped it. When she looked up her expression was thoughtful, even grave.

'I do worry about Dora and Jean, you know.'

'Really?' Connie sat down, tucking her feet under her, preparing for a confidence. The boys finished their cordial and returned to their game while the two dogs emerged from the shadow of the oak where they had been resting in order to be included in the fun. 'Is there something wrong?' Connie continued as Eliza seemed to hesitate before answering.

'There's nothing *wrong*,' Eliza said, frowning, 'but I don't understand their relationship. It's not like being married. They have separate bedrooms. I suppose I shouldn't tell you, this is gossip. But it does worry me because they seem so detached, from each other that is.'

'But they always were, I mean they were rather a curious couple even before they were married.'

'They just seem like good friends.' Eliza looked dubious. 'You know, chums.'

'Perhaps they are.'

As if anxious to ignore the implications of this remark Eliza hurried on:

'And then I would have thought Dora would want children. She is so good with children.'

Connie nodded. 'The boys love her.'

'And she loves them.'

'Do you talk to her about it?'

'Oh no. It's so difficult.'

'Anyway, it's a bit late,' Connie said practically. 'Dora is in her forties, Aunt Eliza.'

'Yes, but it would not have been too late when they got married. It is, I suppose, just possible now, but with separate bedrooms...' She paused and looked searchingly at Connie. 'Don't misunderstand me, they never row or have cross words; they seem very fond. But somehow, I can't quite explain it, but they're not like a married couple.'

At that moment Dora and Carson appeared, walking over from the stables and speculation had to stop. Both looked in good spirits. The boys ran over to them, Toby going to his father, Leonard to Dora who, being a tall, powerful woman, easily lifted him up and, holding him in her arms, continued walking towards her mother.

50

'What a heavenly day,' she said. 'Have you come for a ride, Mummy?'

'Not today." Eliza smiled. 'I wanted to go to Sherborne and wondered if you'd like to come and help me choose curtain material.'

'That's a great idea.' Dora looked over at Carson. 'Could I leave Bonnie here?'

'Of course.'

'I might pick her up on the way back, depends how late it is.' She looked at her watch and then down at her jodhpurs. 'On the other hand, Mummy, I'm not exactly dressed for a shopping excursion. I think I'll go home.'

'Just as you like, dear, though I'd value your opinion.'

'Stay for lunch, oh *do*,' Connie said, jumping up, 'and go into Sherborne another day.'

'Oh, well.' Eliza looked at her daughter. 'I feel tempted. It seems a pity to spend even part of such a lovely day in a shop.'

'Come on, boys.' Dora lowered Leonard to the ground. 'Let's see who can throw the ball furthest.'

'I'll go and tell cook there will be two more for lunch,' Connie said, pleased.

'And I'll go and change.' Carson held out his hand which Connie grasped, and together they wandered back towards the house. Eliza lay back in her chair, eyes half closed. She had been widowed for the second time two years previously when her second husband, Julius, had died. Theirs had been a marriage of convenience rather than love. She had been lonely after Ryder's death and Julius had also been a widower.

He had been a man of great wealth and had left her his fortune, but his death made her feel guilty because she knew that after the suicide of her son, Laurence, she had never forgiven Julius for failing to help him. Such a little sum of money to him would easily have helped Laurence out of his difficulty and he might now be alive.

After Laurence's death she had ceased to feel any affection for Julius, and she often wondered if she had been hard on him, unforgiving, in the way he had been to her son.

Such sad thoughts intruded into her mind and must have shown on her face because she was aware of Dora leaning towards her, an expression of concern on her face.

'What is it, Mummy? You look so sad.'

'I was thinking a bit of Julius.' Eliza patted the chair beside her. 'I think I was hard on him.'

'You were hard on *him*?' Dora exploded. She had idolised her elder brother and had never liked her stepfather.

'I know what you mean.' Eliza put a hand on her daughter's arm. 'But that's the sort of person Julius was. I never thought he would leave me everything and the Heering family nothing. I think he wanted to make up.'

'Well, you deserve it.' Dora pressed her mother's hand. 'You had a tough time and no one deserves it more.'

'I wish you weren't going back,' Eliza burst out, surprising herself by her vehemence. 'You have no idea how much I miss you. How lonely I am in that big house.'

Upper Park was one of the finest examples of Georgian Baroque in the country, and stood on an incline facing north to south with magnificent views of the surrounding countryside. It was on the far side of the market town of Blandford Forum, about fifteen miles from Pelham's Oak. It was a substantial house built for a large family and now there was only Eliza and, occasionally, Hugh, who had resumed his fellowship of All Souls interrupted by the war and spent most of his time in his rooms in Oxford.

'Mother,' Dora looked at her closely, 'did you ever think of moving? It is a big house. You could come nearer to Wenham, or Sherborne which you love. Here you are, doing it all up, new carpets, curtains, and yet there's just you and rather a lot of servants.'

'They're becoming harder to get too,' Eliza said thoughtfully.

'Exactly. I think you should get a smaller place.'

'On the other hand, I do love it. Only I wish you were there.'

Dora said nothing but held on to her mother's hand, her expression thoughtful.

'Oh golly,' she said suddenly, jumping up. 'I must telephone Jean and say we won't be back for lunch.' And she ran across the lawn and disappeared inside the house leaving Eliza alone with her thoughts and two small boys playing with a ball and their dogs on the lawn.

Jean Parterre knocked on the door of his wife's room and, as she called for him to come in, turned the handle. He found her lying on the bed in her dressing gown, a book in her hand. As he came in she put the book down and smiled.

'Hello!'

'Hello!' He went and sat on the bed beside her. 'Had a good day?'

'Yes. When I came back from my ride with Carson Mother was there. She wanted me to go into Sherborne with her to help choose curtain material; but as it was such a lovely day Connie persuaded us to stay for lunch and give Sherborne a miss. We had it in the garden. I rang you but you weren't here. What did you do, dear?' She gazed at him fondly.

'I went for a very long walk. I had a pint of beer and a sandwich at a pub. I must have walked twenty miles.'

He put a hand on Dora's bare leg and, imperceptibly, she moved it away just out of touch.

'Dora,' he said as though he hadn't noticed her gesture, 'when are we going home? We've been here over a month.'

'Are you in a hurry?' She looked at him in surprise.

'I don't call staying away a month and wanting to go home being in a hurry. We have already been here longer than I intended. I fear for the vines without me.'

Jean gave a rather nervous laugh and, rising from the bed went over to the window, hands in his pockets, and stood looking out. 'You know I think one could grow vines here. I believe Julius was thinking of it.'

'Would you like to?'

He turned, surprised at her eager tone, and looked at her. Dora continued: 'Mother is very lonely here, dear. It is a big house for her. She told me today how upset she was at the thought of us going back.'

'You mean *you* going back. Your mother wouldn't miss me.'

'Oh, don't say it like that, Jean.'

'I feel she tolerates me.'

'But you don't try very hard, do you?'

'I try as hard as I can. But she resents the fact that I took you away from her in the first place.'

'I don't think that's true. Mummy has never been possessive about her children. She only wants us to be happy.'

'Maybe she doesn't think I've made you happy?' Jean's expression was sad. 'Have I, Dora?'

'Of course!' She put her hand out towards him and he clasped it. If only she would pull him closer to her, allow him to ... but she never did.

'She is my mother. I do feel a responsibility for her, Jean.'

'But Dora...'

'I do. I'm sorry, but I do. She has had a hard life. Dad died in an accident. Laurence killed himself. She had a lot of worry about money. She married a cold fish, largely I think for security. And now that she's getting on she's alone. Yes I *do* feel a responsibility and that's why I wondered...'

Letting go of his hand, Dora rose from the bed and, draping her gown closely around her, sat on the edge and lit a cigarette. Jean was aware that she was wearing nothing underneath her gown. He wondered if she knew what such proximity to naked female flesh did to him; the thought that it was there but he couldn't touch it. Never had been allowed to touch because that was the condition on which she married him. Friends, companions, but nothing more.

However, this was the last thing on Dora's mind as she sat smoking. Almost carelessly she crossed one nude leg over the other and the gown fell apart even more.

Not for the first time her frustrated husband wanted to take her in his arms and ... well, violence was out of the question which was why he went on long walks and had a mistress in Paris.

'Jean, I wondered...' Dora appeared to be wrestling with something on her mind. 'If you *really* thought you could start growing vines here ... we could come and live with Mother.'

Jean felt a ball of rage and fury explode inside him but, as usual, he hid it as he hid his sexual frustration and instead allowed an expression of mild incredulity to cross his face.

'Are you serious, Dora?'

'Well, I haven't given it a lot of thought. I mean only since this afternoon; but I do miss England. I'm English and I love England. I love my mother, my family. I love being near Pelham's Oak, Carson and Connie. In France, well, we lead a pretty solitary life.'

It was true that they did. Jean had children by an earlier marriage, but they lived with their mother in the south, and he scarcely ever saw them. The home near Rheims was isolated in the middle of vineyards and they had few friends, though many acquaintances in the city of Rheims and the town of Epernay where Jean sold his grapes. Often, though, he went to Paris for several days without her and she felt even more isolated, far away from home.

Dora had served in France in the war. She had nursed near the front line and somehow she could never separate that country from the carnage she had seen. It wasn't so much that she didn't like France as that she was far from comfortable there.

'Maybe we could talk about it?' She rose from the bed and, stubbing out her cigarette, looked across at him as she gathered up some clothes to take into the bathroom.

'There is nothing to talk about,' Jean said, finally giving vent to his repressed anger. 'When you married me you knew you were going to live in France. You made some conditions...' he looked at her meaningfully, 'and that was my condition. We had a marriage without sex because that was how you wanted it, but at least I lived at home.'

'You accepted it, Jean,' Dora replied coldly. 'You said you couldn't live without me. You needed me to make your life complete. Has that changed?'

'Well ... I hoped.' Jean made a vague gesture. 'Yes, I do find it hard, harder than I thought because even now I desire you. I always have.'

58

'Even *now*.' Dora laughed mirthlessly.

'Yes, even after six years of abstinence I desire you and want you. I love you, Dora.'

'Oh, God!' Dora exclaimed running her hands through her short, boyish crop. 'What have we started? I thought this was all ironed out years ago? Now I see how bitter you are.'

'No, Dora, I'm not bitter; but I thought ... yes I thought I could seduce you, or should I say, persuade you? That, eventually, you would give in because you wanted me too. I still wish...'

'Oh, forget it, Jean, *please!*' Dora made for the bathroom, but Jean flung out an arm and stopped her. For a moment as she gazed at him the expression on his face frightened her.

'I do not consent to staying here, Dora. I do not wish to grow vines here or live here. You can come and see your mother as much as you like, but I will not make this place my home. Is that clear, Dora? If you want to be my wife you live with me in France. If not...'

Dora wrenched away her arm and flew into the bathroom slamming the door behind her while Jean, white with fury, rage and also a sense of despair, flopped on to the empty bed and rolled across it, his face to the covers savouring her fragrance, torturing himself with the thought of everything he had wanted and could not have.

It was as if he had risked everything on the throw of the dice all those years ago, and now he knew he had lost. Really lost.

Three

That summer of 1928 was a hard one for Eliza as she wrestled with the problem of whether or not to sell her large house, as her children advised, and get something smaller and more suitable. Finally she made up her mind and put it on the market.

Some of her friends could not believe it. One of them was Lally Martyn who, though not strictly speaking a Woodville, had been part of the Woodville family for a very long time.

She had been a dancer in her youth and at one time the mistress of Guy Woodville by whom she had a son, Roger. In those days, the late 1880s, it had been very difficult for an unmarried woman to keep an illegitimate child, even someone who was a dancer and not as conventional as most people.

But Lally had embraced respectability, as far as she could, given her humble origins. By the time her son, Roger, was born she was ensconced as Guy's mistress in a house in London and, to all intents and purposes, very respectable indeed. Accordingly, after Guy had abandoned her, she had her son brought up by a working class woman in

Camden Town.

Eventually Lally married Prosper Martyn, whose sister, Henrietta, was Guy's mother. He was much older than Lally and a man of great wealth, in business with Eliza's husband, Julius.

Now Julius and Prosper were dead and, living near each other, the two widows became much closer than they had been before, though people had always loved Lally. There was absolutely nothing about her to dislike as she was as good and kind and compassionate as she was beautiful.

In many ways she had changed little over the years. In her youth she had been blonde and petite and now, even though she was not far off seventy, largely because she had spent a lifetime being pampered by rich men, she had retained her looks, her figure and her exquisite sense of style. Her eyes were the colour of cornflowers, undimmed over the years and her carefully coiffured hair was still a rich gold.

She lived in another beautiful house not far from Eliza and was a frequent visitor. She had an adopted son, Alexander, who was eighteen and had just finished his last year at public school.

Lally looked sadly round the gracious drawing room of Upper Park where they had had so many happy times, fantastic parties when the children were around, especially before the war from which they all returned much changed, older and graver. Roger didn't return at all, and his was one of the bodies that was never found. It made it so much harder to bear, thinking of Roger with no known grave.

'I really can't believe that all this ... that we'll never see it again.' She took hold of Eliza's arm and looked at her appealingly.

'Perhaps someone we like will buy it and invite us from time to time,' Eliza said lightly, trying to manufacture a cheerful smile. 'I really think it is the best thing. Dora is convinced it is.'

'But you won't go too far away?'

'Of course not!' Eliza looked at her in surprise. 'I would never leave the area.' She tucked her arm through that of her friend and, throwing open the French windows, led her on to the broad terrace overlooking the perfectly kept lawn.

Here there were comfortable chairs and a large umbrella to shield them from the sun.

Eliza was close in age to Lally, though a little younger. She too had kept her looks but she had never been a beauty in the conventional sense, whereas Lally had. But Eliza was striking; people looked at her twice. Her appearance was slightly foreign, slightly Mediterranean, which was a throwback to Portuguese ancestors of long ago, because she was as English as could be with

English tastes and temperament. She was tall, erect, held herself well. She had flashing, tawny brown eyes. Her dark hair was only slightly streaked with grey. She led a healthy life, plenty of gardening and walking and looked ten years younger than her age.

The two women now sat looking at each other.

'You could come and live with me at Forest House,' Lally burst out. 'There is plenty of room.'

Eliza touched her hand in appreciation.

'My dear, it is sweet of you to think of it, but it would never do to have two people like us living together.'

'You could have your own quarters.'

'Are you lonely, Lally?' Eliza looked at her with concern. 'You have Alexander.'

She gazed across the lawn where a tall, strikingly goodlooking youth was taking a leisurely stroll with Dora. They had been to inspect her horses.

'You know Alexander will not be with me for long. Besides, I don't want him to be a mother's boy.'

'But he *is* a mother's boy.' Eliza laughed softly. 'He adores you.'

'Oh, don't speak of it, Eliza. After Roger ... he is all I have left.'

'But he will come to no harm! There won't be another war, please God, in our lifetimes.

He is a fine, healthy young man. One you should be proud of.'

'And I am proud of him. He has done so well in his examinations. First in his year. At one time it was only sports, but Sherborne brought out the best in him. It turned him into a scholar as well.'

'He's a perfect young man,' Eliza said fondly. 'One who has turned out very, very well. A credit to you, Lally.'

Eliza spoke no more than the truth because Alexander's beginnings had been inauspicious. He had been found on the doorstep of the Martyns' London home in the year 1910 only, according to the doctors, a few days after his birth. There was a note pinned on his shawl commending him to Lally, it seemed, in person by someone who knew her.

His mother had never been found, but Lally had lavished on him all the attention a foundling could wish of a mother, and he had rewarded her.

It was universally agreed that he was a most singular young man, and he was highly regarded by everybody.

Dora and Alexander were now slowly approaching, heads close together. Dora was wearing riding clothes, tall and upright like her mother but, unlike her mother, she was fair, her cropped hair gleaming like a golden cap in the sunlight. She and

Alexander were sharing a joke and their laughter echoed across to the two people on the terrace who looked up.

Alexander wore Oxford bags and a white shirt open at the neck, a cashmere sweater draped casually over his shoulder. He was a slightly languid, very elegant young man with black hair, a lock of which hung over his forehead, high cheekbones and deeply recessed, beautiful eyes which were so dark as to be almost black. He was tall and slightly built, but also muscular and athletic. At school he had first of all excelled at games, scholarship came later.

'Tell us what's so funny?' Lally teasingly called to Alexander as the pair arrived on the terrace and collapsed into chairs.

'Oh, you wouldn't understand, Mother.' Alexander held out a hand and clasped Lally's. 'It's a horsey joke.'

A footman appeared at the open French windows and waited to speak. 'I think some refreshment for Mr Martyn and my daughter, please, Francis...' Eliza said, looking up.

The footman interrupted her.

'Madam, the estate agent Mr Barker has called with a possible client. Is it convenient?'

Eliza immediately grew uncharacteristically flustered.

'It is certainly *not* convenient!' she cried.

66

'Tell him to go away and make an appointment, as I have guests. He can't just turn up at the door.'

'Yes, Mrs Heering.'

'Oh, Mummy, don't be so silly!' Dora chided her mother. 'You want to sell the house.'

'But he has no right to call like this.'

'We don't mind.' Dora exchanged a conspiratorial smile with Alexander. 'If it is someone very nice we want to make a good impression.'

'Well...' Eliza's cheeks glowed pink. 'Perhaps I'd better go in.'

'Would you like me to go, Mummy?'

'Why don't you come with me?' Eliza rose and put out a hand. 'I confess I am terribly nervous about all this.'

'The trouble is you don't *really* want to sell the house,' Lally murmured with a half smile. 'You can't fool me.'

Mother and daughter walked indoors, across the large parquet hall and into a parlour by the front door, which stood open. Inside two men were talking, their backs to the women. As they entered the men turned and the agent, Mr Barker, moved forward.

'I do hope you will forgive this intrusion, Mrs Heering. I know I should have telephoned, but my client is most anxious to see the house, as it has just come on to the market. He is most interested–'

'Mr Sadler and I know each other,' Eliza interrupted coldly as Bart stepped forward and held out his hand, which Eliza ignored.

In the background Dora froze, and looked anxiously at her mother.

'Why, that is delightful.' Mr Barker appeared to relax. 'I didn't realise...'

'We *are* acquaintances,' Bart said with a slight smile, lowering his hand. 'If you would rather I returned another time, Mrs Heering...'

'I would rather you didn't return at all, Mr Sadler,' Eliza said without a tremor in her voice. 'You are not a person to whom I would wish to sell my house.'

'Well!' Nonplussed for once in his life, Bart Sadler's smile vanished. 'I can't see what I have done to offend you, Mrs Heering.'

'You have offended Mrs Heering? Oh dear.' The estate agent began to look agitated.

'I said I have *not* offended her,' Bart said tersely.

'You can't altogether escape the blame for the death of my son, Mr Sadler.'

'Oh, come, come, Mrs Heering. That was years ago. Besides, I had nothing to do with it. I was in no way responsible for the death of your son.'

'Indirectly, through you he died. I think

68

you were,' Eliza said firmly

'Mummy, *please*.' Dora laid a hand on her mother's arm.

But Eliza took no notice. 'You introduced Laurence to a man who was a crook. You should have known he was a crook. He helped to bankrupt my son who then took his own life.'

'I was as sorry as anyone, Mrs Heering. I did not know Wainwright was a crook. I knew nothing about him.'

'Then you should not have introduced him. Good day to you, Mr Sadler.' Eliza turned to leave the room then, as if she had another thought, stopped and stared at the estate agent.

'Please don't attempt to bring anyone else here unless you telephone me beforehand.'

'Of course, Mrs Heering.' Mr Barker grovelled as if in the presence of royalty. 'I *do* apologise.'

'It will save us all unnecessary embarrassment. Are you coming, Dora?'

'In a minute, Mummy.'

Dora watched her mother go and then closed the door after her.

'I apologise for my mother,' she said, looking at Bart. 'It does seem rather unfair after all these years.'

'It is *most* unreasonable.' Bart's voice was petulant. 'I am most upset. Upper Park would suit me very well and we could

69

perhaps have achieved a speedy sale. Maybe you could get your mother to change her mind? She has got the wrong end of the stick. I merely *introduced* Laurence to Dick Wainwright. I lost out on the deal too, because Wainwright never paid me.'

'But you took no risk, I believe?' Dora interjected. 'It's not quite the same thing.'

'We had better say no more, Miss Yetman. Oh, I beg your pardon. I believe you married...'

'It doesn't matter.' Dora waved a hand as she opened the door and ushered the two men into the hall.

'But if you could talk to your mother...' Bart took his hat from the butler and looked pleadingly at Dora. 'Hopefully she will let bygones be bygones.'

'Not a chance,' Eliza exclaimed over the lunch table when Dora told her of Bart's parting wish. 'You think I can forget something like that?' Agitatedly she crumbled the bread on her side plate.

Alexander was leaning back in his chair watching her with an air of well-bred amusement. He had never seen her quite so angry.

'Could you explain what happened, Aunt Eliza?'

So Eliza told him about her son, Laurence, whose prosperous business was

70

ruined by a man called Dick Wainwright who commissioned him to build a factory near Dorchester and then disappeared without payment. The bank foreclosed on Laurence who, in an act of despair, shot himself in the woods beyond his house, Riversmead, leaving a widow and three children.

'There were other things too,' Eliza continued, but Lally shot her a warning glance. 'All I can say is that he was an unsavoury character and the last thing I want is for him to live here.'

'But Mother, once you're gone you're gone,' Dora said reasonably. 'You'll be miles away.'

'Sarah-Jane wouldn't like it either. She has little time for Bart, even if he is her brother. No, I will definitely not accept any offers from that man. I want to feel that a house where I have spent a great part of my life, which has memories for me, is lived in by someone I like.'

'Or approve of, Aunt,' Alexander said solemnly.

'Approve of. Exactly.'

Though pretending to be unruffled by his encounter with Eliza, Bart was furious and vented his rage on the estate agent once they had left the house.

'You've handled it very badly, Barker,' he

71

said as they made their way back to Blandford. 'You made a complete fool of me.'

'I'm extremely sorry, Mr Sadler. I had no idea ...'

'To go storming in without a phone call...'

'But you yourself suggested it, Mr Sadler.' Barker looked at him reproachfully. 'You were so anxious to see the property before anyone else.'

'Don't argue with me, Barker. You handled it badly and should have known better. I'm dispensing with the services of you and your firm, forthwith.' As they arrived at the market place Bart prepared to get out of Mr Barker's car. 'You made an absolute fool of me. I was humiliated.' He turned his back on the unfortunate man crouching behind the wheel and then jumped out on to the pavement, slamming the door behind him.

Mr Barker, perspiring freely, drove on to garage his car behind his firm's office.

All things considered, he thought Mr Sadler was not a client he would be sorry to lose. If Mrs Heering was to be believed, and she was a person of the utmost integrity, well liked and respected in the neighbourhood, there was something unsavoury in his client's past, something not quite trustworthy about him.

Still feeling angry, Sadler watched the car depart and then walked along the market place inspecting the brass plaques outside various doorways.

What was the name of Elizabeth's husband? What did he say his firm was called? He stopped before a shop front which was curtained so as to conceal what was behind the name on the glass panes picked out in large gold letters. Pearson, Wilde and Brickell immediately rang a bell. It was a double-fronted window with the doorway in the middle. Bart stopped and gazed at the names on the brass plates running down by the side of the door. Was his name Pearson? He couldn't recall. Then another name stood out: Graham E Temple LLB no less: a man of letters.

Bart swung open the door and in front of him was a desk at which sat a stenographer with a large typewriting machine in front of her on which she was busily tapping. She stopped as he came in and smiled at him.

'Can I help you, sir?'

'Is Mr Temple in?'

The girl consulted a list by her side. 'I think so.'

'Could I have a word with him?' The girl rose and came round the desk.

'Who shall I say is asking?'

'Mr Sadler. Bart Sadler.' The girl disappeared along a corridor to one side of the desk and Bart gazed round. It was an impersonal place with shelves all along one wall on which were heavy legal tomes and copies of *The Legal Gazette*. There were a couple of leather chairs, a small table with a fresh vase of flowers and a fireplace, now empty. The walls were wooden panelled and looked old. It could be that this had once been a substantial dwelling in this prosperous market town.

There was something solid and satisfying about the premises, and Bart nodded his approval to himself as a man appeared at the entrance to the corridor and stood looking at Bart, at first curiously and then his face broke into a smile of recognition.

'Mr Sadler!' He stretched out his hand and warmly shook Bart's. 'How *nice* to see you again.'

'I don't know if you remember me. We met–'

'Of *course* I remember you. It was at Sir Carson and Lady Woodville's daughter's christening ceremony. You were an old acquaintance of my wife.'

'That's it.' Bart smiled his relief.

'Would you like to come this way, Mr Sadler?' The solicitor courteously pointed to the corridor behind him and then led the way, opening a door at the end through which he ushered Bart. He showed him a chair, offered him a cigar, which Bart refused, and then sat down behind his desk and folded his hands, the smile on his cherubic face wearing an expression of one hoping for rich rewards.

'Now, how may I help you, Mr Sadler?'

'I am looking for property in which to live. I would be glad if you would act for me.'

'I would be delighted, sir.' Mr Temple drew a pad towards him with relish and after writing something on it looked up. 'Delighted. Now have you something in mind, Mr Sadler? Have you found a property, or are you just looking?'

'I have found somewhere.' Bart leaned forward. 'But I am anxious that I should not be known as the purchaser. I have personal reasons for this which I cannot reveal at the moment. Is it possible that you could act for me in this matter exercising the greatest discretion?'

Mr Temple gazed for a moment at his desk, as if perplexed.

'Well, it *is* a little unusual but I daresay we could keep your identity secret, at least until the exchange of contracts. Have you, er, have you seen the property, Mr Sadler?'

'All I can tell you is that I wish to purchase it,' Bart said firmly. 'The price is immaterial. I am quite determined to have that house.'

'And the name of the property, sir?'

'Upper Park, belonging at the moment to Mrs Julius Heering.'

Newman's, the saddlers in Wenham High

Street, had looked after the needs of the Woodville families for over a hundred years. The skills of the saddler had been passed from father to son, although there had been a blip when Albert Newman had been sent to prison for a savage attack on Ted Yewell, one of the Woodville servants, and foster father to Elizabeth Temple. When he came out of prison, Albert went to Australia and settled there and, as he was an only son, for a time it looked as though the business would be sold and pass into other hands. But a cousin, David Newman, professed an interest in the business, which was encouraged by Albert's father who, when he came to retirement, left it to him.

This had been forty years ago, and it was David's son, Clement Newman, who now ran the business, which had changed very little since the day of its foundation, occupying cramped premises opposite the market cross. The sewing was still done upstairs in a room over the shop and there was an all-pervasive smell of old leather about the place, which was pleasing to some, offensive to others.

Dora had all the leatherwork, the saddles, bridles and accoutrements for her horses looked after by Newman's. Clement Newman was also a keen horseman and follower of the hunt, and Dora liked nothing better than a chat with him or one of his apprentices when she went in to bring something for repair or to collect a job that had been done.

Today she'd ridden to the town on her horse, Bonnie, which was now tied up outside the shop by the drinking fountain which William Newman had erected in place of the village pump to mark the accession of Queen Victoria in 1837.

Dora loved visiting the small town, which had changed so little since her birth. The shops in the high street remained pretty much the same – the butcher, the greengrocer, the baker, the bank, the solitary pub, The Baker's Arms, the haberdashers once owned by Connie's guardian and now run by an equally worthy maiden lady in much the same fashion as Miss Fairchild all those years ago. It still sold very much the same goods, with little regard for changing fashions.

So much of the Woodville history was linked to Wenham and its townsfolk that Dora knew almost everyone there and they knew her.

Dora had brought in some bridles for stitching, and stood for a long time chatting to Clement Newman about the prospects for the forthcoming hunting season and then, hearing the church clock strike noon, said she must be on her way.

Mr Newman saw her to the door, said how

glad he was to see her again, how much he missed her when she was away, and how he wished she still lived here.

'So do I, Clem,' Dora said a little sadly, 'so do I.'

Clement was about to help her mount her horse but, at the last minute, Dora remembered she had to go to the bank and asked if she could leave Bonnie tied up by the fountain. Clement assured her things would be fine, but told her when she did set off to be careful and take care of the increasing amount of motorised traffic which was spoiling the character of the countryside and causing hazard all round. Then, as she waved and strode off into the town he stood there watching her before re-entering his shop and getting on with his work.

To get from one end of the town to the other involved countless stops to greet people she knew or who knew her and who asked, if they could, after every member of the family. Dora was popular. Some thought she had been a heroine in the war like her cousin Carson, who had been decorated. Dora had also been brave, a woman with no medical training, nursing hideously wounded and dying men at the front. That had taken a great amount of courage, but she had no medal to show for it.

Her brother, Laurence, had been very

popular and when he died the whole town closed out of respect and everyone who could attended his funeral, except the manager of the bank which had foreclosed, who had been run out of town.

Laurence was still remembered by many people and so was their father, Ryder, a son of the soil if ever there was one and, of course, their mother Eliza, who continued to live in Wenham, was greatly loved and respected.

So by the time Dora reached the bank it was nearly one and as she ran up the steps she cannoned into a woman, began to apologise and then stood still, as if rooted to the spot.

'May,' she said in a curious, flat tone of voice. 'May Carpenter.'

The woman she'd encountered, nearly knocked over because she was so much smaller than Dora, also remained as if struck by lightning.

'Dora!' she exclaimed.

People looked at them curiously as they either entered or left the bank, busy at lunch time, and finally Dora said:

'How *are* you, May?' Her friendly tone immediately breaking the ice. May smiled.

'I was wondering if you'd speak to me.'

'Oh, May, how could I *not* speak to you?'

Dora felt very emotional as she looked at May and put a hand on her arm. 'It really is *very* good to see you.'

'And you. I heard you live in France?' May said after a pause. 'Your husband is a Frenchman?'

'Yes. Jean Parterre. I think you must remember him.'

May nodded. 'Do you like France?'

'May, why don't we find somewhere to talk?' Dora ventured, looking around. 'Look there's a new cafe just opened behind the saddlers. It's only a tea room, but...'

'Tea would be fine,' May said, putting the heavy basket in her hand down on the floor.

'Wait a tick while I get some money.' Dora pressed her arm again. 'Don't run away, will you?'

May shook her head and watched as Dora disappeared inside the bank, her heart full of conflicting emotions.

The two women had nursed together during the war and a close friendship had sprung up. Some people might have called it an unnatural one, but to Dora and May it had been the most natural thing in the world.

They came from very different backgrounds. May, having never known her parents, grew up in an orphanage, had gone into service and then, by dint of character and sheer hard work, had trained as a nurse. In France she had been Dora's superior. Dora, being untrained and a volunteer, did exactly as she was told and came to admire the tough little northerner. In time she came to love her.

After the war, Dora persuaded May to give up nursing and stay with her at Upper Park. It was a relationship, an attraction of opposites, that perplexed Eliza because May had no love of the country pursuits which obsessed Dora, and Dora had none of the domestic skills which May was so good at.

It was with some relief that Eliza learned of May's eventual attachment to a local farmer who she married. After which, until this day, Dora had never seen or spoken to her again.

May waited nervously for Dora to come out of the bank, her emotions in a state of flux. She didn't know what to expect or what they would say, or how they would feel after the passage of seven years since May had married.

But after a very short time Dora hurried cheerfully out of the bank and grabbing May's arm led her back the way she had come, past the shops, past the saddlers to the little tea shop at the back of the town, the proprietress of which looked up with some surprise at Dora as she came in.

'Why, Miss Yetman...' she faltered. 'I'm afraid we only serve tea and buns at lunch time. There's not much call for anything else except on market day when we do pies.'

'Tea and buns would be fine,' Dora said, ushering May to a window seat. 'Won't it, May?'

'Fine,' May said, still feeling awkward, rather shabby, the antithesis of the glamorous woman in riding clothes opposite her, who looked so vibrant, so much younger than her age. 'You look very well, Dora.'

'And May ... you?' Dora looked at her anxiously.

'Well, you know.' May inspected her calloused hands with their broken nails. 'A farmer's life isn't easy. Bernard, of course, is getting on.'

Bernard was so much older than May that Dora could never understand why she married him.

'He'd like to give up,' May hurried on, 'but it's so hard these days to make a living on the farm.'

'Have you children?' Dora asked.

'A boy and a girl. There's Dorothy, five, and Simon, four.'

'Not much help on the farm?' Dora's smile was warm, sympathetic.

'And you?' May hesitated, looking at Dora. 'Do you have children?'

Dora shook her head.

'Well, you're lucky. I mean I love them, of course, but they're a handful, and with Bernard not much help...' Suddenly May's eyes filled with tears, her lips trembled, and Dora's hand instinctively shot across the table and clasped hers.

'Oh, May,' she said, 'I *have* missed you.'

Four

Abel Yetman often used to pop into The Crown in Blandford for a drink before going home. Sometimes he had clients to entertain, sometimes he went with friends or workmates and sometimes by himself.

Abel was a bright, personable young man, but his life had been marked by tragedy. When he was only eight his father, Laurence, had committed suicide and from then on Abel became the mainstay of the family. He had two younger sisters, Felicity and Martha, and his mother had turned from a sensible, contented, hard-working, loving wife and mother to a bitter and discontented woman, something of a shrew, slow to praise and quick to find blame, which made family life at Riversmead very difficult.

Eliza had done her best to help out and had become a steady support to her grandchildren. But sometimes her presence was termed interference by Sarah-Jane and resented and gradually the two women, who had once been close and united in the great love they shared for Laurence, grew apart.

Abel had left school at the age of sixteen

and immediately became apprenticed to a builder, as his father and grandfather had been before him.

This made his mother even more discontented as she had wanted him to shine academically, to be a doctor or a lawyer, a member of the professions. Building, she told him, had done neither his father nor his grandfather any good. It had killed them both and she was pretty sure it would soon kill him. However, like many children with parents who are in some way inadequate, Abel compensated for his mother's coldness. He was practical and pragmatic, remaining determinedly cheerful, robust and hard-working. By the age of twenty-one he was a master builder and he started a small business, Abel Yetman Ltd, in the same town that his father and grandfather had before him. He employed very few men in order to keep overheads low. His premises were small. His special skill was carpentry and he went in for high quality work. In a very short time he had acquired a reputation for quality, for reliability and cost competitiveness. He delivered on time. His services were in demand and he was beginning to think that now was the time seriously to consider expansion.

Abel was entertaining a new client who was modernising a house he'd just bought.

They finished discussing the details, the costs involved, the schedule for work and, well pleased, Abel was about to order another round of drinks when his client looked at his watch and said he must go. Abel had half an hour to fill before meeting another client so he ordered a pint of beer for himself and, while the barman was getting it, saw his client to the door and shook hands.

Then he walked back into the hotel and when he reached the bar he took his pint, paid for it and prepared to go and sit at the back of the bar to read the evening paper. But, just as he was doing this, he caught sight of a familiar face. Bart Sadler was sitting at the far end of the bar, also engaged in reading the evening paper. At that moment he looked up and Abel slid his beer along the bar counter and, going over, put out his hand.

'Hello, Uncle Bart.'

'Why, Abel,' Bart said with surprise. 'How nice to see you again. I hardly recognised you at the christening.'

'I remember you, just a little, from the past.'

'But you were very small at the time.'

'About eight. But you were often at our house.'

'Ah yes.' Bart sighed and put his glass to his lips. 'Yes, those days are over, I'm afraid.'

He glanced sideways at his nephew. 'Your mother doesn't like me any more. She blames me for the death of your father.' Bart grimaced. 'Which is quite wrong. In the first place I didn't know that Dick Wainwright was a rogue and secondly ... well, I thought Sophie Lamb could look after herself. She was old enough.'

'Sophie Lamb? Aunt Sophie?'

'Yes, I suppose you call her Aunt Sophie. Ah, I can see by the look on your face you don't know what I'm talking about.' Bart sighed deeply. 'Well, I stepped out with Aunt Sophie. People said I took her for a ride; but that was quite wrong. She was a mature woman and knew what she was doing. However, what with one thing and another, I thought it best to shake the dust of Wenham off my feet. I went to South America and I'm glad I did because there I made a fortune.' Bart sat back on his stool and with an expression of satisfaction lit a cigarette. 'But in recent months I think I've made the wrong decision to come home. No one seems to want me around here and I may well go away again.' Bart blew a long stream of smoke into the air. 'Which is a pity.'

'It seems unfair if you did nothing wrong. I'm sure Father would not have blamed you.'

'Your mother had to blame someone. She

couldn't blame him and Dick Wainwright had vanished. As for Sophie Woodville, as she was then, she married very well and lives, I believe, happy ever after.' Bart lifted his glass and drained the contents. 'Cheers, Abel.'

'Cheers, Uncle.' Knowing his mother's nature, Abel thought his uncle was more sinned against than sinning and decided that, despite all he had heard about him, he rather liked him.

Abel was a young man always prepared to see the good in people rather than the bad.

'I don't suppose you're free for dinner tonight, are you?' Bart looked approvingly at his nephew. 'I could do with some company.'

'Well,' Abel looked again at his watch, 'I am to see a client and then I was going home; but I could ring Mother...'

'Capital, do that,' Bart said, slapping him on the shoulder. 'The steak and oyster pie here is very good.'

'Uncle Bart is very lonely,' Abel said to his mother at breakfast the next morning having listened to her reprimands about the folly of his outing the night before.

Sarah-Jane said something like 'pah' and hurled a spoonful of porridge on to his plate.

'He thinks he has been treated badly,

misunderstood. I rather liked him.'

Sarah-Jane said nothing but her back, turned to her son as she cooked his bacon and eggs over the stove, seemed to speak volumes.

'He said he might leave the area.'

'Good riddance.'

'Or he might build a house here.' Abel's tone grew excited. 'If so he might like me to undertake it for him.'

His mother turned round, her expression waspish. When she spoke her tone was sharp.

'If you take my advice you will have nothing to do with Bart Sadler. He might be my brother, but he is no good. I would also like to know how he came about his so-called fortune.'

'He told me. In tin and copper.'

'Well.' Sarah-Jane shook her large spoon at him. '*If* you take my advice, which I'm sure you won't, being a stubborn male, you will get the money first. Bart Sadler, in my opinion, is not to be trusted.'

'Is it about Aunt Sophie too?' Abel asked slyly, and Sarah-Jane spun round again.

'Oh, he told you about *that*, did he?'

'He said he walked out with her.'

'"Walked out!"' Sarah-Jane sniffed. 'He did a lot more than "walking out". He all but ruined her reputation. If it hadn't been for Hubert Turner...' Sarah-Jane turned back to the stove and scooped the eggs and bacon on to a hot plate which she deftly conveyed to the breakfast table, 'I don't know what would have become of your aunt. But enough of this tittle-tattle.' She glanced at the clock on the wall. 'You had better eat your breakfast and hurry up, else you'll be late for work.' She then brought her cup of tea over to the table and, sitting opposite Abel, looked solemnly at him. 'Please, Abel, have nothing to do with Bart Sadler. I truly believe he's a bad penny.'

Eliza sat looking at the husband of a woman of whom she had once been very fond, her niece, Elizabeth. He fiddled rather nervously with a sheaf of legal documents which he had taken out of his briefcase, trying to put them in order, and she observed that he was sweating. She let him get on with his task, watching him, saying nothing.

It was true that Elizabeth had been very wronged in her life, and Eliza felt some responsibility for this. After her mother abandoned her, and acting, she thought, in Elizabeth's best interests, she had her brought up by trusted family servants, Beth and Ted Yewell, as their daughter.

In the light of hindsight it seemed wrong and when Elizabeth found out her true parentage she was unforgiving, but unfortunately towards Beth and Ted, who now lived in retirement on an estate cottage and whom she never saw. Nor was she inclined to forgive the Woodvilles with the exception of Carson, who had known nothing of the deception. Eliza was relieved she lived so far away from Elizabeth and now saw little of her. She was too like her mother, Agnes, for comfort.

Eliza was glad when Elizabeth married Graham Temple, a man who gave her the respectability, the lift up in the world she had always wanted. For one thing it enabled Connie to claim Pelham's Oak as her own domain and not have the prospect of having to share it with a woman she didn't particularly like or get on with. The marriage between Connie and Carson nearly didn't take place because of Elizabeth who, Carson had insisted, was owed something by the family who had wronged her. Had it not been for the death of her first husband and remarriage, Elizabeth might still be queening it over Pelham's Oak and Carson and Connie would never have got married at all.

Carson was a gentle, compassionate man with a social conscience who had also given a home to Jean Parterre, and taken Deborah in when she strayed and had let Elizabeth and her family live in his house for two years.

Finally, Graham had his papers in order and, pushing his spectacles up his nose, gave her a broad, reassuring smile. He was a reassuring sort of person, or so Eliza had thought until now. He was not particularly distinguished in appearance being rather short, stout and, although he was only just forty, almost completely bald except for a fringe of blond hair at the back and a few carefully combed wisps remaining on top. But he had moved rapidly up the ladder of promotion at Pearson, Wilde and Brickell and was now a senior partner. He also adored Elizabeth, gave her the comforts she had always wanted, and was good to her three children by Frank Sprogett, in addition to giving her two sons of their own.

No, one would never have thought Graham Temple capable of deception or duplicity, but Eliza couldn't help feeling that there was something about all this that was not quite straight. They were facing each other across the table in the small parlour off the hall where she kept the household accounts and carried out her business, and when he handed the papers across to her she took them and began to examine them carefully.

After a while she looked up. 'These papers say your firm are the purchasers.'

'My clients did insist on confidentiality, Mrs Heering. I told you that.'

Eliza pushed the contract back across the table.

'Then don't expect me to sell you my house. I have already had one person I didn't like. I'm surprised at you, Graham.'

Eliza rose as if to signify that the interview was at an end. She walked across the room and then stopped, straightening the belt of her dress. 'How are the family?'

'Very well, thank you, Mrs Heering.' Graham got up, palpably distressed. He ran his finger round his collar and swallowed. 'I can tell you the name, Mrs Heering. There is no problem in that. A Colonel and Mrs Brent. They are not at the moment in this country and wish my firm to act for them.'

'And where *are* they at this moment?' Eliza walked back slowly across the room.

'In Barbados, Mrs Heering. Colonel Brent is in sugar.'

'And they want to buy a property they haven't seen?' Eliza snorted derisively. 'Really, I can hardly believe it.'

'They had the details, Mrs Heering. I assure you they are very respectable people. They are prepared to pay the asking price with no quibble. I have every authority to complete the purchase on their account.'

'Then why are they so secretive about it?'

'I have no idea. Some clients do insist on confidentiality. It is perfectly legal.'

'I shall have to consult with my daughter,'

Eliza said, looking at the clock. 'She will be back any minute. I'll telephone you, Graham, and tell you what we decide, but I think the answer will be "no".'

'Thank you, Mrs Heering,' Graham said humbly, secretly hoping now that she would not go ahead. He had always been a man of honour and this was the first time in his professional life that he had lied to a client. It was a form of deception. He went hot and cold all over as he thought what the consequences of his folly might be. Too late to back out now. He had been seduced by a bribe from Bart that would go straight into his pocket. He gathered up the papers any old how and stuffed them into his briefcase.

Eliza saw him to the door, managing a smile as they shook hands. 'Give my love to Elizabeth. Tell her I'd like to see her.'

'Of course, Mrs Heering. Thank you,' Graham muttered, making a sideways exit, nearly falling down the stairs in his eagerness to get away.

Eliza stood thoughtfully for a long time at the top of the staircase watching him drive away.

Something not quite right. She'd say 'no', whatever Dora advised.

She then called her dogs and, putting on a coat and boots, went down to the greenhouses which had been her husband's pride and, perhaps, also his consolation in his last years. Sadness again overtook her at the thought of Julius. She wished now she had made more of an effort to understand him. In many ways he had been a kind man, particularly at the start of their marriage.

It was easy to say that, she thought as, leaving the dogs to wander round outside, she walked through the long greenhouse with its now empty benches, once so full of rare specimens, fine plants, which he had imported from the East. She emerged at the other end where the black Labradors, Tim and Murgatroyd, who were three-year-old brothers, joined her.

There were forty acres of land round Upper Park. It was like a small village with its outbuildings, stables and cottages where the grooms, gardeners and some of the indoor staff lived. It was a happy, busy place and suddenly Eliza realised how fond she was of it. She had, after all, lived there for more than a quarter of a century since her marriage to Julius in 1902. She realised that she was very attached to the place, despite its size, the number of servants needed to run it. After all she paid them well, looked after them and, as long as they stayed, she could well afford to keep them.

She never felt lost or lonely here. So far, thank God, she was in good health. And then wouldn't it be nice for Hugh and Dora to own it after her death? It would give them a sense of security, or they could do what they liked with it, sell it if they wished. Sarah-Jane and her grandchildren were well provided for after her death as she had provided for them in life.

In the autumn sunshine Eliza strolled through the lovely grounds on which Julius had lavished so much time and money; the landscaped gardens, herbaceous borders, stretches of emerald green lawn, ponds stocked with carp, huge goldfish, and fountains merrily spraying fine jets of water into the air. It was really rather nice after half a lifetime of hardship to be a wealthy woman, able to contemplate the future with equanimity. Wealth was certainly the cushion everyone said it was and, in a way, she wished she'd had it before so that she could have helped Guy, and certainly Laurence. As it was she had bought Rivers-mead back from the receiver for his family after his death.

She could certainly be happy here, and to sell, especially to people she didn't know, seemed absurd. Or even to people she knew.

She turned back towards the house and saw that Dora's car stood in the drive by the front door. Her step quickened because Dora would be sure to give her good advice. Hopefully, to agree with her now that Upper Park should be taken off the market, even if she had suggested putting it on in the first place.

Eliza ran up the stairs, removed her dusty boots and coat and walked quickly across the hall to the drawing room. Wagging their tails, the dogs padded after her. She heard voices from the other side of the doors, women's voices. For a moment Eliza paused briefly to listen before turning the handle and entering.

Dora rose and came to greet her mother, pointing to a woman who had been sitting opposite her.

'Mummy, you remember May?'

'Of course I remember May.' Eliza carefully composed her features and shook hands. 'How are you, May? How *nice* to see you again.' May took her hand, but otherwise seemed tongue-tied.

'May and I met a few weeks ago, Mummy, in the town. I think I told you.'

There was a distinctly false note in Dora's tone and Eliza felt a flicker of apprehension. After the unpleasant interview with Graham she felt this was not going to be a good day.

'Perhaps you did, dear. I can't remember.'

In fact Eliza knew that Dora had certainly not mentioned May. It was not something she was likely to forget. May had lived in the house after the war for nearly two years and Eliza had quite come to dislike her.

'Mummy...' Dora looked awkwardly at May, 'could we have a word?'

'Of course, dear.' Eliza smiled at May who avoided her eyes and studied the ground. Her feeling of apprehension growing, Eliza followed her daughter out of the room and across the hall into the small parlour where she'd had her meeting with Graham. Dora carefully shut the door behind them.

'Mummy...' Dora paused, leaning against the door.

'Something's up, isn't it?' Eliza gazed steadily into her daughter's eyes.

'Mummy, May and I are going off for a while. May hasn't been well ... she's very unhappy. Bernard is a pig. We thought he would be, didn't we, Mummy?'

'But, darling, it's no business of *yours*...' Eliza began, but Dora interrupted her.

'It *is* my business, Mummy. You know how I feel about May. Always have...' Seeing an expression of anguish in Dora's eyes, Eliza began to feel thoroughly alarmed.

'But, darling, she's married, she's got children I believe, young children. She can't just *leave* them.'

'Well, she is, just for the time being. Otherwise she thinks she'll crack up, have a breakdown. She can't cope any more.'

'But, Dora, think of the scandal it will cause!'

'Oh, to hell with the scandal, Mummy. My only concern is May. You can see how pale she is, and thin–'

'And what about Jean?' Eliza suddenly had a feeling of outrage as she looked at her daughter's troubled face. Trust May to come back and upset the applecart!

Dora collapsed into a chair. As usual she wore trousers and she flung one leg over the other.

'You might as well know, in fact I'm sure you've guessed. We don't have a marriage, Mummy, not in the way that other people do. There *is* affection, or was. It's waning a bit.' Dora studied the floor. 'That's why there are no babies, Mummy. Jean knew it when he married me.'

'No sex?' Eliza's voice was scarcely above a whisper. Dora nodded.

'We were great chums. You know how well we got on. He didn't want to go back to France without me. But it doesn't really work. I know he's tense and frustrated. I think he has a mistress; but I can't do anything about it, I'm afraid. It's the way I am.'

'Never, at any time at all?'

'Never at any time at all.' Dora rose and went over to her mother and put her arms around her. 'I'm terribly sorry, Mummy. I know you're upset. I should have told you before. You see, I thought at one time May and I would live together for ever. Then she met Bernard...'

'But why did she marry him if you felt this

way about each other?' Eliza drew away from Dora, who resumed her seat as if she was suddenly very tired and, indeed, her decision to go away with May had not been easy.

'She thought she was missing out. She thought she wanted children. Now she realises she was wrong and she wants to be with me. We're going away together. Frankly I don't know for how long at this moment in time.'

'But Dora–'

'Just until the fuss dies down, Mummy. It won't be very nice for you, but I'm sorry.'

'Don't worry about me,' Eliza said with a note of bitterness in her voice. 'I'm used to scandal. I seem to have been dogged by it most of my life.'

Then she walked to the window and stood for a long time looking out. The autumn leaves were beginning to fall. The landscape seemed suddenly bleak. Soon it would be winter.

She was going to be very lonely without Dora.

Wenham hadn't known a scandal like it since the rector's stepdaughter, Deborah Woodville, went off with an unknown workman and had a baby by him. Some memories went even further back to when Eliza Woodville eloped with Ryder Yetman in the year 1880 and they lived openly together for a long time before they were married. In between times, Sir Guy's widow, Agnes Woodville, married a man who was supposed to have a title and money and proved to have neither. He ran off with all her jewels, and some said she had never recovered from the shock as she lived a very reclusive life these days in a small house not far from the church, and seldom received visitors.

If the Woodvilles were not so prominent, so important, not so much would be made of their misdemeanours. But they *were* important, they *were* prominent, and whatever they did was magnified ten times over and became the talk not only of the town but of the neighbourhood, as far as Blandford and beyond.

Bernard Williams had lost no time in trumpeting to the world that his wife had left him with two young children and gone off with Dora Parterre who, of course, was as Woodville as they come, Eliza's daughter. Like mother like daughter some people murmured, and not only to themselves. The gossip went on furiously: at street corners, across hedges, over garden gates, at meetings of the Women's Institute and, particularly, at church gatherings which seemed to attract all the most spiteful gossips in town.

Although both women had been very popular in the community, and Eliza remained so, there was no gainsaying the fact that there was bad blood in the Woodvilles, a reckless streak.

Dora, after all, was a married woman too and should have known better. Her stock in the community fell. May was not in the same class as the Woodvilles and Dora had demeaned herself. After all, the little Williams children, Dorothy and Simon, only five and four, had been left motherless, in the care of a father who was nearly sixty and cantankerous to boot. Everyone knew that May's life with Bernard Williams could not have been easy, but she had chosen it. No one had forced her, and even if she didn't care for him one would have thought she would have cared for her children, poor mites.

In vain, Eliza tried to tell everyone that Dora had only taken May away for a holiday, as she was on the brink of a nervous breakdown, but it wouldn't do. It wasn't enough, not where children were concerned. Dora and May were unanimously condemned.

Elizabeth Temple had managed to avoid scandal in her life, even if her existence was the cause of one. By the time it was discovered who her mother and father were she was over thirty and a lot of people had guessed anyway because she looked so like her mother, with airs and graces that did not become a mere serving girl. Scandals only whipped up attention if they were fresh, and the Guy Woodville and Agnes Yetman scandal was very old indeed.

'Well I never,' Elizabeth said when Graham first broke the news. 'What a to-do that will cause.'

Often, these days, Elizabeth, to her chagrin, was the last to hear gossip because she did not live in Wenham and regarded herself far above the ordinary folk. In a way she lived in a world of her own, a fantasy world, but it suited her. She had worked so hard all her life that she enjoyed doing nothing, or as little as she could given that she was mother to five children.

'It has already caused a "to-do",' Graham said, sitting down beside his beloved who was polishing her nails, feet up on the drawing room couch. 'People can't talk of anything else.'

'I expect they can't,' Elizabeth said with a sniff, and regarded her spouse. 'I'm not surprised at Dora. I mean that marriage of hers was a sham, anyone could see that.'

'How do you mean, "a sham", my dear?' Graham asked innocently.

'Well ... she was so mannish. Always in trousers and riding boots. Didn't she remind you of a boy? She did me. And that May was living with her at her mother's home after the war. I knew there was something funny about it then. Eliza couldn't stand her.'

Graham Temple scratched his shiny bald pate in bewilderment. 'I don't really understand...'

'Oh, Graham...' Elizabeth gave him a meaningful nudge, 'grow up. Sometimes for a solicitor you strike me as very unworldly.' She looked impatiently across at the clock on the mantelpiece. 'Now, hadn't you better go and have a wash? Bart Sadler will be here in about half an hour.' Elizabeth put her nail buffer on the table beside her and looked at her husband. 'I must say I shall be *very* interested to hear what Bart has to say about the scandal.'

This was not the first visit of Bart Sadler to the Temple household since his return to Wenham, or rather to Blandford where he was still living at The Crown, a lonely and rather isolated man who was already regretting his return to his native land. He came for dinner at least once a month. Elizabeth liked him – they enjoyed a mild flirtation behind Graham's back – and her husband hoped to get lucrative business deals from him. He was good with the children and it seemed that here was a place where he could relax.

104

After dinner he sat in the drawing room facing his host and hostess, smoking a large cigar.

'So,' he said, looking at them from beneath his dark brows. 'And what do you think will happen next?'

Dora and her goings-on had been almost the sole topic of conversation at the dinner table, and the subject continued over cigars, brandy and coffee.

'I think Dora will keep out of the way for a while,' Elizabeth said, 'and then she'll come back to her mother.'

'With or without May?'

'With, I would guess. People will soon forget. They have short memories.'

'And what will happen to May's children?'

Elizabeth shrugged. 'I shouldn't think the father would let them go to their mother, ever again if you ask me.'

'I have heard that they might go to his sister who lives near Yeovil, on a farm, I think,' Graham said.

'You're *very* well informed.' Elizabeth looked at him sharply.

'Bernard is suing for divorce. My firm has been instructed.'

'Is *that* so?' Bart's eyes narrowed.

'Please don't quote me on this,' Graham said hastily, conscious that he was guilty of indiscretion.

'Poor creatures.' Bart shook his head. 'It is

always the children who suffer.'

He applied the flame of his lighter to the end of his cigar which had gone out and puffed hard for a few moments. 'Do you think Mrs Heering will be any more interested in selling her house now that her daughter has left her?'

Graham began to sweat again at the thought of his part in Bart's deception. It was something he would dearly like to have resolved. It was not illegal to keep the name of a purchaser confidential, if he or she so wished, and the legal documents were in order. But he hadn't left it at that. No, he had told Mrs Heering a lie and he wished he hadn't. If the sale went through it could cause no end of trouble.

But Bart wasn't deterred. 'I think you should press her with it now,' he said, thumping the arm of his chair. 'Now is the time to strike.'

'Do you want to *buy* Upper Park?' This was the first Elizabeth had heard this news and she looked at him with interest.

'It is my dearest wish; but she doesn't want to sell it to me.'

'Whyever not?'

'Because of Laurence. She says I killed him.'

'Maybe *I* could talk to Aunt Eliza.' Elizabeth looked at him speculatively.

'Oh, please don't, Elizabeth.' Bart held up

his hand. 'She can't stand me. She has a personal dislike. The offer so far is secret through Graham's firm.'

Graham studiously avoided Bart's eyes.

'I expect she dislikes you also on account of Sophie Turner.' Elizabeth looked at him slyly. 'I remember before the war hearing people say you put her in the family way.'

'Oh, people will say anything.' Bart sounded offhand, but Elizabeth continued to look at him, the same sly smile on her lips.

'Well?' she challenged him.

'I can't say anything.' Bart shook his head. 'I'm too much of a gentleman.'

'Then the rector's elder son *may* be yours? Everyone says he looks like you.'

'As far as I know he is the son of the Reverend Turner,' Bart said virtuously. 'But to return to the subject, Graham, now may be the time to strike. Catch her when she's vulnerable. Without her daughter Dora for support Eliza Heering will feel very lost indeed. She might even wish to move away from the scandal.'

'What will you do if she finds out it's you?' Elizabeth, as if relishing the situation, moistened her lips.

Bart leaned forward and looked at her. 'Sufficient unto the day is the evil thereof, my dear Elizabeth. Once the purchase is completed there is nothing she can do.'

107

Five

It was hard to believe it of Dora, yet at the same time, paradoxically, not hard. She was compassionate yet she was impulsive; she was also a little selfish and all her life had had a rather hard wilful streak, which had perhaps helped her to survive the rigours of her life in the war. All these attributes of her character also helped to explain her current behaviour. She was sorry for May; impulsively she decided to take her away. But she also loved May and wanted her for herself, and in this she showed little regard for May's children or the effect of her behaviour on her family.

Carson, Connie and Eliza sat round the fire in the drawing room at Pelham's Oak while a gale blew outside, reminding them that winter, if not upon them, was very near.

Eliza had just told them she had accepted the offer for Upper Park and was expecting to sign the contract soon.

'You're sure you're not being too hasty, Aunt?' Carson looked anxiously over at her while Connie sat back in her chair, her expression thoughtful. So far she had taken little part in the conversation.

'Well,' Eliza said, 'it was what Dora and Hugh advised me to do. Now Dora has gone off and I don't know when I'll see her again. I don't even know where she is at the present time.'

'But she has surely telephoned you?'

'Oh yes. She telephones, but they're touring. I think they're looking for property.'

'Then it does sound rather final.' Now it was Carson's turn to look thoughtful.

'Oh, it's final. She's determined, but you see, Carson, if Dora does come back I don't want May here too. This is a factor in making me decide to sell.' Eliza firmly pursed her lips. 'I don't like May. I didn't like her when she stayed with us before. She behaved as though she owned the place. She was rude to the servants and I can't stand that sort of thing.' Eliza shook her head. 'No, May and I didn't get on. Dora is my daughter and I love her and there will always be a home for her but,' she shook her head several times, '*not* May Williams.'

'And what does Jean say about all this?' Connie stopped to poke the fire.

'I haven't asked and he hasn't been in touch with me.'

'But he knows?'

'I'm not sure.' Eliza looked across at Carson. 'Did *you* know it wasn't a proper marriage, Carson?'

109

Carson shook his head. 'I had no idea. Neither Jean nor Dora would talk to me about that kind of thing. But I am a little surprised at Jean because I know him to be a very physical man. He likes women.'

'But Dora didn't seem to like men. She never had a boyfriend. That's why I was so relieved when she unexpectedly married Jean. Oh dear...' Eliza, as if on the verge of tears, produced a handkerchief from the pocket of her cardigan, and screwed it into a tight ball in her hand. 'I so hoped there'd be ... grandchildren, and that she'd be ... happy.'

'But she *is* happy, Aunt Eliza.' Connie moved over to Eliza and put a comforting arm round her shoulders. 'If she is happy with May then she's happy. We can't live other people's lives for them.'

'I think it's a good thing to get away.' Carson rose and, taking his pipe off the mantelpiece, began to fill it from a tobacco jar on a side table. 'I think you *should* move, Aunt Eliza. Begin a new life. Anyway you weren't always terribly happy at Upper Park, were you?'

Eliza shook her head. 'No, there were some terrible times.'

'Well, there you are.' Carson pressed the tobacco firmly into the bowl of his pipe and, taking a spill from the hearth, began to light it. After a few puffs he removed it from his mouth and stood on the hearthrug, one hand behind his back.

'I think you should come back to Pelham's Oak.'

'Pelham's Oak!' Eliza looked at him in astonishment.

'For a while. Put your furniture in storage and spend a few months here, thinking. Don't you agree, Connie?'

Connie loved her husband and she loved Eliza, but ... this was another of Carson's impulsive acts with the best intentions, but who knew where it would end? Would she like it if Aunt Eliza made it a long stay? Emphatically no, she wouldn't.

But Eliza was already reading her thoughts. She leaned over and touched Connie's arm.

'Don't worry, darling Connie. I won't.'

'Oh, but Aunt, I didn't mean...' Abashed, Connie looked across at Carson.

'No, I know what you mean. This is your home. People have a habit of dumping themselves on Carson, and I don't want to be one of them. I don't know when the Brents will want to move in. I mean, if they are abroad they may not come back for some time. Anyway, I can rent somewhere if I can't find a suitable house immediately, or stay in a hotel. I may go abroad for a while, take a cruise ... who knows?' Eliza's eyes momentarily gleamed with an almost girlish

111

sense of anticipation. 'I might start to live again. Nothing is holding me back.'

But the Brents apparently *did* want to move in, and in some hurry. The contract was signed shortly before Christmas and Eliza was asked if she could vacate by the beginning of February. Really, there was so much to do, and she had been so busy, that she hadn't had a chance to think about what she was going to do or where she was going to go. The staff were all informed and were extremely sad. However, it was possible, she was told, that the Brents would want to keep them on. Nothing would be known until the new owners arrived, possibly in the middle of January.

In the end, Eliza and Hugh decided that she should have a break and they went to Tangiers for Christmas, travelling by train to Marseilles and crossing the Med by sea. In all they were away three weeks and it was with some sense of relief, and with renewed energy, that Eliza returned to Upper Park in mid January and began to make final preparations for the move. Precious carpets were rolled up, paintings taken down and items of valuable antique furniture carefully prepared for storage. At each stage a different part of her life with Julius was remembered, sometimes with pleasure, sometimes pain. In addition to Carson's invitation, reinforced by Connie, Sarah-Jane had invited her to stay at Riversmead. Sophie Turner at the Rectory, even Elizabeth, had extended an invitation.

No one wanted to see her without a home to go to. It was gratifying to know how much the family cared, how important her well-being seemed to them.

But in the end Eliza accepted Lally's invitation to stay at Forest House, the house that many years before Ryder had built for Julius and where, as a result of an accident, he had died. Julius had sold the house to Prosper and Lally Martyn before he married Eliza, never having wanted to live there himself.

For a long time Eliza had been unable to visit Forest House, but gradually, over the years, although she didn't love Ryder any the less, the memory of that dreadful day in 1895 when they brought his body back to Riversmead faded and, after the war, but more particularly after Prosper's death, she laid the ghost and began to visit Lally quite often.

It was true that it was a very big house, a very beautiful one, and the fact that it had been built by Ryder was a memorial to him rather than a tomb.

One day towards the end of January, with everything at Upper Park packed in cases or wrapped in sheets and ready to be moved to a warehouse, she wandered round the rooms that Lally had set aside for her: a bedroom with bathroom, a spacious sitting room, and another room for anyone she wished to have stay, Hugh or Dora, and thought how fortunate she was. Lally had even had the rooms redecorated for her, had gone out of her way to make her welcome and comfortable, had filled them with fresh flowers and, as Eliza flung open one of the bedroom windows and leaned out, it was almost as though she caught a breath of spring. There were snowdrops at the base of the giant Sequoia on the edge of the lawn, and above it the sky was cerulean blue, almost as it had been in Tangiers.

Downstairs, Lally, an anxious expression on her face, was waiting to greet her.

'Is everything all right?'

Eliza almost fell into Lally's outstretched arms and hugged her for a few moments, tears glistening in her eyes. 'Oh, Lally, you're so good to me...'

'But I love you, Eliza.' Lally stood back and, taking a dainty handkerchief from her sleeve, dabbed at Eliza's eyes. 'And I want you to feel that this is your home and you are welcome here for as long as you like. You can come and go as freely as you wish.'

Eliza drove back to Upper Park feeling more optimistic and peaceful than she had been for weeks, maybe even months, since the suggestion to sell had first come up.

She had enjoyed her time in Tangiers, and Hugh's suggestion that they should go abroad a couple of times a year was an appealing one. She had a large fortune and could do what she liked and there was no need to shackle herself with a huge house. It would be nice to spend some of her wealth on foreign travel. She would eventually buy something that could be easily maintained by a couple of maids and a cook, and a small garden would be a boon.

Hugh had suggested she could also buy a flat in London, but the capital was almost as foreign to her as Tangiers. Even as the wife of Julius Heering, prosperous businessman, she had only ever been there half a dozen times in her life.

No, a small house in the country and two or three visits abroad with Hugh would be wonderful, especially as they were closer now than they had ever been. Of her three children, Hugh, the scholar, the classicist, reluctant war hero, had always been the most elusive. He was kind and considerate to his mother and, with his vast knowledge, an erudite companion on tours abroad. It would also enable her to try and get to know her enigmatic son better.

Eliza reached the gates of Upper Park and was surprised to find them open. There was a car parked outside the portico and this too surprised her because in the state the house was in she was not expecting visitors. She drove round to the garages at the back of the house and one of the servants appeared from the kitchen door and ran to assist her.

'Visitors, Grieves?' she asked the butler.

'The gentleman says he is the new owner, madam.'

'Oh!' Immediately Eliza looked flustered. 'Colonel Brent?'

'He didn't give his name, madam.' The butler's expression remained impassive.

'Did you let him in?'

'No, madam. I said you were not at home so he asked if he could take a stroll in the grounds.' Grieves appeared embarrassed. 'I didn't quite know what to say as he is the new owner, madam. I didn't wish to appear rude.'

'I quite understand your dilemma,' Eliza replied after a moment's thought. 'All the same, Colonel Brent is not due to take possession until February the first.'

Eliza felt irritated, angry, but she could hardly ignore the new owner however she might wish to. Besides, there was a sense of curiosity about what, after all this secrecy, he would be like. He might after all be very charming, an asset to the neighbourhood.

'Which way did he go?' she asked the butler who pointed in the direction of the greenhouses.

116

'I told him I was not expecting you back until the afternoon, Mrs Heering. He said he would be gone by then.'

Asking Grieves to garage the car Eliza bound her scarf more tightly around her neck against the keen wind and walked in the direction of Julius's beloved greenhouses. She found herself hoping that the new owners were keen gardeners. It was not her favourite hobby and she felt in a way that, although well tended by the gardeners, they had somehow missed the loving personal care of a true devotee.

She approached the first of the three long greenhouses and saw through the windows the figure of a man wearing a hat and coat, hands in his pockets, shoulders hunched, staring ahead of him, as if deep in thought.

He seemed lost in a reverie and didn't hear her as she quietly approached.

'Colonel Brent?' She composed her features into a pleasant smile of welcome but, as the man slowly turned to face her, Eliza's hand flew to her mouth.

'Bart Sadler!' she cried, the smile replaced by an expression of outrage.

'Mrs Heering,' Bart acknowledged with a chilly smile.

'I think there's some mistake. I was told the new owner was here.'

'*I am* the new owner, Mrs Heering.' He appeared to relish the information.

117

'I was informed a Colonel and Mrs Brent were the new owners.'

'That was the mistake, *I* am the new owner,' Bart said firmly. His smile had now vanished.

'Then this has been an outrageous deception.'

'Well, it is a house I very much wanted and you wouldn't sell it to me. I had no option but to deceive you.'

'Then you instructed Graham Temple in this criminal act?'

'It is not criminal, Mrs Heering, to purchase a property through one's solicitors acting confidentially.'

Eliza drew herself up until she almost stood on tiptoe.

'We shall see about that. Meanwhile, I'm ordering you off this property. You have no business here.'

'Until February first,' Bart said, suddenly bowing his head. 'I'm sorry I was trespassing but I happened to see the car leave your gates as I was passing and I was tempted to go in and inspect the property I have just bought.'

'I will not allow you to buy this property, Mr Sadler.'

'It is bought, Mrs Heering. Signed, sealed and paid for. The solicitors will transfer the money to your bank the day I take possession. That is, I believe, in slightly over a week's time.'

'If I were a man I'd knock you down.' Waves of cold fury sweeping over her, Eliza bunched her fists inside her pockets.

'Then I'm lucky you're not, though I think I could defend myself.' As Bart looked at her his expression changed, and he held out his arms appealingly towards her.

'Mrs Heering ... Eliza. Why do we have to fight? Why do you have to fight *me*? I am an innocent man. I am not the rogue you think I am. Believe me, I regret the day I introduced Laurence to Dick Wainwright. But it was not a malicious deed. I only wished to help him. It hardly amounts to a killing, does it, Mrs Heering? I only wish now to retire quietly in the countryside where I was born. I am very interested in horticulture and have some fine specimens on order from South America. I believe your late husband was a botanist too. I love this house.' He swept an arm expansively towards it. 'I wish to restore it, to enhance its beauty. Upper Park, I assure you, will be quite safe with me.'

'We shall see about that. I am quite unmoved by your words, Bart Sadler. I think you are a rogue and a cheat as your behaviour in buying or trying to buy, this house proves. I am glad I discovered your deception in time. I shall fight you. I shall not take a penny from you. I am going, as a

119

matter of fact, this very moment to consult my solicitors.'

Whereupon Eliza turned on her heel and walked swiftly across to the house.

Dora pondered over the letter in her hand for a long time and then laid it on her lap and looked out of the window at the tree-covered escarpment that led to the rock formation known as Simon's Seat overlooking Wharfedale. In the garden in front of her window daffodils were in bloom and newborn lambs tumbled about in the adjoining fields.

Yorkshire was May's home county and, after travelling through the country in a leisurely manner, they had arrived at Skipton, where they stayed for some weeks in a hotel, going out each day to explore the celebrated Yorkshire Dales.

One day they came across a house on a hill near Appletreewick overlooking the Wharfe, and, swinging on the gate, was a TO LET sign. To one side of the house was woodland. To the other a steep, tree-covered hill. In front the river meandered its way through the valley, past Barden Tower, on its way to join the River Ouse at Selby.

The following day they arranged to rent the house, Dora paying the first three months' rent and a deposit, and they moved in straight away.

It was spacious, comfortably furnished with spectacular views. The garden was a little neglected but May soon had it in shape. She was very domesticated and they employed a maid and a cook to look after them, and a man to help in the garden. All staff lived out. May saw to all the household tasks, arranged the menus with cook and did most of the shopping or ordering by telephone.

There were already stables and Dora bought a horse and joined the local hunt although it was the end of the season. It was a comfortable life and should have been carefree. But it was hard for either women to shed the worries of the past: May fretted about her children, and Dora about her mother's homelessness and about Jean.

Dora looked up as May came in and held up the letter.

'Mother has dropped her case against Bart Sadler. The lawyers say there is no possibility she can win. He's moved into Upper Park.'

'I'm sorry.' May flopped down in the chair opposite Dora.

'It has been an awful time for Mummy.'

'It has.' May nodded sympathetically.

'I feel I should have been with her, May.'

May rose from her chair and, crossing to Dora, put her arm round her neck, bent to kiss her cheek.

'Dearest, there was not much you could do. She seems to be very happy with Lally.'

'I think she is, and comfortable. And it was not as though the house meant all that much to her. I mean the last years of her life with Julius were not very happy, at least I didn't think so. Not like Riversmead where she was so happy with Daddy. Anyway, she has given up, paid the legal bills and decided to be forward-looking. But her letter sounds sad.'

She put an arm round May's waist. 'May, I do think I should go over and see Jean. I could stop on the way and see Mummy.'

'But why must you see Jean?' May looked at her aghast.

'Because he *is* still my husband. I'm going to ask for a divorce, or an annulment as we never slept together. I'm going to move out all my stuff. We've got to decide something, May. It can't be left in a state of suspension.'

May left Dora's side and, going over to the window, stood looking out at the view, at the river below them in the valley, the lambs skipping in the field, the myriads of tiny little leaves appearing on the trees which seemed to cloak the landscape in a soft green haze. Life burgeoning all round, and she and Dora together. It should have been idyllic.

But she didn't like the thought of Dora returning to Jean. It seemed like a threat.

'We're so *happy* here!' she burst out. 'I might never see you again.'

'Don't be absurd,' Dora said robustly. 'I shall only be gone for a couple of weeks.'

'What makes you think he will let you go so easily?' May swung round to face her.

'Darling, he can't *keep* me. He can't *force* me to stay.'

'But he loves you. You told me.'

'I think "loved" in the past tense. I can't believe he really loves me in the way he used to. I think he is really angry with me now, if his letters are anything to go by.'

May ran over and, kneeling by Dora's side, took her hand.

'Then don't go,' she pleaded. 'He may harm you.'

'*Harm* me?' Dora looked at May with astonishment. 'Jean is the gentlest of people. He would *never* harm me. I think he's incapable of harming anyone...' She put out a hand and stroked May's brow.

How she adored her, little May, so small and fragile, so much in need of her protection. Yet in the war it had been May who was strong. May who gave orders and Dora who took them.

She clasped her hand.

'Don't distress yourself, dearest. I'll soon be back. Would you like to live here permanently? Shall we try to buy this house? Shall we ask the agents if the owner will sell? I'm sure Mummy would give me the money.'

May nodded her head slowly. 'Then perhaps one day the children can come and stay. I miss them, you know.'

'Of course you miss them, I know that.' Looking into her eyes Dora continued stroking her forehead as if trying unsuccessfully to smooth out the wrinkles that lined it. 'You'd be a very unnatural mother if you didn't.'

'If Bernard will let them.' Sadly, fearfully, May looked past Dora and out of the window again.

She didn't add, 'and if the children want to come.'

Because what sort of mother was she, really, to have abandoned them?

Jean Parterre wandered slowly along the vines that lined the hillside as far as the eye could see.

All his. His *pinot noirs,* the finest grapes for the making of the finest champagne, lovingly tended by his workers and by him because, since Dora went away, the time had hung heavily on his hands.

He knew now that she wasn't coming back. She had gone off with May Williams whom she really loved. May had won and he had lost. The vines too were in leaf and soon, warmed by the summer sun, the grapes would ripen and grow plump until the *vendage* in the autumn when they would be put into huge panniers and sold to the *negociants* in Rheims and Epernay. So excellent was his produce that they always fetched the best prices.

Jean turned to study the terrain around him, the River Marne snaking below. Those banks which had trembled to the sound of so many terrible battles in the war were now replanted and replenished. But scattered throughout the countryside were the many cemeteries that were the last resting places of the war dead, and now and again a rotting corpse was dug up from the newly replanted fields and, occasionally, someone was killed by an unexploded shell.

The war had deeply scarred Jean. Luckily his estates had hardly been touched. Even some of his vineyards remained intact. He had, however, lost his family. His wife had gone off with another man and taken his children.

He had felt like a lost soul without roots and had travelled to England where Carson took him in and gave him a temporary home, while, useful with his hands, he had helped restore Pelham's Oak which had been badly in need of repair.

There he had met Dora Yetman and had fallen in love with her. They had gone off together to look for Deborah, Dora's young cousin who had eloped with a workman. They hadn't found Debbie but they had found each other. Jean knew that Dora loved him then, but not yet in the way he loved her.

He had thought in time that would come, with love and gentleness on his part, hopefully with willingness to learn on hers. However, he was wrong. He was loving and gentle, but Dora did not want to learn.

If, as she told him, she was a virgin when they married, then she was one still. In time desire turned to frustration and sometimes rage, though he tried not to show it. But slowly their relationship changed. She began going home to her mother more frequently, staying longer. They found it hard to communicate when they were together, and there were long painful silences, a lack of rapport that could sometimes last for weeks. He had a woman in Paris but she was not Dora. He wanted Dora. He wanted her back, but now Dora had been away for nearly nine months. She was living in Yorkshire with May. She would not return.

The only comfort he had were his vines.

In the late afternoon, following his inspection and a good lunch at a restaurant in Epernay, Jean returned to his house and the first thing he saw was Dora's tourer outside the front door. It was early spring but it was a warm day and the earth seemed to shimmer in the heat.

He drew up beside Dora's car, jumped out, slammed the door and ran into the house.

'Dora!' he shouted. 'Dora, you're back!"

He waited for her answer. There was none. The house seemed peculiarly deserted, even more than when he'd left it than now when he knew someone was there.

He employed no indoor staff now that Dora had gone. A woman came part time to clean, do the washing and sometimes cook him meals. Otherwise he led a withdrawn bachelor-like existence.

He stood outside the main salon, the door of which was ajar. He was sure he'd closed it when he'd left just after eight. Madam Jules might have left it open after doing a bit of cleaning, some washing. She often left at lunch time.

He pushed the door open and there she was: Dora, perched on the window-sill, a cigarette in one hand, the other tucked under her arm: a meditative pose, languid and elegant. Her expression was inviting, almost coquettish, perhaps a little bit apprehensive. Dora was very good at concealing her feelings. She wore trousers and a tailored jacket, red shirt open at the neck. Jean thought she looked wonderful.

'Dora,' he murmured. Her smile, he

thought, was provocative. Quietly he shut the door, still wondering if he was seeing a vision, a figment of his intense imagination that so often had summoned up the memory of her physical presence.

He advanced towards her, still murmuring: 'Dora.'

'I see I've given you a shock, Jean.' She jumped up stubbing out her cigarette, and he came up to her and gently kissed her cheek, briefly touching her arm.

'It's *very* good to see you,' he said. 'I've missed you so much.'

'Jean...' She paused, looking into his eyes. 'I haven't come back for long.'

'Oh!' He turned and, sinking into one of the deep leather armchairs, lit a cigarette, blew out the match and put it in an ashtray. His hands were trembling.

'Jean,' she went on, coming to sit by his side. 'It's very difficult to say this ... but I've come to get my things.'

'You're leaving for *good*?'

She nodded. She thought she saw tears in his eyes and turned her head away. He was so very vulnerable, so sweet, so patient. She'd forgotten just what a good sort he was. In many ways he was a victim of her selfishness, and suddenly she felt ashamed.

It was possible to think that she was spoiling two lives, Jean's and May's, people she had bent to her will.

'Stay just a few days?' Jean implored her. 'You don't know what it's like here without you.'

'Well, it will take me a few days to get everything together,' she said prosaically, suddenly feeling tired. This interview wasn't going the way she expected; being away from Jean so long seemed to have made a difference. Suddenly it was as it had been between them when the times were good, when they'd been like buddies, comrades-in-arms.

For several days it was as though she'd never been away. They seemed to grow into their old routine effortlessly. The weather was good, the Champagne countryside at its glorious best, the fruit burgeoning on the vines. She accompanied him on his tours of inspection, waited for him while he talked to the *negociants,* did some shopping in Rheims, went to look at horses as though she had never been away.

They'd lunch or dine somewhere nice. She took a critical look at the house, noting what repairs were needed. It really was looking shabby, like an old bachelor establishment. Jean needed a woman around, even a woman like her.

She put off getting her things together. May telephoned several times and she told her what a lot she had to do. She'd turn round and see Jean gazing at her with that sad, wistful expression. At night she lay for a long time wakeful, looking out at the stars through the open window.

After a couple of weeks like this Dora knew that if she didn't go away now she never would. Over dinner one night she told him.

'I must go, Jean. It's not fair to May.' She put a hand over his and saw there again in his eyes traces of tears.

'I love you, Dora.'

'I know.' She bent her head. 'And I love you. But I love May too, and she is very vulnerable. Through me she left her family. I don't really think I thought it through, but at the time it seemed the right thing to do. The only thing to do. I can't leave her in Yorkshire. Oh, Jean.' Dora bowed her head over his hand, on the verge of tears herself.

But finally everything was packed into cases, the wardrobes and drawers cleared. Still she didn't seem to want to go. She knew she was divided, torn in half between her love for May and her renewed love for the man she'd married five years before. The time they had spent together was reminiscent of those days when they'd gone after Debbie, the awareness of a coming together, an understanding that slowly burgeoned into love.

The night before her departure they dined

at home, a meal prepared for them by Madam Jules: *escargots*, a casserole made with plenty of rough red wine and a bottle of good champagne.

'I came to ask you for a divorce,' Dora said after a long silence that had followed the end of the meal. 'But I can't.'

'I don't mind sharing you with May as long as you come back.'

'Six months with May, six months with you?' Dora gave a wry grimace. 'It seems odd, to say the least. I don't think she'd wear it. But ...' Dora threw down her napkin and, rising from the table, held out her hand. 'I suppose there *are* odder arrangements.'

'If I knew you were coming back,' there was a catch in Jean's throat as he spoke, 'I could survive. Otherwise ... I think I will die.'

She thought he'd said something like that to her before. Maybe he meant it. Maybe it was true and he would die of a broken heart. Dora stooped to kiss him lightly on the forehead and then, her own heart charged with emotion, fled the room.

Upstairs her bedroom looked very bare. All the luggage had been taken downstairs to the hall. She knew now that she would leave some behind. She wanted an excuse to come back. She loved this house, she loved the Champagne area of France and, well, she loved Jean. In many ways she felt closer to him than she ever had before.

She took ages washing, doing her teeth, running a comb through her hair. She stood for a long time in front of the window before climbing into bed. In three days she'd be in Yorkshire with May. Then, as usual, she lay looking out at the stars.

There was a slight click and the door gently swung open. She looked sideways and in the light of the moon she saw Jean at the door.

He stood gazing at her and stretched out a hand. He crept towards her bed and slowly turned back the sheets and got in beside her. She didn't try and stop him. For a moment they lay together and then her hand sought his.

'Like that night in the Lakes?' she said. 'Remember?' She was referring to the time they'd taken refuge at an inn in a snowstorm and they had slept together to keep out the cold, but nothing else had happened.

'I remember,' Jean said.

Only, tonight it was different.

Six

Sarah-Jane Yetman sat upright in her chair, stiff as a ramrod, her eyes with their hard, unforgiving expression bearing down on her brother. Her lips were pursed and her hands were clenched tightly together in her lap. Her whole body bristled in an attitude of profound disapproval.

'Sarah-Jane,' Bart's tone was firm but conciliatory, 'it's not a bit of use carrying on in this way. I have been back over a year and I mean to stay in the neighbourhood of Wenham. I have bought a fine house. Your son is engaged on work for me and is doing very well. I want to be friends with you. All the other members of my family accept me but you.'

'There are good reasons,' Sarah said.

'The only reason that I know is because I introduced your husband to Dick Wainwright with, I hoped at the time, the possibility of gain for us both. I did not kill Laurence. He killed himself. It is very unfair of you, of everyone in this town, to blame me for it.'

'There was also the matter of Sophie Woodville,' Sarah-Jane said with a sniff.

'That was nothing to do with anyone but the lady in question and myself.'

'You brought a scandal on the neighbourhood.'

'It was not a scandal. There is no harm in walking out with a woman of age who is in her right mind.'

'It was said that you promised her marriage, and for that she...'

It was true that it was Laurence Yetman who had caught him and Sophie Woodville, then a widow, *in flagrante delicto*. There was no denying that he had, perhaps, treated Sophie less well than he should.

'Yes, she went to bed with me. It was her own decision. But that woman was obsessed with a sense of sin. She was hysterical. When I saw what she was really like I knew I could never have married her, and I'm glad I didn't. Anyway, she is happy as the rector's wife. Why rake over old sins?'

'They *say* that the elder boy is yours.'

'Well, they have no proof, have they?'

'Except that he has your looks *and* a temperament to go with it. Unruly, untamed.'

'I thought him a good-looking youth,' Bart said with an air of smugness, 'but that is as far as my interest in him goes. I have no other. I think I have behaved well, and others have behaved badly.'

'Huh!' Sarah-Jane snorted. '*Then* when

134

you came back you had to diddle Eliza Heering out of her home.'

'It was *not* a diddle.'

'But it was not honest.'

'It *was* honest.' Bart, eyes flashing, met her gaze. '*She* was not honest. I had the money, why should she not sell me her house? Can you answer me that?'

'It was her right to sell it to whom she wanted.'

'She was prejudiced against me. She had no objection to selling it, apparently, to someone she had never seen.'

'Well, Bart.' Sarah-Jane rose from her chair and walked to the window which overlooked the river and the wood beyond, where Laurence had shot himself that fateful November day in 1912, the memory of which still haunted her on a bad day, and there were many of those. She turned to look at him. 'Well, Bart Sadler, I see you have an answer for everything. Nothing fazes you, does it?'

'I only want to be given a chance, Sarah-Jane,' he pleaded. 'I want to be accepted by you and your family. You are *my* family. I want to belong.' He got up and going towards her put out his arms. 'Believe me I am not the man I was. If I was a little ruthless, a little selfish, that has all gone. I have been through many painful years. I have suffered and I have learned. Through

135

good fortune and listening to wise advice about my investments I made a fortune. I love this part of Dorset. I am a Dorset man born and bred. I want to die here and be buried here but, hopefully,' his face broke into a smile, 'not yet. I would like to marry and raise a family. I don't think I am too old.'

'Bart Sadler!' Sarah-Jane exclaimed. 'You are a man of fifty-three. *Marry* at your age?'

'It is not too old for a man to marry. Maybe I won't find the right woman but, whatever, I intend to make Upper Park into a fine residence, to entertain there and I would like you to be there, Sarah-Jane, among my guests.'

Sarah-Jane saw her brother to the door. There seemed little more to say. She was mollified by his approach, his manner, his desire to renew the bonds of family. Precious bonds. They stood at the entrance to the house facing each other. Finally Sarah-Jane put out her hand, her expression gentler.

'Thank you for coming to see me, Bart. It took courage for I have not treated you very well. I will think about what you've said. I will think very carefully indeed.'

'Thank *you*, Sarah-Jane.' There was an unusual note of humility in Bart's voice.

Then he took her hand and pressed it.

Bart walked down to the bottom of the garden and stood for a while looking at the river, aware that his sister's eyes were still on him. Then he turned back to look at the house and saw she was still at the top of the steps. He raised his hand and waved and she waved back. Then she went back inside and shut the door.

Bart stood for a while longer, hands in his pockets and, as the day was clement, the sun every now and then peeping from behind the clouds, he decided to walk along the river bank before strolling back to the market place where he'd left his car, being unsure of his welcome at Riversmead.

But on the whole he thought the meeting with his sister had gone well. He was glad that he had gone, as he had detected a softening in her attitude. And why not? She knew he was not really responsible for Laurence's death, except in the most indirect way. It was rather like selling a man a car which subsequently ran him over. It was not the fault of the seller. It was as remote as that. Laurence was of age, a man of experience, and knew he was taking a risk.

As for Sophie Woodville, he looked towards the rectory which stood at the top of the meadow in front of him.

It was true he had treated her ungallantly towards the end when her religious scruples

137

got the better of her and made her prone to hysterical outbursts. Besides, a marriage between them would never have done. She was far too stern and pious and if he had stayed in these parts, married to Sophie Woodville, he would never have gone abroad and made his fortune. He doubted whether he would have been faithful to her either.

At the bottom of the field, woodland lined the water's edge and he carried along the path that led between the trees until he reached an ancient boathouse and broken jetty, now never used. There was even the hull of a rowing boat half in and half out of the water, and sitting on the end of the jetty was a woman who appeared unaware of his presence and remained where she was, her head bent, staring into the water. She had both hands on the jetty and seemed lost in reverie.

He was about to pass on as quietly as he had come when, with a start, she turned and stared at him.

'I beg your pardon,' he said, pausing. 'Did I give you a fright?'

He thought for a moment she was not going to reply, but her manner made him curious and going up to her he lowered himself down to sit beside her, his feet too dangling over the water.

'I think you must be one of the Woodville

138

girls, if I am not mistaken,' he said with a smile. 'My name is Bart Sadler, Sarah-Jane's brother.'

'Oh!' the young woman replied sharply, looking at him.

'I see my name means something to you?' He gave a wry smile.

'Well, I have heard of Bart Sadler,' she admitted.

'Nothing good, I expect?'

She didn't reply but began staring moodily again into the water. She was fair-skinned with thick golden hair which was tied in a bunch and hung untidily down her back, little tendrils clinging to her brow. Her eyes were the colour of aquamarine and her firm, beautifully moulded mouth had a downward turn which made her look rather discontented, not momentarily, but as though it was her usual expression. She gave the impression of someone who smiled little.

She was, however, extraordinarily pretty and from what he could see of her figure Bart deduced that she was tall and slim with fine long legs dangling beside his own, and with a well-developed bosom underneath her simple pinafore dress which was buttoned up to the neck. She wore woollen stockings and laced boots and, altogether, could have stepped from a painting of a young woman of half a century before, somehow old-fashioned and out of place.

Or maybe with the rectory just above her she was not out of place at all.

'I see you don't remember me, Debbie. Is it Debbie?'

She nodded and turned to examine him, screwing up her eyes.

'Yes, I think I *do* remember you.'

'I used to come and play with you at Pelham's Oak.'

'Yes, I remember now.' Debbie suddenly lost her expression of discontent and grew more animated. 'You used to come and play in the nursery.'

'And sometimes take you out with your sister in my pony and trap.'

'Have you come to see my mother?' Deborah asked. 'I think you used to be friendly with her too.'

'I was a great *admirer* of your mother,' Bart said cautiously, 'but who would not be? How is she, by the way?'

'She's very well. Very busy, of course, about the parish.'

'And you? Still unmarried? I can't believe it.'

Bart noticed a blush suffuse Deborah's cheeks and she avoided his eyes. 'No young man?' he went on. 'I find that impossible. What is the matter with all the men around here?'

She still didn't reply, her eyes remaining

140

fixed on the swirling water below her.

'Ah, I mustn't ask impertinent questions.' Bart rose as if to resume his walk. 'And how is your sister, Ruth, if I recall?'

'She's a teacher, she's very well, thank you.'

Bart stood gazing down at her.

'And do you *do* anything?' Deborah shook her head and seemed again intent on studying the flow of the water.

'Well, I hope I see you again, Deborah,' Bart said conversationally. 'Do give my best to your mother and stepfather, and sister too of course.'

Deborah didn't reply, looking as though she had forgotten he was there, and Bart, instead of resuming his walk, retraced his steps the way he had come.

In for a penny in for a pound, Bart thought, as he walked slowly around the outside of the house whose purchase was now complete. It was surrounded by scaffolding, up and down which workmen of various kinds were busily scampering. The warm Dorset brick of which the house was built was being repointed, the roof was being repaired, and the white Chilmark stone, with which it was faced, was being washed and cleaned. The gargoyles, lions rampant and other heraldic figures adorning the four corners of the square house were under-

141

going repair and restoration.

In the extensive gardens and shrubbery more men were at work digging, hoeing, planting, and the greenhouses, the late Julius Heering's pride and joy, were being reglazed and repaired, with a complex system of irrigation and heating installed. It would take six months, for the inside of the house too was undergoing complete refurbishment, the wooden panels revarnished, repaired and restored, the ancient parquet flooring scoured and re-waxed and all the paintwork renewed, while the ornate plasterwork on the ceilings – lozenges, quatrefoils, fleur de lys – were re-gilded. The huge crystal chandeliers in the hall and reception rooms were being cleaned and polished until they shone like diamonds.

Yes, it was all costing a fortune; but then he had a fortune. He, Bart Sadler, son of a tenant farmer, who had hewed stone for a living, had gone to South America a relatively poor man and returned a rich one. The money honestly made, as far as excessive profits in business transactions are ever honestly come by.

He had gone to America in 1912, the year his affair with Sophie floundered when he realised that he didn't love her, didn't want to marry her, that all he had intended was the seduction of a virtuous woman. Excessively virtuous and exceedingly prim.

Yet how she had burned! What ardour she had shown. The memory of their fevered love-making, even after all these years, could still make a *frisson* of excitement run through him.

Sixteen years was a long time to be away, but he had always yearned for the cool valleys and pasturelands of his native county. At first he had toiled in the mines, but the intelligence of the people in charge was so inferior to his that he soon rose up the ladder of command until, wheeling and dealing his way around, backed by a study of the world-wide markets for copper and precious ores, he came into a position to buy out his former employers.

The war helped. He had not, as he told Sophie, tried to get home. He had no taste for battle or throwing his life away in the futile disputes of far-away countries. They were no concern of his and when, after the war, he learned the scale of the fatalities he was very glad that common sense had taken the place of patriotism.

But when he returned home there was not the welcome he expected. People had long memories. He was not liked. It had got round that he was a schemer who introduced people to dubious men of business and, indeed, he had been singularly unfortunate in his meeting with Dick Wainwright and subsequently introducing him, for what to him was a meagre profit, to his brother-in-law Laurence.

It was Laurence who had caught him with Sophie, a fight ensued and that was the last time he'd set eyes on either of them until the baptism of Carson's daughter, when he'd seen Sophie after all these years, and also a youth purported to be his son. But if he was his son Bart had no paternal feelings towards him. He could never prove it or recognise him, and the past was the past. Over, as far as he was concerned.

But the future? He thought of the young girl sitting on the water's edge. Happily, she looked nothing like her mother, but must have resembled her father, the saintly George, who Sophie was forever talking about and who died in some far-off place when his children were young.

Bart completed his tour of the outside of the building and was about to go inside when two men came down the steps slowly, heads together, studying a large plan or map that they had in their hands. One was the architect, Solomon Palmer, a talented young man recently qualified, who had been engaged on the recommendation of Abel Yetman, his companion on the steps. Bart hailed them and as they looked up Abel folded the plan and, saying something to his companion, ran down the steps.

'Good morning, Uncle Bart.'

144

'Good morning, Abel, Solomon.' Bart turned to the fresh-faced young architect not long out of college. 'And how is the work coming on?'

'It's ahead of schedule, Mr Sadler,' the architect said, excited by his first important commission, anxious to please. 'You will be able to move in by midsummer.'

Bart smiled with satisfaction and placed a hand on Abel's shoulder.

'You've done well, Abel. To transform this place within six months is a miracle.'

'Maybe you'll recommend us, Uncle Bart,' Abel said, pointing to his companion. 'We mean to set up in a partnership to undertake house restoration, conversions and offer a complete architectural and building service.'

'That sounds a capital idea,' Bart said. 'I like the sound of it.'

Solomon shot out an arm and looked at his watch.

'I must go, if you'll excuse me, gentlemen. I have another appointment.' He held out a hand. 'Do go inside and look round, Mr Sadler. I'm sure you'll be pleased with what you find.'

'I'm pleased already.' Bart vigorously shook his hand. 'I think you've got a great future ahead of you.'

He stood with his nephew as Solomon Palmer got into his car, which was parked in front of the house and, after performing a U-turn, disappeared down the drive.

'A fine young man,' Bart said approvingly. 'How old is he?'

'He's younger than I am, Uncle. About twenty-four. He only qualified last year.'

'Have you known him long?'

'No. The architect I worked for on my last house was retiring, and I looked around for another. Someone knew Palmer who had recently come to the town. He was looking for work and I was in search of an architect. This is our second job. The first one was much smaller, but we worked very well together. Solomon specialises in the restoration of old buildings, but of course he is quite happy to work on new ones.'

'Now, young man,' Bart put an avuncular arm through his nephew's as they started up the steps to the hall, 'tell me about Deborah Woodville.'

'Deborah Woodville?' Abel seemed surprised by the question. 'What do you want to know about her?'

'Why is she not married? She's a very pretty young woman. Some might even call her beautiful.'

'She is very comely,' Abel agreed rather woodenly. 'I prefer her sister.'

'But the two are alike, are they not? The beautiful Misses Woodville. I knew them quite well when they were small.'

'Did you? I didn't know that.'

'I was acquainted with their mother. She was a very handsome woman, but different from the girls. I imagine they took after their father,' he glanced at Abel, 'your saintly Uncle George.'

'Whom I didn't know at all. I was only three when he died. Actually, Uncle, I am very interested in my cousin Ruth. She is not only beautiful but she is kind, good and intelligent.'

'Ah!' Bart seemed interested in this news. 'She's a schoolteacher I believe?'

'Of course we grew up together...'

'And is she as interested in you as you are in her?'

The young man blushed. 'I think so, Uncle.'

'Why then that is very good news. We might have a wedding in the family.'

'Oh, nothing is arranged,' Abel said hastily. 'But ... well,' he studied his feet, 'I can but live in hope.'

'And why did Deborah not appeal to you?' Bart halted in the middle of the stairway and looked closely at his nephew. 'She is very beautiful too.'

'It is Ruth I prefer,' Abel said and paused. 'Deborah is, well ... she has a past, you know, Uncle.'

'Oh, *has* she?' Bart looked immediately interested. 'Do tell me about it.'

147

'I shouldn't.'

'Oh, but you should.' Bart engaged his arm with his nephew's again, as they proceeded up the steps. 'I love gossip. It just so happens that I went to see your mother this morning and after I went for a walk along the river bank. I came upon the elder Miss Woodville sitting on the jetty, her feet nearly in the water. I thought she had a very sad expression. She was not at the christening last year, was she?'

'She seldom goes out.'

'Because of her past?'

Abel nodded. 'It is something to do with that. She has a child, Uncle, out of wedlock. He is now about seven years old.'

'And who was the father?'

'Some workman, not a local man. She ran off with him and disappeared for six months. When he knew she was having a baby he deserted her. She was found by Uncle Carson and for a time she went to live with him until the baby was born. Now she lives with her mother, but she never goes out. She is never seen in the town. She still thinks people talk about her.'

'And where is the child? Does he live with his mother?'

'He is being cared for by a relative of Mr Turner who lives in Bristol. He goes to school there and is well taken care of.'

'And does his mother ever see him?'

'I don't know. I don't think so. But Aunt Sophie and Mr Turner visit him.'

'What a very sad story,' Bart said thoughtfully, pausing once more as they entered the house. 'Sad for everyone concerned.'

'It is,' Abel agreed. 'They say Deborah never got over it, and will spend the rest of her life as a recluse.'

Dora lay in bed and gazed at the ceiling. For a second the room seemed to spin round and she was aware of that awful feeling of queasiness that she had so often these days. Sometimes she was actually physically sick.

May had noticed her pallor and commented on it, watching her with concern like an ancient mother hen.

The spring days had lengthened into summer and, in many ways, her relationship with May had grown a little stale. She felt sometimes that they were like a pair of castaways who had landed on an island far from anywhere, and all they had for company was the beautiful but essentially passive scenery of the Yorkshire Dales.

They went for long walks, shopping expeditions into Skipton or Harrogate, but Dora tired easily. May, convinced she was not well, begged her to see the doctor.

But Dora knew what was the matter with her. Her one and only experience with a man had had a totally unexpected and unpredictable result. At the age of forty-five she was convinced she was expecting a child.

Her first thought, as the suspicion grew, was to get rid of it. Not very nice, but there were ways and means of doing this. A call to a few friends in London, a visit to an establishment in Harley Street where one entered and exited by the back door. This kind of thing happened all the time.

And yet, and yet...

The longer she pondered the more difficult she knew it would be to get rid of it, both emotionally and physically. Then her thoughts flew to Debbie and the stigma that had accrued to her as the unwed mother of a child. But Debbie was much younger and she, Dora, was married. There was nothing at all reprehensible or shameful in having a baby by one's husband, however unusual the circumstances.

But did she really want a child at her age? It would create enormous problems and the thing was: how to tell May?

Her mother had always said that May was a rather ordinary, difficult woman with a chip about class on her shoulder. Dora hadn't seen it at the time May lived with them at Upper Park, but now that they had been closeted alone together for almost six months, her mother's opinion of May

150

seemed more realistic than hers.

She had once seen May not only as a capable superior in a front line hospital, someone she looked up to and admired, but as someone whom she loved. Now she knew how little they had in common.

Her love for Jean had been different but, maybe, in time it had eased her away from her obsession with May, the despair and isolation she had felt when May married Bernard.

But since her return from France nothing had been the same.

There was a tension between the two women which this new situation, Dora thought, would do nothing to resolve.

In her dilemma she rather longed for the wise counsel of Jean. How happy he would be, and how wrong it would seem to get rid of his child. Her thoughts often went back to the days they had spent together, the renewed feeling of intimacy that had grown between them, leading to the final culmination: the single act of marital love.

It was hard not to recollect her thoughts about that experience: confusion, bewilderment, resistance but not the radical distaste she had expected. It had been neither thrilling nor satisfying, it had been very brief, and afterwards they had lain together and slept in each other's arms, and it had seemed right.

But, afraid of being ensnared and entrapped once more, Dora had left almost immediately without, however, taking the bulk of her belongings back with her.

It was very difficult to think of a way out of this dilemma, to know what to do, and Dora found herself longing for the wise counsel of her mother, or the sensible advice of Jean.

There was a tap on the door and May popped her head round.

'Tea, dear?'

'That would be lovely.' Dora propped herself up on her arms as May entered, carrying a tray on which there were two cups, a teapot and milk jug.

She put it on the table beside Dora's bed, poured and, as she handed her her cup, she looked at her with concern.

'I do wish you'd see a doctor, dear. You look so peaky.' Cup in hand she perched on the bed close to Dora.

Dora lay back and sipped her tea, her expression thoughtful. She had always had a reputation for being forthright and straightforward, someone who didn't procrastinate, who called a spade a spade. What was the matter with her now?

'I think I'm going to have a baby,' she said, finishing the tea and putting the cup back on the tray. 'Thanks, that was lovely.'

She looked across at May, who was staring

at her, her expression aghast.

'I guess it must be a shock,' Dora went on. 'It is to me too. After all I'm forty-five. I didn't think such a thing was possible at my age.'

'When? How?' May managed to gasp. Then, more censoriously: 'Above all, *who*?'

'Who is easy. Jean, my husband–'

'But I thought you were going to...' May's eyes narrowed spitefully. 'You really are a terrible *liar*, Dora. I can't believe what I'm hearing.' She finished her tea and moved along the bed as though to put distance between herself and her friend, and clasped her knees tightly with her hands.

'I am not a liar.'

'You said it was a leave-taking. A parting of the ways. It was all over.'

'That's what I thought when I went there. I really object to being called a liar.' Dora looked coldly at May and the distance between her and her friend seemed to widen.

'I should have known when you came back without all your things.'

'Well, he *is* a very nice man. I mean...'

'What you mean is beside the point Dora,' May cried, jumping up. 'I feel utterly betrayed and humiliated by you.'

'Well, I don't see why you should.' Dora reached for a cigarette and then decided against it. Smoking in the morning made her feel even queasier.

'You've deceived me.'

'Nothing of the sort. I–'

'You said you'd never slept with him!' May stamped her foot on the floor like an adolescent in a fit of temper.

'I hadn't. On this occasion we did. Once.'

'I'm expected to believe you?'

'I don't care if you believe me or not. It's true.' Dora turned back the bedclothes and sat on the side of the bed, facing her friend. 'Look, May, once upon a time you had no compunction in leaving me for a man. I thought we were going to spend our lives together. You deceived *me*.' She stood up and flung her dressing gown around her shoulders. 'Now, if you don't mind I'm going to take a bath.'

When Dora came into the living room an hour or so later after a leisurely bath she realised the house was empty. May would have gone off on her shopping expedition. She felt uneasy at what had occurred, thought she'd handled it badly.

Spontaneity was not always a good or kind thing. She hadn't meant to hurt May, but now she knew it had helped her make up her mind.

She wanted the baby, and she would have it. If she hadn't she could have slunk off and had an abortion without telling May. The very fact that she'd told her had sealed her fate, and May's. What would happen now?

It was a lovely June day. The scenery was beautiful and she was about eight weeks pregnant. She went and sat on the terrace in a basket chair, her feet up, a large sun-hat on her head. There was no sound but the buzzing of bees among the lavender in the garden. The green sward of lawn swept down to the meadow, at the bottom of which lazily trundled the river. Birds swooped in and out of the trees on the far bank and up on the hill towards Simon's Seat. Occasionally the bleat of a sheep or moo of a cow broke the silence.

Perfection. Dora lay back and closed her eyes, yet she knew that everything was, in reality, far from peaceful.

Around her raged a storm.

Seven

'Alexander has such a fine seat on a horse,' Eliza said admiringly, shielding her eyes from the sun. In the paddock at the end of the garden Alexander was practising the intricate steps of the dressage supervised by Dora who sat on a chair by the fence.

'He has come on enormously since Dora has been coaching him.' Lally looked at her son with pride. For he was her son, whatever the nature of his true parentage. She had had him since a few days of his birth, and he was as precious to her as her own flesh and blood.

'Poor Dora,' Eliza sighed.

'Poor Dora! Why?' Lally looked at her.

'What is to become of her? I am so anxious about this baby. The danger to a woman of her age is considerable. I feel so apprehensive.'

Lally reached for Eliza's hand. They sat in the shelter of a tree, with rugs over their laps as, although the weather was fine, there was an autumnal breeze in the air.

'I wish she had told Jean,' Lally said firmly. 'Not to tell her husband is absurd. It is wrong.'

156

'But she is not sure if she wants to return to him.'

'It is *still* wrong. After all it is his child. Besides, at this time a woman needs the protection of a man.'

Eliza grew alarmed at Lally's vehemence.

'But you don't mind having her here?'

'Of course I don't mind having her here. What a thing to suggest! I love Dora and always have. She is no trouble. It is the future that I am concerned about.'

And, indeed, what was the future to bring? Lally was right. To have a baby at forty-six was quite an age. Dora was now five months pregnant, and had returned to her mother in July, following a row with May. May had grown very vindictive, according to Dora. Her attitude and comments had got her down until she felt they were undermining her health. One day while May was out she had simply left, driven away without a word. Cowardice, perhaps, but she had been unable to face any more scenes. So, as she'd always wanted, she went home to Mother.

Once at Forest House, and with several hundred miles between them, she immediately wrote to May offering a settlement that was not unlike a divorce. She would continue to pay the rent of the house and give May an allowance until she decided what she wanted to do, take a job or return to her husband. After all, she was a

157

qualified nurse whose services would be in demand at any hospital.

Or rather it wasn't Dora who was paying. As usual it was Eliza. Eliza who stumped up for everything, Dora having no income of her own.

In Lally's opinion, much as she loved her, Dora was spoilt. She was indulged by her mother who not only could refuse her nothing, but had the wherewithal to do it. In Lally's opinion it did a grown woman no good at all to be so dependent on her mother.

But it was true that Dora, who no longer rode, had been of enormous help to Alexander. She was a fine horsewoman and a fine coach and the two spent hours together during the vacation as Alexander prepared to take up a place at Trinity College Cambridge in October.

For Alexander it had been a golden summer. He had gone to Paris and travelled through France, Italy and the Balkans with some school friends to Greece.

And then when Dora came down she helped him choose a new horse and began to coach him in the art of dressage at which she excelled. Now as he performed the complex steps she rose from her chair and, getting closer to him, began to direct him, her arms swaying backwards and forwards as though she was directing a ballet, which dressage in so many ways resembled.

'Dora seems very much to want this baby,' Eliza murmured. 'I'm quite surprised.'

'But Dora's always loved children and been good with them.'

'I thought she and Jean had no marriage. It just shows how wrong you can be.' Eliza sat back. 'I'm glad, though. It is fulfilling for a woman to have a child, however much heartbreak goes with it. And I will be always there to support her or, rather, when I am not here my money will enable her to lead a good life and give her child one.' Eliza sighed again. 'How I wish I had Upper Park to leave her. Lally,' looking across at her, Eliza seemed to hesitate, 'I am presuming too much on your hospitality. Now that Dora is to have a baby in four months' time I feel I should find us a house.'

'But I *love* you being here.'

'And I love being here. But it is not the same as a home of one's own, especially after the baby comes.'

'I understand.' Lally nodded, her eyes on the two in the far paddock. 'By the way, an invitation came this morning ... I think you had one too.' She glanced at her friend.

'I threw it in the waste paper basket. The cheek of the man. Shall you go?'

'I don't really know what to do,' Lally said. 'I believe the house looks beautiful and you know he will have invited all your family:

Carson and Connie, Elizabeth and Graham, Sarah-Jane and, of course, Abel who worked on the house.' She paused and looked at her friend. 'Sometimes I think bygones should be bygones.'

'Please feel free to go if you wish,' Eliza said frostily. 'Don't for a moment be influenced by me. Personally I shall never step inside Upper Park again, nor have I any wish ever to meet Bart Sadler. Whatever people say about him, and it doesn't take long for them to change their tune, I consider him a rogue and a cheat.'

Not too far away from Forest House someone else was also studying the invitation with perplexity and, indeed, apprehension.

Mr Bartholomew Sadler
requests the pleasure of the company of
the Rev Hubert and Mrs Turner
together with
the Misses Deborah and Ruth Woodville
at a soiree to be held on October 1st
1929
at Upper Park, Nether Upton, Wenham,
Dorset to celebrate its restoration

7.30 pm for 8 pm
Carriages from 1 am

RSVP
White Tie

When it had been placed on the breakfast table, together with the rest of the mail, it had of course been Hubert who had opened it and, with a cry of pleasure, announced its contents to his assembled family. Ruth was very pleased, Deborah said nothing and the boys were suitably downcast that they had not been asked. Their father reminded them that they would be back at school and, anyway, this was an occasion strictly for grown-ups.

'You will have to get a new dress for the occasion, my dear,' Hubert had said, looking at his wife. 'I can't remember when you last had something new.'

'And I need a new dress too, Father,' Ruth told her stepfather. 'And Debbie...'

'I shall not be going,' Deborah said.

'But you must, my dear.' Hubert leaned towards her. 'You are *specifically* invited. I think it will be fun.' He looked round hopefully, but saw only one pair of interested eyes.

'But I don't want to go,' Debbie replied.

'It will do you good.'

'I shan't go either.' Sophie sat back, a sense of relief at Deborah's attitude which so mirrored her own.

'But *why*, my dear?' The rector looked downcast. 'It will be the event of the season.'

'Besides I'm *dying* to know how Upper

Park looks.' Ruth's cheeks were flushed with excitement. 'Abel says it looks very fine. Aren't you curious, Mother?'

'Not a bit.' Sophie popped a piece of cold toast in her mouth. 'You can tell me what it's like.'

'I really must *insist* you accompany us, dear.' The Reverend Turner was normally a mild man but on this occasion his tone was firm. 'It will look very *bad* if you don't accompany us.'

'Why will it look bad, dearest?' Sophie's expression was rebellious.

'Because you are the rector's wife. People *expect* it of you.'

Deborah had been surprised by her mother's obvious dismay at the invitation and this made her recall the conversation she'd had some months before with Mr Sadler at the water's edge. Being of a secretive nature she had never told a soul about the encounter. Now she began to wonder, and her memory travelled back in time to the far-off days when, as a small child, Mr Sadler used to come and play with them while they lived with their mother at Pelham's Oak looking after Grandpa. She had been eight or nine at the time, Ruth two years younger and, although it was so long ago, the harder she thought the clearer her memory became and she seemed to recall

162

the expression on her mother's face as she looked at Mr Sadler and how her eyes lit up when he entered the room, and how close they sat together on the driving seat of his cart.

Sophie looked up from the invitation as Deborah entered her sanctum, a small room off the hall where she did her accounts and planned her work for the parish. In front of her on the table was the invitation and Sophie's eye seemed to fly to it guiltily and she tried to hide it by leaning an elbow on it.

Deborah sat down by the window and looked at her mother.

'I've been thinking I *should* go to Mr Sadler's party, Mother.'

'But why on *earth*...' Suddenly Sophie appeared covered with confusion.

'Well, it is *most* unfair of me to keep you away.'

'I assure you I don't wish to go, Debbie. I am very happy to stay at home with you. There, dear, the matter is settled.'

'But Father is so upset. After you left the dining room this morning I could see how upset he was. He said that there were so few occasions we went to as a family. Besides, everyone we know will be there, Uncle Carson and Connie, all the Yetmans...'

'How do you know that?'

'Abel told Ruth. His mother has finally

become reconciled to her brother. And if she can forgive him, Mother,' Deborah looked at her levelly, 'I think *you* should forgive him too.'

'There is nothing to forgive,' Sophie said, clearly still flustered in a way Deborah, who sometimes resented the iron control of her mother, had never seen before. Her mother was usually the one without emotion: so cool, calm and collected in any emergency or crisis.

'I don't know what you mean. Mr Sadler was a mere acquaintance in the past. Nothing more. I can assure you of that.'

Bart Sadler, resplendent in full evening dress, stood in the splendidly restored entrance hall of his newly refurbished home flanked by members of his immediate family, similarly attired. Sarah-Jane was there with Abel on one side, her daughters Martha and Felicity on the other. Also there in the receiving line were his farmer brothers, John and Tom, with their wives Hettie and Ethel, his elder sister Maureen and her husband Ernest who was a prosperous boat builder in Poole.

Bart's mother and father had had seven children in all. Another brother, Cuthbert, was in America and two of his siblings had died young.

His many nephews and nieces, for the

Sadlers were a prolific family, stood awkwardly about, not yet quite accustomed to the newly enhanced status of an uncle who had always been regarded as a bit of an outsider, if not the black sheep of the family. Many of them scarcely remembered him, some had never known him.

As a family the Sadlers were close, but Bart had always been the one who stood apart, didn't fit in. They were not even sure, in those far-off days, if he was honest and the scandal about Laurence Yetman, even if some of the facts were exaggerated, had left a nasty taste.

But now all was forgiven. Uncle Bart was a rich man, the owner of a very fine property, one of the finest in the district. He had had a gracious house restored to a very high standard, and everything about them glittered and shone, symbols of opulence as well as good taste.

Through the open doors a long buffet table could be glimpsed, small gilded supper tables and chairs scattered about. Liveried waiters moved discreetly among the guests with glasses of champagne. In the background a muted string orchestra played quietly. In the drive cars came and went depositing their guests from as far away as Bournemouth, Salisbury and Exeter. Everyone, it seemed, who Bart had ever known, however remote, had been invited and most had wanted to be there.

The guest who least wanted to be there, Sophie Turner, moved slowly along the line waiting to be welcomed by the host. In front of her was Hubert, behind her Ruth and Deborah. The three women had gone to Bath to be bought pretty dresses by Hubert Turner, who was determined that his family would not be shown up by the rest of the company.

Ruth, pert and pretty with fashionably short hair, had chosen an elegant gown of rose chiffon over taffeta, with a simple bodice, long sleeves and a straight calf-length skirt. The effect was one of sophistication, in contrast to her sister Deborah who, despite being two years older, contrived to look like a country maid with her long hair coiled into a large bun at the nape of her neck, festooned with tiny artificial flowers similar to the posies embroidered in her long dress of pale yellow organdie. The style was that of a simple shepherdess, with a round neck and buttons down to the waist, charming but too young for her, as though she wished to remain a child. Sophie wore a long dress of blue silk with no frills and flounces and a high collar which, combined with her plain hairstyle – no visit to the hairdresser for her – and the severity of her expression, enhanced by the pair of steel-rimmed spectacles perched on

166

the bridge of her nose, made her look like a particularly hardhearted schoolmistress.

Bart took a long time welcoming Hubert, whose face was wreathed in smiles as he turned to bring forward his womenfolk. Sophie perfunctorily shook hands, grim-faced, not even looking into the eyes of the man who had once been her lover. A very slight, quizzical smile played on Bart's lips as he let go her hand, and took that of Deborah, who did smile, and he murmured something to her which made her smile even more and she nodded, remembering the day they had met on the jetty.

'I am so glad you could come,' Bart whispered, squeezing her hand. '*And* your mother too, oh, yes, and your sister.' He turned to Ruth as if reluctant to let go of Deborah's hand, but at last he did.

'I have not seen you, Ruth, since you were about six years old.'

'Except for the day of the christening.'

'Oh yes, but I don't think at that time I realised who you were. I had just come home. How splendidly you two young girls have come on!'

Along the line Abel Yetman waited for Ruth with all the eagerness of a suitor, his head slightly forward from the line of people standing with Bart.

However, there were very few stragglers left. It was after nine and people had already begun eating, so Bart carefully shepherded the rector, his wife and family, through the doors into the reception room with its blazing chandeliers, tables groaning with food, and the string orchestra, tucked almost out of sight in a corner, playing airs from *Rosamund* by Schubert.

Sophie stood at the entrance to the room, scanning it for familiar faces. In fact there were very few. The normal citizens of Wenham, the people she encountered every day, farmers and their wives, shopkeepers, members of the parish, were not among those invited to such an important occasion. Now that the ordeal of greeting Bart was over she felt she could relax.

In fact it hadn't been too bad. She had avoided his eyes, believed he'd smiled at her, but she had gone quickly on to plant a kiss on the cheek of Sarah-Jane next to him. The comforting presence of a friend and near neighbour had helped to settle her, banish her fears. Why, after all, be afraid of the past, things that had happened so long ago? Tonight, she decided, after all, she would make an effort to enjoy herself. Carson and Connie she espied in a corner talking to the Chairman of the Town Council, Councillor Green. Elizabeth, looking extremely elegant in a most fashionable gown of silver cloth sparkling with sequins, was trailed by her husband gently mopping his perspiring brow, his evening dress looking a trifle on the tight side, his red neck bulging above his white, carelessly tied cravat.

But neither Eliza nor Dora were there nor, apparently, Lally, though somewhat to her surprise she saw Alexander, who was chatting to a pretty young girl Sophie didn't know. Without interrupting Hubert, who was still talking animatedly to Bart, she made her way across the room where Carson and Connie, seeing her, excused themselves with some relief to Councillor Green and greeted her with an embrace.

Connie had good dress sense. She bought her clothes in Bristol and London, occasionally in Paris, and had chosen for this evening a cool, stylish off the shoulder evening gown in pale green crepe-de-chine. Her style and elegance matched her husband, who looked almost absurdly handsome in evening dress. Sophie, who had not seen them for some time, enquired after the children, who were all well except little Netta who, she was told, had had a bad cold.

'It is quite amazing to see the turn-out,' Carson said pointing to the concourse in the room. 'I didn't know Bart knew so many people.'

'No Eliza,' Sophie said. 'No Dora.'

'Lally wouldn't come without them. Eliza is still very bitter about the way she was

169

deceived over the house. Frankly, Aunt Sophie, I don't know about you, but I think we should bury the past after all this time.'

Sophie looked sharply at Carson but could detect no *double entendre* in his meaning. Carson was a straightforward, simple man and, anyway, she doubted whether the scandal about Bart Sadler and herself had even reached him in those far-off days before the war when he was, for the most part, working in London.

'I believe Aunt Eliza got a very good price for the house,' Carson continued when Sophie seemed reluctant to reply. 'Bart was so keen to have it; much better than she might otherwise have got. We all advised her to sell. Why not to Bart Sadler?' He looked around. 'A man who has done so much to beautify it. I don't believe it looked like this even when Julius first bought it and spent a lot of money doing it up.'

'So you too are going to be friendly with Bart?' Sophie's tone was cynical.

'Why not? I have no war with him. I think the business with Laurence was exaggerated but, as I say, Aunt Sophie, we can't bear grudges for ever.'

'Possibly not.' Sophie turned once again to look at the crowd and found herself face to face with Alexander who greeted her and Connie with a kiss.

'Why did your mother not come?' Connie

enquired. 'Surely *she* has no quarrel with Bart Sadler?'

'Mother didn't wish to come because of Aunt Eliza. She may not agree with her, but she feels for her. I must say I think the whole thing is very silly. Aunt Eliza was looking for another property, anyway, and now that Dora is to have a baby she will have to find something soon.'

'Isn't Dora ever going to return to her husband?' Connie asked. 'I would have thought he would be thrilled and delighted. Does he *know?*'

Alexander's reply was tactful. 'Dora never tells anyone what is on her mind; but she is an excellent teacher of dressage and I have enjoyed her company.'

Carson looked with interest, almost with a sense of fond pride, at the young man with whom he had always shared a special bond. Young Alexander, lacking a suitable father figure, had hero-worshipped Carson, always deferred to him and sought his approval for everything, maybe because he was a man in a family largely consisting of women. The two men bore a certain resemblance except for the fact that Alexander was dark-haired and dark-eyed, whereas Carson, though not so much now as in his youth, was fair-skinned, with blue eyes. In build and stature they were similar, and they seemed to have certain characteristics in common.

'You're going up to Cambridge next week, I hear?'

'Yes, Uncle.'

'And looking forward to it?'

'Very much. Mother says I can take my horses and she will pay for stables. I shall join the polo club.'

'And we'll come and see you, and you can take us punting on the Cam,' Connie cried with delight.

'I'd love that, Aunt Connie.'

'I think you have a brilliant future ahead of you but,' Sophie placed a hand anxiously on his arm, 'do take care, Alexander.'

The smile vanished from the young man's face.

'But what do you mean, Aunt Sophie?'

'The world is a dangerous place. You will soon learn.'

Deborah stood against the wall, feeling a little fearful and out of place. She was that dreaded species: a wallflower. She should not have come. It was mischievous to have forced her mother too, and she felt she had inflicted pain. However, the meeting between her mother and Bart Sadler had been uneventful and her mother now seemed quite happy chatting over supper to Connie, Carson and Alexander at the far end of the room. She could have joined them if she wished, but she didn't. Abel had

172

immediately commandeered Ruth, and her stepfather was surrounded by a number of earnest-looking men, local notables or elders of the church, who Deborah didn't know.

In fact she had come tonight because she thought she would know so few people. The gossips of the town who would never let her, or anybody if it came to that, forget their pasts would be tucked up in bed long ago.

Deborah had never been to an occasion like this, never seen men in white ties and tails and women in long evening dresses, even if some of them seemed uncomfortable and out of place, the women stitched into their gowns, the men prised into their suits. She had never been in a place as splendid as this, been offered champagne and plates piled high with delicious and unusual food.

She noticed that the members of the string orchestra were stealthily moving with their cumbersome instruments, and thought that was the end of the musical entertainment but, after a few minutes, the music began in another room and shortly after that Bart Sadler appeared through the crowd and, smiling down at her in a very kindly manner, put out his hand.

'Would you like to dance, Deborah? May I rescue the little shepherdess? Incidentally your dress is charming.'

'But...' Deborah went scarlet, shook her

173

head. 'I can't dance, Mr Sadler.'

'Neither can I.' He took her hand and with practised ease steered her through the crowd, through the double doors that led into the hall from where she could see the reception room from which the music came. One or two couples were also sauntering in that direction.

'You must call me Bart,' Bart whispered to her, his lips very close to her ear. '"Mr Sadler" makes me feel *very* old.' And as if enjoying the joke he tucked her hand in his.

They entered the room at the end of which the orchestra were now seated on a raised podium and the music was very different from Schubert: a slow foxtrot. A few couples were on the dance floor and, slipping his arm round her waist, Bart, with an almost casual familiarity, began to move in time to the music and to take her with him.

'*Very* slowly,' he murmured into her ear, his hand tightening round her waist. 'No one will notice if we trip up. Are you enjoying yourself?' He leaned back and studied her carefully.

'I don't believe you can't dance.' She was aware of his arm skilfully steering her and found it was easy to keep in step with him.

'Well, let's say I'm out of practice. You're very pretty, you know. You don't give yourself a chance, Deborah. A lovely young girl should have more fun. Look at your sister how *she's* enjoying herself.' He nodded in the direction of Abel and Ruth, who were gazing into each other's eyes as they moved in time to the music, oblivious of everything else.

'Ruth and Abel are going to be married,' Deborah said.

'Are they? That's exciting.'

'Yes. I suppose so.'

'Has it been announced?'

'No, but they have an understanding.'

'Do you like Abel?'

'Very much.'

'And you, Deborah, what plans do you have for the future?'

'None,' Deborah said, looking straight at him with an air of disarming frankness. 'I don't have any plans at all.'

'We must change all that,' Bart said and drew her ever so slightly closer to him.

Sarah-Jane was mildly enjoying herself, much better, anyway, than she had expected. For one thing it was nice being with her family again. Although they didn't live very far away she so seldom saw them. She hadn't seen her sister Maureen for years so, in a way, Bart was doing a good thing by bringing them all together. It was nice to sit over one of the supper tables with the family having a good chat, and the champagne was flowing. None of them could get over how well Bart had done. Extraordinary really. You couldn't help wondering if he had come by it all honestly, but no one was asking.

She heard the dance music from next door and her foot tapped in time to the rhythm. She really hadn't let herself go or enjoyed herself so much for years. In fact for many years, almost too many to count, she had felt isolated and alone despite the presence of her family, a devoted son like Abel and her two thoughtful daughters, a conscientious neighbour like Sophie, the frequent visits and a lot of financial help from her mother-in-law Eliza, and the support of all the people of the parish who had tried hard to sustain her over the years.

Sarah-Jane Sadler had been an attractive, good-humoured, pleasant-natured farmer's daughter when she married Laurence Yetman in the year 1903. In temperament, husband and wife were very alike: uncomplicated, hard working. They had three children and a happy family life until the year 1912 when Laurence Yetman went up into the woods with his dog and shot himself in the mouth.

It was almost impossible for Sarah-Jane to cope with such a tragedy. In the morning she had lain next to the warm, vibrant body of a loving husband. By noon he was dead, his lifeless body carried back to his home.

Some people react in unforseen ways to disaster and everyone would have expected Sarah-Jane to be among the copers; but she wasn't and only now, many many years later, did she show signs of even emerging from the chrysalis which had cocooned her from those she loved and the rest of the world.

Maybe it was forgiving Bart that was the catharsis. Yes, Bart was not really responsible for Laurence's death. Laurence had killed himself. He could have survived bankruptcy with her support, the help of his mother and family, all of whom loved him. She began to see that act of suicide that happened so long ago as one of selfishness, a lack of trust in herself and the family, a weakness that robbed her of her youth, almost of her own life. Years had been lost to grieving over Laurence.

Now talking to her family, drinking the heady wine and hearing the music, she suddenly felt like dancing. She felt, truth to tell, a little bit tipsy. On the outskirts of the family group, listening but not really participating because he didn't know anyone, sat a young man with curly brown hair, warm brown eyes and an engaging, rather shy smile. She only knew him through her son Abel with whom he worked, and they had once entertained him to dinner at Riversmead.

'Like to dance?' she said over her shoulder, smiling at him.

'Why, Mrs Yetman.' The young man appeared confused and half rose putting a hand nervously to adjust his white cravat.

'I know I'm too old for you. There are lots of pretty girls, but I just feel like a turn on the dance floor.' She looked at her brothers with their wives, her sister with her husband. Abel with Ruth. 'They all have partners.'

Solomon Palmer gallantly extended his hand and grasped hers.

'I'm not very good.'

'I haven't danced for years,' she said as together they walked towards the door. 'I'm very out of practice.' She stood for a moment in the hall looking at the great double staircase leading to the first floor, its highly polished balustrade and ornate twin newel posts reflecting the myriad lights of the glittering chandelier suspended from the ceiling. 'It's a magnificent place, isn't it?'

'It is,' Solomon said enthusiastically, trying to toss a wayward piece of hair out of his eyes. His face was very youthful, almost as though he had no beard; his features strong and clearcut. Sarah-Jane thought him very handsome. Neither of her daughters had a beau. They had been sent away to school after their father died, Eliza paying the fees, and thought themselves a bit superior to the local men, most of them the sons of farmers and tradesmen. Martha was twenty-three, Felicity twenty-one. Neither of them were beauties but they were nice-looking, well-educated young women. The trouble was, of course, so many suitable men had died in the war. Maybe, Sarah-Jane thought momentarily, stifling a feeling of guilt, she should have suggested that Solomon danced with one of her daughters. But he had looked so lonely and a little shy. Anyway her daughters were nowhere to be seen, probably busy enjoying their supper with cronies from the town, or people introduced to them by their uncle, Bart.

'I think you're very clever.' As they took to the floor Sarah-Jane looked up admiringly at Solomon. He was very tall, lean and gangly. She liked tall men. Laurence had been tall, strong and well-built.

'Clever?' Solomon looked down at her, his expression puzzled.

'My son tells me you were entirely responsible for the restoration of all this.'

'It wasn't very difficult. I mean most of it was in place. Mrs Heering had taken good care of the property. It simply needed a bit of a facelift.'

'I still think you're clever. I'm so *glad* you're in partnership with Abel.'

As the old-fashioned waltz started and

they closed up and began to move sedately round the dance floor Sarah-Jane experienced on her back a sensation of heat as Solomon's hand seemed to rest on it with a familiarity, almost an intimacy that reawakened in her feelings and desires remembered from when her husband was alive, and too long dormant.

PART TWO

An Old Love Rekindled

Eight

Jean Parterre sat for a long time outside the open gates leading to Forest House, shoulders hunched, arms folded, pondering his next move.

A feeling of exasperation had led him to seek out his wife who, since her departure the previous spring, had been evasive. He had written, he had telephoned, he had cabled. Only silence. He knew now that she had left Yorkshire in the summer and was staying with her mother at the home of Lally Martyn, whose house he had visited many times in the past.

It was a splendid residence, built in the Dutch style as it had been intended for a Dutchman, Julius Heering, and it had first been called Amsterdam Hoos. But Julius, because of Ryder's accident, had never lived there, and the first inhabitants had been Prosper Martyn and his wife Lally.

It was surrounded by woods, the short drive leading directly to the main door.

But now that he was here at last Jean was afraid. His hand trembled. He was fearful that something awful had happened to Dora and no one had told him. That he had

183

deeply offended, maybe traumatised her by making love that night. But it was not rape, it had not felt like rape and he had thought, hoped, that he detected a response in her, a woman he dearly loved, to his caresses. After all she did not flee the bed afterwards, but stayed with him until morning. His only hope now was that she had never returned for the rest of her things, nor sent for them. Nor had she filed for a divorce.

So, summoning all his courage, Jean had embarked with his motor car and here he was on a cold November day with the landscape bleak around him, and a hint of snow in the low-lying clouds. He, a man who had bravely faced the Bosch, dared not approach by the drive, so he parked the car off the road in the shadow of trees and slipped through the gates in the hope that he would be unobserved.

He was. It was lunch time and, perhaps, the staff were busy serving Eliza and her daughter, maybe Lally.

What should he say? What would he do? Maybe he should go back and find a telephone, at least warn them of his presence?

Instead he slipped round the side of the house, following a path that led, he knew, to the extensive gardens behind.

There was a large conservatory at the back full of rare tropical plants and a huge vine that provided a tranquil arbour of greenery in the summer when the sun beat hotly down on the glass roof. Shady in summer, it was also a pleasant place to sit in wintertime and, peering in, he saw Dora lying in a long wicker chair, her feet up, half covered with a rug of some description. There was a book on her lap and she appeared to have fallen asleep.

But she looked very pale and his first thought was that she was ill. Covered with a rug, a woman of her age! She hadn't contacted him because she was ill and didn't want him to know. He pressed his face against the glass and tapped on it with clenched knuckles.

Startled, Dora's eyes flew open. She raised herself in her chair and looked up. At first she couldn't fathom where the noise was coming from and so he tapped again.

'Dora!' he mouthed through the glass and, turning sharply, she saw him. Her hand flew to her lips as, for a long moment, they stared at each other. Then Jean rapidly rounded the huge glass edifice and went inside.

Dora was alone. Beyond her an open door led into the vast atrium of a hall from which a circular staircase led up to a huge glass dome, making it always a place of light, sun-dappled, cheerful even on the gloomiest day.

Jean stood at the doorway and looked at

the woman in the wicker chair, who hadn't risen but remained where she was, those startling blue eyes fixed on him. Her golden hair had been cut in the fashionable Eton crop and more than ever she resembled an androgynous figure in a pre-Raphaelite painting, neither male nor female.

Slowly he approached her.

'You should have told us you were coming,' she said.

'You never returned my calls.'

Silence.

'Dora, are you all right? I've been very worried about you. You've no idea how worried I've been.'

'I'm sorry.' She looked up and gave a wan smile. 'I'm going to have a baby, Jean.' She patted her stomach. 'Quite soon now. I should have told you. Mother, everyone, said I should have told you but, in a way, I'm a coward. I kept on putting it off. I was afraid, you know...'

'But if you were afraid,' he said gently, pulling up a basket chair to sit down close beside her, 'all the more reason for telling me.'

'No, not afraid of having the baby – I leave all the worrying to Mother – but afraid of, you know, entanglement, possession, all the things I never wanted to get married for and on account of which I left you.'

He reached out and tried to take her hand,

186

but she kept hers tucked under the rug. She seemed somehow to have shrivelled up, out of reach.

'Is the baby... ' he paused and his mouth felt terribly dry, 'ours?' he ended in a whisper.

'Of course, you silly thing.' Now she put a hand out and took his. 'You don't think I'd go in for that sort of thing too often, do you?'

'I thought you were very angry with me.'

'I was confused.' Her nails dug into his palm. 'I didn't know what to do about May. I felt terribly guilty about her. Still do.' Dora threw him a look of anguish. 'She left her husband and children because of me, you know. He won't have her back. In a way I've ruined May's life; but things seemed different when we were together. I know I ruined yours. You've no idea how ghastly I feel about it all.' For a moment she looked so distressed that Jean actually felt sorry for her, as though she was the one who had suffered, instead of causing so much suffering to the two people she professed to love best. But how could you feel angry with someone you adored in the way that still, despite everything, he adored Dora?

'Also, of course, it was some time before I realised I was pregnant. *That* was a shock, I can tell you! I'm forty-six soon, you know.'

'But you're all right?' he asked anxiously.

187

'Fit as a flea. I get a little tired. Mother and Lally are both out today, so I had sandwiches and a glass of milk.' She pointed to a tray by her side. 'I was just having a snooze.' She looked at him sharply. 'Have you eaten?'

'Darling, I'm so *glad* you're all right,' Jean said and, placing his head on her knees, he started to weep. 'You've no idea how terrible I've felt. How much I missed you.'

'Silly old sausage,' Dora said, a note of fondness in her voice as he clutched her. 'Silly old man.'

And for a time they sat there, Dora stroking his head, making soothing noises.

She realised now that very soon she would have two babies to care for, not one. And that nothing would ever be the same again.

Bart Sadler placed an avuncular hand on Abel's shoulder. With the other he sketched an imaginary building to the left of the newly refurbished greenhouses. They were standing at the drawing-room window looking out on to the wintry landscape, the thick layer of frost that still covered the ground, although it was nearly noon and a bright January day.

'I am going to breed horses, Abel. Arabians. Or shall I say I am thinking of it? I want the finest stables in the county. That is your next job. I think we take the existing stables down towards the park and then I want a paddock and a training ring, and all the paraphernalia,' he went on, waving his hand expansively in the direction of the extension to the stables.

'Breeding *horses*, Uncle Bart?' Abel stroked his chin.

'Don't you think it a good idea?' Bart looked concerned.

'Is it something you really know anything about?'

'Not yet. But I shall. I shall endeavour to find out everything I can about horse breeding, and employ the best advisers. How about Dora?' He looked across at Abel. 'She knows everything there is to know about horses, doesn't she?'

'She knows a lot. Whether about Arabians or not I have no idea. But she has just had a baby, Uncle Bart, and I understand she is to return to France to live with her husband.'

'Well, well, I'm delighted to hear the news, but sorry I shan't have the benefit of her advice.'

'My advice, Uncle Bart, if you really want it...' Abel began slowly.

'And I do,' Bart interrupted him.

'...is to stick to what you know. You are a very successful businessman. Metals, is it not? You also have a knowledge of stone, having been a mason for many years. Much as I would like the work of designing and building new stables for you I think you should stick to what you know.'

'But it is for a hobby, not a business. I have money to spend, you know, and I fancy that to get ahead in a rural county you have to know about horses.' Bart looked approvingly at his nephew. 'Thank you for your honesty, Abel. I like an honest man. But I still want you to go ahead and build me stables. Now, why don't you bring your fiancee to dinner, and invite her sister too? Next week some time?'

'Why,' Abel looked gratified, 'that is very nice of you, Uncle Bart. Ruth, I'm sure, will be delighted. I can't answer for Debbie. She scarcely ever goes out.'

'Try and persuade her.' Bart winked at his nephew and pressed his arm. 'Tell her it will do her the world of good.'

'And when is the wedding to be?' Bart asked, raising his glass towards the couple who, wreathed in smiles, sat together to his left. On his right, occupying sole position, was Deborah who too was smiling, relaxed for the first time since she'd come into the house an hour before.

'In the spring,' Abel said, looking at Ruth. 'A big wedding in Wenham Parish Church.'

'I would consider it an honour if you would have your reception here,' Bart said.

'Oh, but Uncle Bart...'

190

'I think Mother would want it in the Rectory,' Debbie murmured. 'I think she would be very upset to have it anywhere else.' She had been on the point of saying 'here', but managed to stop herself at the last minute.

'Well, we shall have to work on your mother,' Bart said with a smile.

'It would be splendid to have the reception here,' Abel said, gratified. 'Very generous of you, Uncle.'

'And Ruth, what do you say?' Bart turned to the bride-to-be, noticing that the sparkle had left her eyes.

'Well...' she was looking at her elder sister to whom she usually deferred, 'if Debbie says Mother wouldn't like it...'

'But it is not for your mother's wedding, is it, Ruth?' Bart said with an edge to his voice. 'It is yours and Abel's. You will have many guests and, large as the Rectory is, I don't think you could do justice to the numbers who will come. Nor, I think, would you provide the kind of fare I would have in mind. Not that I think your stepfather is frugal,' he added hastily, 'for I know him to be a generous man and, I believe, not a poor one. But it is something I would like to give the happy couple as my gift, and also a way of saying "thank you" to Abel for all he has done for me.'

'We shall have to ask Mother.' Ruth still

191

had an eye on Debbie. 'Although it is *most* kind of you to suggest it.'

'I think we should have it here,' Abel said eagerly. 'I can't think of a better place to start our married life, or a better way. We must try and persuade your mother who, I'm sure, will be grateful to Uncle Bart for his generosity.'

'Remember, I'm an old friend of the family,' Bart rang the bell for the butler to serve the next course, 'as well as a relation. Nothing would give me greater pleasure than to give my dear nephew and his bride a good start in life.'

It had been a splendid dinner, course upon course, accompanied by fine wines served by attentive servants tip-toeing about. The flickering pinpoints of light from dozens of candles in silver candelabra were reflected in the highly polished, huge mahogany table, the cut-glass decanters and crystal wine glasses.

Bart Sadler and Abel had worn black ties, she and Ruth their party best, though Deborah knew that hers didn't amount to much, a blue woollen dress with belt and collar, buttoned up to the neck; a true daughter of the rectory. Like her mother she had no interest in clothes, but Ruth had gone to Yeovil to buy a new frock, had had her hair done, wore make-up, which Debbie had never touched, and sparkled in her finery, aglow with her new-found happiness.

However, Deborah was aware that Bart paid her a lot of attention. He looked at her often, smiling, the kind of intimate smile that was a little disconcerting, as though they shared some kind of secret. And maybe they did; that day at the jetty about which she had told no one. Nothing much had happened, but it seemed to mark the beginning of an understanding that was cemented at his party the previous October, when he had danced several times with her, so often, in fact, that people commented on it.

But he was so very old, older than her stepfather, who was some years younger than her mother. As he had courted her mother, and she knew that he had, they must be about the same age. It was unthinkable ... but he was so very kind to her, so very nice. He made her feel rather important, which no one else in her family bothered much to do. She was an embarrassment to them, a woman who had once run away with a common labourer, lived with him and borne a child.

It was only because they regarded it their Christian duty to forgive all sinners that they had taken her back, and that was not until after the birth when the baby had been spirited away.

But of course everyone knew. Baby or no baby, everyone knew.

The butler, followed by a footman, brought in a huge silver tray with a silver coffee pot and began to pour into tiny delicate porcelain cups that had already been arranged on a side table. The footman carried a tray on which there was an assortment of bottles and glasses.

Bart and Abel had brandies, Ruth had a liqueur. But Deborah knew that, unused as she was to drinking, she had had enough. Any more would go to her head and she would make a fool of herself. She didn't want that.

Abel and Bart smoked large cigars and sat back in their armchairs with a brandy in one hand, a cigar in the other. They were chatting about plans being drawn up by Solomon Palmer for the stables. Ruth smoked too, black Sobranie cigarettes. Her mother would have had a fit. It wasn't that Deborah didn't dare try them. She thought they might make her sick. Although she was the one who had created scandal, run away and had a child, she was far from being the sort of woman of the world she knew her sister aspired to be. Already Ruth could see herself as the wife of a prosperous builder, living in the fine house which Abel talked of building.

Debbie aspired to nothing. Since her

return home in disgrace she lived in a shell, and she knew that, in many ways, she was terrified of emerging from it.

The air was thick with smoke and the fumes of fine brandy. Deborah looked around and could hardly believe that she could be in such sophisticated company in such a place. Why, she had hardly ever gone out in her life!

Bart got up and began to wind up the gramophone that stood on a table.

'I thought we might dance,' he said looking around, his cigar at a rakish angle in the corner of his mouth. 'Anyone like to dance?'

Immediately Abel sprang up, both hands towards Ruth who also bounded out of her chair and, as the racy strain of *Bye, Bye Blackbird* began, the two started to bob around the room to sounds of laughter from Debbie, while Bart made selections from a pile of records by the side of the machine. He then turned to Deborah and, hand extended, gently drew her from her chair, put his arm round her waist and they too began to jog around the room until the record finished and was replaced by tunes from *No, No Nanette*.

Bart then changed the mood of the music. *What is this Thing called Love?* was a slow, romantic number from the hit Cochran musical *Wake Up and Dream*. The engaged couple danced closer and closer until they ended up in an embrace on the dance floor. Deborah found her head resting on Bart's shoulder, his hands very tight round her waist as he drew her closer to him. She raised her head and looked into his eyes and, as he bent forward she thought he was going to try to kiss her. Luckily, she averted her face and the kiss landed on her cheek.

Suddenly the memory of the pair of them sitting on the jetty came to her; sitting side by side gazing into the depths of the river, with unexpected sense of comradeship, and she realised that she was getting into very deep water with Bart Sadler.

Sophie, face white with fury, gazed at the letter that Hubert had passed to her without comment.

'I certainly will *not* let Ruth hold her reception at Bart Sadler's,' she said. 'What an impertinence!'

Her reaction was not unexpected and Ruth and Deborah sat at the breakfast table, hands out of sight, mouths clenched, preparing for the storm.

'Bart *is* Abel's uncle,' Hubert broke the awkward pause, 'I'm sure he didn't mean to be impertinent, dear. I think it is a very nice letter.'

'"*May* I have the pleasure"...' Sophie's voice assumed a note of mockery. '"I can't *tell* you how delighted I would be if..." "My wedding present to the young couple". What rubbish this man writes!'

She then tore the letter in two and pitched the pages towards the waste-paper basket, but they missed their target and landed on the floor.

'I think he means well, dear,' Hubert said lamely. 'What does Ruth think?' He looked anxiously at his step-daughter, who was gazing at her plate.

Finally she raised her eyes to look at her mother. 'I think it's very kind too. It was well-meant.'

'I told him you would not like it.' Deborah also recovered her courage. 'He brought it up at the dinner party–'

'And *if* I'd known there were only *four* people at that party I would not have allowed you to go, Deborah,' her mother rounded on her. 'I understood many more people would be there.'

'I don't see how you could stop me, Mother,' Deborah, who had hardly ever contradicted her mother in her life, found herself retorting. 'I am twenty-seven years old this year. I shall soon be an old spinster of thirty, and then forty and fifty. I–'

'Deborah, I don't *know* what's got into you!' The colour mounted on Sophie's cheeks. 'I think you had better go to your room and calm down.'

'I am very calm, Mother.' Deborah stood up. 'I am calm, but I am angry. Mr Sadler has made a very generous offer which you misinterpret in order to undermine him. What sort of reception do you think you can have in this shabby old place? We have not one room big enough to hold more than fifty people.'

'I'll ask Carson,' Sophie clenched her jaw. 'Please sit down, Deborah, and don't make a scene. You would like it at Pelham's Oak, wouldn't you, Ruth?'

Ruth didn't reply but, as though shocked at her sister's outburst, continued to gaze at her plate.

'I think we'd better consider this matter carefully, my dear.' Hubert went over to his wife and put his hand on her shoulder. 'You are a bit overwrought.'

'I am not overwrought, Hubert,' Sophie said, dashing his hand away. 'On the contrary. If Ruth considers this a "shabby old place" I thought she might prefer Pelham's Oak which is, after all, the Woodville family home whereas Upper Park is not.'

'That *is* a point.' Hubert turned placatingly to his stepdaughters.

'But Abel is not a Woodville, Father,' Ruth said. 'He is a Yetman, and I am going to take his name.'

'The bride traditionally has the reception

in her home, or a place chosen by her parents.' Hubert looked for assistance to Sophie who sat staring at the table as if in an effort to control herself, both fists tightly clenched against her face.

'Besides,' Hubert went on, his tone conciliatory as befitted a man of the cloth, 'if it is held at Upper Park, Eliza won't come.'

'Neither will I,' Sophie looked across at her daughter, 'so you can please yourself. I am saying no more.'

She then rose from the table and, taking the rest of her mail, left the room.

'There!' Hubert dejectedly sat down next to Ruth. 'You've upset your mother.'

'Why *does* she hate Bart so?' Ruth demanded, her face pale with anxiety. 'She loses no opportunity to be rude to him or unpleasant about him. What has he done to her?'

Hubert said nothing while Deborah raised her eyes over Ruth's head and gazed out of the window.

'I think we'd best do as Mother wants,' she said after a while, also getting up. 'Pelham's Oak, after all, will be very nice, that is if Uncle Carson agrees, and I'm sure he will. You'd like that, Ruth, wouldn't you?'

But Ruth's mouth remained in a stubborn line as if she were thinking of the luxuries, both of food and surroundings, that Upper

Park would have to offer compared to the slightly more homespun, but nevertheless perfectly acceptable, facilities of the family home at Pelham's Oak.

Deborah went to her room and contemplated herself in her mirror. With both hands she scraped back her hair, bared her teeth, looked deep into her eyes.

Plain. Decidedly plain, and shabby. Twenty-seven next birthday, and what had she to show for her life? A son she never saw and wished didn't exist, whose unseen presence continually troubled her. A mother whom she loved but whose rigidity and piety she not only didn't understand but found increasingly alien. She had a darling of a stepfather, and no one could complain about him: kind, tolerant, understanding, a man one couldn't help but love and admire. His was the compassionate side of Christianity; her mother's was based on rigid Old Testament morality of an eye for an eye and a tooth for a tooth, of reaping as you had sown.

It was said that her mother had had a hard life; that both her own parents and her husband's had opposed her first marriage. That she had suffered in the inhospitable land of Papua, New Guinea, where her husband had died of a fever in her arms.

When she had returned to Wenham she

was impoverished, forced to live first of all with her parents, from whom she seemed to have inherited their own ascetic idea of the Christian faith, and unwelcome by the Woodvilles who refused to see her until the death of Lady Woodville. Then their grandfather had decided he needed help, and decided to forgive his daughter-in-law, who took her children with her to look after him. In many ways living at Pelham's Oak with a dear, tolerant grandfather had been the happiest time of Deborah's childhood.

But when he remarried, Sophie and her children were told they were not wanted, and it was then that kindly Hubert Turner had stepped in and given them a home and their mother a new name.

Deborah sat on the bed and looked at the floor. She remembered Bart Sadler coming quite often to Pelham's Oak, her mother's eyes lighting up when she saw him. She even began to look pretty which even her greatest admirers admitted she never had before. Those eyes never lit up now. It seemed that, behind her steel-framed spectacles, they remained veiled from the world, seeing but unseen. Her mood, her thoughts, were never really known or understood. As a person in the town she was admired rather than liked.

And then, of course, she, Deborah, had added to her mother's woes by running off with Michael Stansgate, an ignorant workman of no fixed abode who had seduced her in a side chapel in her stepfather's church, a place she felt she had desecrated to this very day.

Her mother and she had wanted to have the baby adopted, but it was Hubert who tried to be more far-seeing to the day they might regret such as an action, and had suggested that his clergyman cousin and his wife, who had two children of their own but were not well-off, might value the income that would accrue if they fostered a baby boy, at least for the foreseeable future.

Deborah often thought of the boy, now nearly eight years old. Would he ever forgive her if she did want to see him? What would she say and how would she explain what she had done? What worth was her life? What use?

Then she thought of Bart, and his suggestion when they parted that night, holding hands surreptitiously in the doorway, that they might meet again.

It gave her a secret hope. To be wanted, even by an old man like Bart, made her feel important and necessary.

But there was always her mother in the way.

Her mother was not at lunch. It was a Saturday and Ruth was spending the day with Abel. Their father had gone to Salisbury on church business, so Deborah ate alone in the dining room waited on by the housemaid, Polly, who was a cheerful soul, given to gossip.

If anyone wanted to find out what was going on in Wenham, Polly was sure to know the answer.

'What do people say about Bart Sadler, Polly?' Deborah asked as, after finishing her lunch, she began to peel an apple for dessert. Polly, who was clearing away, stopped in her tracks.

'Why, they say he is a very wealthy man, Miss Deborah.'

'Yes, but what else?'

'Well, Miss Deborah, he has been gone from Wenham for very many years. Most people scarcely remember him.'

'Do they *say* anything about Mr Sadler and my mother? I mean, before she was married to my stepfather?'

Deborah gazed at Polly whose placid, cheerful face suddenly went pink.

'Some people have a cruel tongue, Miss Deborah. Mischievous I call them and those are the people you should not listen to.'

'Yes, but what do they *say*, Polly?' Deborah insisted. 'You can tell me. I promise not to pass it on. I simply want to know.'

'Well, Miss,' Polly nervously crumpled her white pinafore between both hands, 'they *say* that your half-brother, Sam, very much resembles Mr Sadler. But I pay no attention to them kind of remarks myself, and neither I think should you, Miss.' And with that Polly, trembling with confusion, fearing she had gone too far, rushed out of the room, leaving the dishes behind.

Deborah tapped on the door of her mother's sanctum and listened. No sound. She tapped again.

After a while, 'Who is it?'

'Deborah, Mother.'

'I've got a headache, Deborah, could you come back later?'

'I just want to say "sorry".' Deborah turned the handle and popped her head round the door. Her mother was sitting in her armchair with her feet up on a stool, and did indeed look very pale.

'Can I get you something for your headache, Mother?' Deborah asked sympathetically. 'You look all in.'

'I'll have a cup of tea in a minute.' Sophie passed a hand across her brow. 'That will do me good.'

'We've agreed to have the reception at Pelham's Oak. After all it *is* the home of the Woodvilles.'

'I'm glad.' Sophie put out a hand to show her gratitude and suddenly Deborah felt humbled because of all the hateful thoughts and feelings she had entertained about her mother, especially recently.

'Why don't you like Bart Sadler, Mother?' she asked. 'Why *do* you dislike him so much? He's very kind.'

'You may think so, but *I* don't think he behaved very well in the past. He *did* introduce Uncle Laurence to a wicked man, and people thought some of the things he did were not...' Sophie paused as if in an effort to find the exact word, 'quite right. He had a rather unsavoury reputation.'

'But, Mother, he used to come and play with us at Pelham's Oak when we were small.'

'That's before we found out what sort of man he was. Now I wouldn't have him in the house, and Deborah...'

'Yes, Mother?'

'I would *very* much prefer it if you didn't see Mr Sadler again. I mean if he asks you to dinner I want you to decline. I know Abel is involved with him work-wise and when Ruth is his wife I suppose she will have to entertain, and be entertained by, her husband's business friends. But I noticed you dancing with him the night of his party and I thought, well ... contact best avoided, Deborah.'

As if her confidence was restored, trust between mother and daughter re-established, the colour began to return to her cheeks and she looked across at Deborah and smiled.

'Do you understand what I'm saying, dear?'

'Yes, Mother.'

Sophie gave a deep sigh and settled back in her chair. 'That's a good girl. Now, why don't you go and ask Polly to bring us some tea? I'm sure we could both do with a cup.'

Nine

Traditionally, the bride looks beautiful and Ruth Woodville on the day of her wedding in May 1930 did not disappoint. She was tall, slim, with hair the colour of ripe corn and deep-set, translucent, violet-blue eyes.

Her bearing as she had walked up the aisle on the arm of her uncle, Carson, for her stepfather was to marry her, was regal, every inch the Woodville, and everyone commented on the likeness between uncle and niece.

Ruth seemed to have no nerves, to be confident in herself and her choice of a bridegroom, and the pair exuded happiness as they came out of the church into the sunshine, to be greeted by a shower of confetti thrown by the waiting, excited crowd who comprised almost every inhabitant of the town.

Again it was one of those days when, in honour of the Woodville family, everything came to a standstill. The bank closed, the shops were shut, only the Baker's Arms remained open in the hope of attracting those revellers who wanted to slake their thirst before and even after the ceremony at the church, before moving on to the reception.

Afterwards, as was by now the custom, all the townsfolk followed the family back to Pelham's Oak, a long, almost unending stream of cars, carts, bicycles and wagons. Some were on horseback, a few hardy souls, usually the less sober ones, even walked, though they were usually picked up en route and given a lift.

Deborah had been chief bridesmaid to her sister, in charge of a host of younger ones: Toby and Leonard Woodville as pages and six bridesmaids who included Elizabeth's children Mary and Betsy, respectively thirteen and twelve.

The bridesmaids' dresses were blue, a shade which brought out the colour of Deborah's eyes, her appearance every bit as striking as her sister. She was two years older than the bride but from the glances of the many young men who attended the reception in the great cream and gold drawing room at Pelham's Oak, few doubted she would be long in following her.

And, indeed, to her surprise, Deborah was enjoying herself. She was devoted to her sister and with the pain of losing her went the joy, the knowledge that until Abel had built them a new house, as he planned to do, she would be living nearby.

The best man was Abel's business partner

Solomon Palmer, who was observed to be paying a lot of attention to the chief bridesmaid as, in fact, a good best man should. However, when one compared them side by side heads nodded, tongues started wagging. What a good pair they would make. Deborah so fair and, on this occasion at least, vivacious, her blonde good looks offset by the handsome young man at her side.

But wouldn't Deborah's past put off a man in search of a respectable bride? That was what no one knew.

Sophie was so glad that that awful suggestion of having the reception at Upper Park had been squashed flat from the start. She had enjoyed the day, been determined to enjoy it despite the knowledge that somewhere in the crowded room lurked Bart Sadler. He had also been in the church but at the back, tucked out of sight of the mother of the bride, who was in the front pew.

Sophie was determined not to let her day be spoilt by Bart. After all not only was Ruth off her hands, happily married to a worthy man of whom everyone approved, but Debbie appeared finally to have emerged from the chrysalis which had kept her so tightly enmeshed for many years, which had stifled her young womanhood and darkened those most precious years of youth.

Debbie had been a continuing sorrow and worry to Sophie, not so much for what she had done but because the prospect of a ruined life was a hard one for a mother to bear.

Solomon Palmer was, indeed, a most suitable young man. She knew nothing about his family but he was now a business partner of Abel who valued him highly. His talent was obvious and his prospects must be considered good. Besides he was a fine looking young man and only a little younger than Deborah. Sophie made a mental note to remember to ask him to dinner as soon as was decently possible.

Eliza had also noticed the attentions paid to Deborah by Solomon and, sidling up to Sophie, gave her a meaningful look.

'Perhaps *another* wedding soon?' She looked towards the table where Deborah and Solomon sat deep in conversation.

'That *would* be nice.' Sophie sighed. 'I would love to see her happily married. But it's early days.' She looked past Eliza to Dora who was talking animatedly to a group of people from the parish who she hadn't seen for some time: Mr Trendle the verger, Mrs Baker the schoolmistress, Councillor Hardy of the Town Council, and Mr and Mrs Marsden, two local worthies who had retired many years ago to the town.

'Dora looks so well,' Sophie said. 'And so

happy. The baby's beautiful, I hear?'

'You must come and see her.' Eliza put a hand on Sophie's arm.

'I will. I want to, now that the wedding is over. There has been so much to do. How long are they staying?'

'They're going back next week. Jean is anxious about his vines.'

Jean was never very far away from Dora, as though afraid that once again she might vanish. He stood rather awkwardly behind her, half listening to what she was saying, his eyes wandering restlessly round the room, mentally recalling the years he'd spent in this very house as friend and factotum to Carson. In those days he had been a restless man suffering the after effects of war, rootless, without family, his first wife having deserted him. Carson, as well as friendship and support, had offered him a home, security and finally he had married Carson's cousin who had now, in the most un-expected way, given him a child.

Jean's cup would have been very full were it not for the fact that his feeling of insecur-ity had returned. Much as he loved Dora and adored their baby he felt uncertain about the future, about Dora, wondering whether she, having left him once, might not one day be tempted to do so again, taking their daughter, Louise, with her.

The afternoon wore on, but the crowd,

enjoying itself, did not diminish. What else was there to do on a warm spring afternoon, with the buds unfurling on the massive oak on the lawn and a sense that the earth, cold and barren in winter, was springing so magically and mysteriously into life again? Some strolled into the grounds carrying drinks or plates of sandwiches precariously balanced; others joined a game of croquet started by some of the younger members of the family on the lawn. Some pairs slunk away, emboldened by wine to canoodle in the woods. Upstairs windows were flung open and heads appeared as those still indoors strove for a breath of fresh air which came wafting from outside.

Elizabeth Temple was prominent, as usual, though it was impossible on this occasion for her to usurp Connie's place. She fussed about the bridesmaids who were stuffing themselves with ice cream until one of them was sick and had to be escorted hastily from the room, weeping over her ruined dress. Of course it had to be Betsy Sprogett who brought disgrace on herself and, indirectly, her mother, who always tried so hard to be just that bit better than the Woodvilles, better behaved, better dressed, anxious to forget that she had been reared by servants of the family of which she never quite felt a part.

Lally, looking gorgeous in a dress of

212

lavender chiffon and a large picture hat, was squired by Alexander who was nearing the end of his first year at Cambridge. Tall and good-looking in his morning suit he was the object of many a flirtatious glance from some of the young women present. But Alexander seemed impervious to female wiles: polite, charming, courteous but, so far, not susceptible. He looked rather disdainfully about him, as if the company were slightly inferior to that which he was used to; young society women with considerable fortunes whose brothers, from Sherborne and Trinity, were his friends. If he concentrated on anyone it was his mother, who was never without a glass or a plate or an ashtray for her cigarette ash, assiduously held for her by her dutiful son.

Connie, well pleased with the day's arrangements, finally had a moment to sit down and enjoy a glass of champagne. It had taken days, weeks, of effort to organise an event which had been rather thrust upon them. They had assumed the reception would be at the Rectory, but when Sophie explained the circumstances they readily agreed to hold it at Pelham's Oak.

The last wedding reception had been hers, the day she married Carson after a period of uncertainty, some doubt and indecision on her part. It was not that she didn't love Carson, but she knew she would always have to share him with other people. There was something compulsively philanthropic about Carson. He had given a home to Elizabeth and her family, a temporary home to Debbie whose baby was born there. Before that there had been Jean Parterre who stayed two years. Then there had been his stepmother, Agnes, who had only left when Connie had provided a house for her. It seemed at one time there would be no room for Connie unless she wanted to run a home for those friends or relations of Carson, who seemed to consider it a duty to offer succour to his fellow men.

Carson would never say 'no'. He was too altruistic, too good-natured. He had even offered Eliza a home when Upper Park was sold because, after all, she had been born at Pelham's Oak. Thankfully, as far as Connie was concerned, although she loved Eliza, she had declined. In her wisdom she had perhaps seen that Connie wished to have her husband, her home and her children to herself.

Connie sat by the open window, glad of the gentle breeze that blew in from outside. She was very tired and she hoped that they would all soon begin to go.

Abel and Ruth seemed to be making a farewell tour of the room, circulating among the crowd who pressed in upon them. They were, indeed, a charming, well-suited couple. Connie looked at her watch. In about an hour, after changing, the bridal pair would be driven to the station to get the boat train for Dover and then to France and Italy.

She felt a hand on her shoulder and found Carson looking tenderly down at her.

'Tired, darling?'

'Exhausted! I feel as though I'd arranged all this myself.' She took his hand.

'It's gone awfully well.' He flopped down beside her.

'Lovely to see everyone here, too. You love these family gatherings don't you, Carson?'

Carson nodded. 'I'm so glad Jean and Dora were able to come. Doesn't she look well?'

As if she'd heard her name Dora looked across at Carson and gave a little wave. Jean lifted his hand and the pair of them drifted across to Carson and Connie.

'What a happy day.' Dora sat on the chair next to Connie, vacated for her by Carson. 'It's so *warm.*'

'Who's looking after Louise?'

'Catherine, one of Lally's maids. She's very good with her. But we must be getting back. Feeding time.'

Carson said: 'We want you to come for dinner, or lunch if you prefer, before you go back. Bring Louise. Netta will be enchanted by her.'

'Stay the night,' Connie added. 'It will be like old times for Jean.'

Jean shook his head. 'Kind of you, but we only have a few days left with Eliza and she so adores the baby.'

'But maybe we could come for lunch.' Dora stooped to kiss Connie who started to rise. 'No, please, don't get up. We'll just slip away.' And, with a smile, she took Jean's hand and went off into the crowd, pausing to take farewell of bride and groom.

Bart Sadler had kept a low profile during the day's proceedings. He nearly didn't go to the wedding but thought it would look at the worst cowardly, at best as though he was sulking. So he sat at the very back of the church and did not hang around outside, appeared in no pictures, but went to his car which he'd parked at the far side of the town, thus making sure he was one of the last to arrive at the reception.

Again he slunk in at the back, missing the receiving line, which had been his intention. He had hardly spoken to anybody but stood on the far side of the room, away from the windows, smoking a cigar, drinking a glass of champagne, observing.

She was just as beautiful as her sister, more so in his eyes. She had a maturity which Ruth lacked, also an air of sadness, the reason for which he thought he understood. In a small town a social misdemeanour like hers assumed gigantic proportions, as he knew only too well. In a way they were both the black sheep of their respective families.

In her pale blue dress, a wreath of artificial roses on her pale gold hair, she looked exquisite. How typical of the men in this backward rural area to leave such a jewel unclaimed, just because of her past. There were a number of pretty young girls in the room and most had the attentions of admiring males who plied them with glasses of champagne and offers of food. Inspired by the occasion there was a lot of understated amorous activity going on; perhaps future liaisons in the process of being hatched?

The daughters of Sarah-Jane Yetman, Martha and Felicity, Abel's sisters, personable though not nearly as beautiful as Deborah Woodville, were surrounded by a cluster of young men.

When he had first come in Bart had noticed that young Solomon Palmer seemed to be paying Deborah a lot of attention, but he drifted away to the side of Sarah-Jane, the bridegroom's mother, and now Deborah seemed to have taken sole charge of the young bridesmaids after the disgraced Betsy departed with sick all down her dress, her hand wrathfully clasped by an outraged, red-faced Elizabeth.

Towards the end of the afternoon, after all the toasts were drunk and speeches finished, and just as the bride and groom were about to leave, Bart managed to make his way surreptitiously around the room so that he stood almost next to Deborah. By now all backs were turned as the focus of attention was on the bride and groom.

'Hello!' Bart mouthed to Deborah, who gave him a distant sort of smile.

Bart sidled up to her.

'Enjoy the day?'

'Oh, lovely. Didn't Ruth look gorgeous?'

'Well,' Bart put his head on one side, 'I think you looked better.'

'Oh no,' a hand flew to her mouth, 'Ruth is *much* much prettier than me.'

'That's a matter of opinion.' Bart looked at her with unconcealed admiration. 'Do you think we could have dinner together again, Deborah?'

'I'd like that ... but–' She glanced over to her mother who was standing with the rector and Carson, as though discussing arrangements for the departure of the bridal couple.

'Deborah,' Bart said gently, 'you can't have your life dominated by your mother.'

'I know, but...'

'I am aware that she doesn't like me, but she can't stop you from seeing who you want. Can she?'

Deborah appeared more and more confused.

'She can't, Deborah,' Bart spoke urgently, 'and if you want to see me, and I think you do, there is no harm in it. You should be able to without being chaperoned by your sister or your new brother-in-law. Now, would you have dinner with me, say, Thursday?'

Deborah coloured and shook her head.

'I can't, really.'

'Why not?'

'It would be so hard to get away, without Mother knowing.'

'Very well then, lunch. You can get away for lunch, can't you?'

'It *might* be easier,' she said cautiously.

'I'll pick you up on the corner of the road by the bridge at, say, twelve-forty-five?'

Deborah remained silent, as if tongue-tied.

'You needn't dress up.' Sensing victory, Bart hurried on. 'It will be as though you're merely going for a walk.'

'Friday would be better. Mother, I know, is away that day, at a church function in Bristol.'

'Friday, then.' Bart reached out and furtively squeezed her hand. 'Don't forget, and don't be late.'

Deborah shook her head.

'And don't be *afraid*,' he hissed.

'Remember, your life is yours not your mother's.'

With their three children, Connie and Carson had settled into an easy tenor of life at Pelham's Oak and, in the days following the wedding reception, things gradually returned to normal. The reception rooms were cleaned, the furniture polished or dusted and put back into place, the long trestle tables taken to one of the outbuildings for storage until the next time they would be required. The large house ran smoothly, aided by its devoted staff under the guidance of Connie who, despite the money that had cosseted her against the harsh rigours of life, was a frugal and expert housekeeper.

It was understood that she was in charge of the arrangements indoors while Carson controlled everything that happened out of doors, from the care of the gardens and grounds to the running of the farms and the tenancies of the various properties on the estate.

One could not wish for a happier, more peaceful life, Connie thought as she opened the mail in the breakfast room which had been laid on this particular morning for three, as Dora was out riding with Carson. The children ate earlier in the nursery, as Connie and Carson tended to breakfast late after he had had his morning ride and she had checked the lunch and dinner menus with cook, and gone over the day's household duties with the butler and head housemaid.

Arthur, the Woodvilles' devoted butler for so many years, had retired to a comfortable flat in Bournemouth and his successor, David Rose, was a local man who had trained at Kingston Lacy, the stately home of the Bankes family near Wimborne, first as footman then under-butler.

Connie finished sorting the post and put Carson's beside his plate, curious about one letter which was addressed to him in a rounded, ill-educated hand. By contrast the rest of his correspondence was, as usual, largely to do with business.

Her own mail was sparse but this morning contained a letter from her friend Francesca Valenti who had been such a help to her after her guardian died and she settled, she thought for ever, in Venice. Francesca and her husband kept an eye on Connie's property there, a flat in one of the palazzi on the Grand Canal, and her letters were always full of news and gossip about the Venetian scene.

Connie had just finished reading her letter when Carson came in, still wearing jodhpurs from his morning ride, followed by Dora, cheeks flushed, eyes sparkling with

221

good health.

'Did you have a good ride?'

'Wonderful!' Dora flung her arms impulsively round Connie. Then, looking at Carson, 'Oh, I shall miss you both so much.'

'And we miss you.' Carson held her chair back for her. 'I wish you lived nearer.'

'Jean promises that we will come over in the summer before the *vendage*. And, of course, I can come at any time,' Dora paused, 'only I must be careful. I never want to upset Jean again. He has been so sweet to me, so giving. Really I don't deserve such a good husband.'

'You do.' Connie clasped Dora's hand reassuringly.

'No I don't.' Dora sat back, her mouth in a stubborn line. 'I behaved abominably, both towards Jean and poor little May. Where is she? Does anyone know?'

Carson shook his head. 'I know that Bernard Williams wouldn't have her back, nor would he let her see her children. Someone said she was in London.'

Dora, hand on her chin, gazed solemnly at the table. 'She gave up the Yorkshire house and just vanished. I was paying her an allowance, but she stopped claiming it and I had a note from the bank that her account had been closed. I feel very *bad* about May.'

'Surely what she did was voluntary?' Carson went over to the sideboard where

222

breakfast awaited them on silver chafing dishes.

After his ride, Carson enjoyed a good breakfast and appreciatively lifted one cover after the other inspecting the contents. 'Can I serve you, Dora?'

'What about Connie?'

'She eats nothing at breakfast. Oh, a piece of toast.'

'Well, I like a cooked breakfast.' Dora got up and stood beside Carson examining one dish after the other: kedgeree, devilled kidneys, eggs fried and boiled, sausages, mushrooms. 'There's enough to feed an army,' Dora observed with a smile.

'Our cook was used to a large family in her last post. She never quite seems to have got the hang of ours. She longs for the days of the stately home with lots of people. As she knew you were coming for breakfast she made the most of it. But the portions are small.'

'Enough to feed an *army*,' Dora said again returning with a well-filled plate.

David entered unobtrusively with toast in a silver rack for Connie and a coffee pot. While they ate he filled their cups.

'That's all for the moment, thank you, David,' Connie said, selecting a piece of toast. Then to Dora, 'I do agree with Carson. May was old enough to know what she was doing. You mustn't feel too guilty.

After all *she* chose to leave the children.'

'She said her nerves were in shreds. I was very worried about her. I think Bernard was very difficult. However, I'm sorry May has cut off contact, which is obviously her choice. Meanwhile I have to rebuild my life with Jean and Louise.'

Carson had started sorting through his mail and was looking at the envelope mentally singled out by Connie, a frown on his face as he too examined it.

For some reason Connie found herself watching him anxiously. However, Carson put the letter down without opening it and continued with his breakfast. When he had finished he sat back, poured himself another cup of coffee in a leisurely manner and then slid a paper knife through the envelopes before him, leaving the handwritten one until the end.

Finally, he opened it and Connie watched him as he perused a closely written, single sheet of paper. Because of his busy, healthy outdoor life he always had a good complexion, but she could have sworn he paled as he came to the end of the letter and put it thoughtfully on the table in front of him.

'Anything wrong, darling?' Connie's tone was carefully offhand.

Carson didn't reply, but leaned on his elbow gazing out of the window, as if he

224

hadn't heard.

'Carson?' Connie asked again and now Dora had put down her knife and fork and was looking at him curiously.

After a while Carson shook his head.

'It's nothing,' he said briskly, gathering up his letters. 'I'll be in my study if I'm wanted.' Then as if remembering Dora he stopped and smiled.

'Same time tomorrow, Dora?'

'I'm not sure. I don't think so.' Dora looked up at him. 'You know we're leaving the day after. I feel I have to spend more time with Mother.'

'Anyway, you're dining with us tomorrow night.' He smiled at her again and left the room.

Connie felt uneasy. But she knew better than to question Carson about the contents of the letter.

Dora carried on with her breakfast and when she had finished sat back and lit a cigarette.

'More coffee?' Connie asked.

'Thanks.' Dora passed her cup. 'Carson seems rather upset by that letter. I wonder what was in it?'

'Oh, I don't expect it was anything,' Connie replied casually. 'Probably some ... well, I don't know.' She shook her head. 'It had a London postmark.' She looked steadily at Dora. 'Carson and I have no secrets from each other. I'm sure he'll tell me in due course.'

Carson sat in the train bearing him to London, the letter he had received a few days before in his hand. He had wanted to leave immediately but he also wanted time to think, to decide what to do. On one hand he could ignore it. Forget Nelly had ever existed though, as he was a kind and compassionate man, this would have been a very difficult thing to do.

But to have rushed up to London would have worried Connie, and then there was the imminent departure of Dora and Jean. So he decided to wait until they had gone. Then, without telling his wife the reason, he announced he had to make a trip to London to attend to some business. He would stay the night at his club and be back the following day.

Again, Connie knew better than to question him.

Carson read the letter, written in very carefully rounded, unformed handwriting, through again.

'Dear Sir Carson,

'I hope you will forgive me writing to you. It is about Nelly. She is very sick. She asks all the time about her son what she left on the doorstep of a lady before the war. She believed the lady was related to you. She has never forgiven herself, sir, and has always pined for the baby. She was forced to give him away as she had no means of support.

My reason for writing is Nelly believes you are the father of her child and you may know his whereabouts.

You do not know me, sir, but I have been a friend of Nelly's for many years. We were in service together until Nelly got sick. Now we are both out of work.

She read about you in the papers when you was married, saw your picture, and said how little you'd changed. She remembered you well. I hope you will not blame me for writing, but I think it would help Nelly to die in peace if you was to be kind enough to help her.

Respectfully,
Massie Smith.'

Nelly: dark hair, oval face, deeply recessed black eyes, the face of a quattrocentro Madonna. She had been a barmaid he met in a pub in London to which he used to repair to cheer himself up, when he had worked in the Martyn Heering business as a clerk in a warehouse by the river and had hated it. They had had a passionate affair.

Once, he had even considered marrying Nelly, but then he had considered marrying so many women with whom he, a deeply susceptible young man, had fallen in love. There was Prudence, a farm girl to whom he had promised marriage; and he had even considered marrying Elizabeth, not knowing at the time that she was his half-sister! Happily fate spared him to marry his one true love, now his dear wife: Connie.

Carson tucked the letter inside his breast pocket and sighed deeply. He was very unhappy. Instinct had told him to throw away the letter, to forget about Nelly, but he could not. He would never have been able to live with himself afterwards. His conscience would have pricked him for the rest of his life.

But what to do? He had longed to confide in Connie, yet he dared not. Nor had there been the time, Dora and Jean on the verge of leaving, a dinner party for them and farewells to make. He nearly confessed all to Dora but he knew it would worry her and this was something he had to face up to himself. For Nelly was the mother of Alexander, whom he had always suspected was his son. Now he knew.

Truth will out, but for him at this moment, a worse situation could not be imagined. He closed his eyes and tried to sleep, as he had had precious little sleep the night before.

Carson took a cab to the street in Stepney

which contained a row of drab-looking houses, most with torn net curtains across the windows, some without. One or two had the woodwork painted and fresh curtains at the windows, but the one in front of which he stood looked forlorn and neglected. An overflowing dustbin stood outside the front door with a mangy cat rubbing itself up and down against it as if to try and appeal to Carson's good nature for a home or, at the very least, a scrap of fish or bacon.

Carson knocked on the door, removed his hat and stood waiting. Round him gathered a crowd of curious adults and children, a couple more cats, and a dog or two. Even those with long memories could not recall the last time a cab had drawn up outside the house in the street.

The door opened a crack and a face peered round it, a rather frightened, elfin face with large hazel eyes and a pitted, unhealthy-looking complexion.

'Sir Carson?' she whispered and, as Carson nodded, she opened the door and anxiously drew him in. Then she stood for a second, bawling obscenities to the crowd gawping round the door and with a rude gesture told them to be off.

'Some people have no manners,' she said as she slammed the door shut. 'You'd think they'd never seen a gentleman before.'

'Probably thought I was the rent

collector,' Carson said with a smile.

'Oh no, sir. You should *see* the rent collector. Face like a ferret. I can tell you *he* ain't no gentleman.'

'You must be Massie,' Carson held out his hand.

'It was *ever* so good of you to come, sir.' Massie appeared overcome with confusion and agitatedly wiped her hands on her pinafore as she led him into a small back room. 'I can hardly believe it.'

'Well, I got your letter and came as soon as I could. You see,' Carson looked round for somewhere to put his hat and finally threw it on a chair which had seen better days, 'I had always suspected Alexander was my son. For one thing he looks so like Nelly, and then he was abandoned at the house of my aunt which Nelly had once visited. But I could not find Nelly, though at the time I tried.'

'Alexander.' Massie's eyes widened. 'Then you *do* know where he is?'

'I do indeed. At this moment he is at Cambridge University, a fine young man whose adoptive mother has given him the best start in life he could possibly want. Now, where is Nelly?'

'You will be very shocked, sir.' Massie wrung her hands again.

'Is she really dying?' Carson whispered.

'It's the tubercular, sir. She is a shadow of

what she was.'

'Has she had treatment?'

Massie gave a derisive laugh.

'Well, we know what's wrong with her, but treatment ... the doctor said she was past treatment. I give her cough mixture occasionally when her cough is bad. The doctor said her lungs was like leather. Charged her ten shillings for the information too.' Massie sniffed. 'Said he wanted to see her again, but at that price ...'

'I'd like to see her,' Carson said urgently and Massie stood back to allow him to pass up the stairs. Heart racing, Carson stood outside the closed door, knocked and then pushed it open.

Nelly lay on a bed in the corner, her hands on the coverlet, her eyes closed. She seemed to Carson unnaturally still, but as he stood looking down at her she opened those wonderful dark eyes whose brilliance seemed, perhaps, accentuated by her condition.

'Nelly,' he whispered as his eyes filled with tears.

'Carson,' she said in a voice so weak he could hardly hear her. 'I knew you'd come.' And, as he sat by her side, she took his hand and brought it unsteadily to her lips.

Ten

Sarah-Jane Yetman sat on a stool in the shade at the back of the house shelling peas. The country was enjoying, if that was the word, a heatwave and it was nice to be in the cool out of doors. There was no breeze at all; the landscape shimmered in the intense heat of the sun, and even the birds were silent. At her feet her Labrador, Rufus, lay panting, and the cats kept to the shadows cast by the house. The air seemed strangely, almost eerily, still.

She was quite alone. The cottage at the side of the house where Ted and Beth, Elizabeth's foster parents, used to live, was now occupied by Ruth and Abel until such time as the house Abel was building for them was finished, perhaps towards the end of the year. Her two live-in maids slept in the attic.

Carson had given Ruth and Abel a piece of land not a mile from Pelham's Oak as a wedding present and today they had both gone to see how work on the project was progressing. The house had been designed by Solomon Palmer, in keeping with the traditional architecture of the great house on whose land it was being built. It would be a large house reflecting the style of a successful businessman in which Abel intended to live.

Martha had gone to London to work as a secretary in a newspaper office in Fleet Street, and Felicity had decided to be a nurse and was training at the ancient hospital of St Bartholomew in the City. Martha lived in a women's hostel in Bloomsbury and Felicity in the nurses' home. Both sisters saw each other regularly and this was a comfort to Sarah-Jane who had never been to London in her life and thought of it as a large, dangerous place, especially for young women.

Sarah-Jane was glad that Felicity had decided to settle down, if she had. She had tried a number of jobs and nothing appealed. In Sarah-Jane's opinion what Felicity really wanted was to get married, whereas Martha was more of a career woman and hoped one day to join the journalistic staff on the newspaper, although it was a career that offered few opportunities to women.

Sarah-Jane was glad of the proximity of Ruth and Abel, though they would soon be gone, and what then? She would have a large house, with a separate cottage and outbuildings, entirely to herself except for the two maids. Time had always hung heavily upon her hands, and she knew she would be lonely. She had been a widow for eighteen years and, although she would have liked to have married again, the opportunity had never presented itself.

In many ways she was an unhappy, unfulfilled woman who had never really recovered from the shock of her husband's premature death. Everything had seemed so perfect; everything was going so well and then–bang! It all vanished.

She knew that, although she had been a good, conscientious mother to her growing children, she had also lacked patience and, perhaps, understanding. She was critical, cantankerous, and the wonder was that they, especially Abel, remained so loyal and faithful to her. The girls had rebelled more than her sons, which was perhaps why they had gone away and he remained at home.

But not for much longer. Sarah-Jane rose, straightened her back and was about to pick up the dish of shelled peas when she heard a crunch on the gravel and Solomon Palmer peered round the corner of the house.

'Oh, Mrs Yetman...' He seemed surprised to see her. 'I hope I haven't disturbed you?'

'Not at all. Abel's not here, I'm afraid. He and Ruth have gone to look at the house.'

'Ah!' Solomon put a hand to his mouth. 'Do you know when he'll be back?'

'I'm afraid I have no idea.' She paused and

looked at him. He seemed very hot. 'Would you like a cold drink? I was just about to get some lemonade.'

'That's *very* kind.'

'We could have it out here in the shade.'

'I feel I'm disturbing you,' he said.

'You're not disturbing me at all. Do take your jacket off and roll up your sleeves. I shan't be long.'

Sarah-Jane went into the kitchen and suddenly her heart felt lighter and she began to hum a tune. It would be nice to have someone to chat to. The time went so slowly. People popped in, of course, and she went daily into the town to shop. Ruth often came over to keep her company, although these days she was so busy planning the house, the furnishings, decoration and fittings for when it would be finished. Sometimes her mother went with her and sometimes she went alone, or took a friend or her sister. Very rarely her mother-in-law.

Sarah-Jane made a jug of lemonade, put some biscuits on a tray and took it back into the yard where Solomon was sitting, now in his shirt-sleeves. He was lying back in his chair, his eyes half-closed. He started as she appeared and smiled rather shamefacedly.

'I'm afraid I was day-dreaming. I should really be at work.'

'Well, you rest while you can in the shade. This heat takes its toll.' Sarah-Jane set the

235

tray on a table, poured the lemonade and passed him his glass. 'Of course we're not used to it.'

'True.' Solomon nodded and, reaching for the glass, drank thirstily.

'My, that was good.' He wiped his mouth on the back of his hand.

'Have some more.' Sarah-Jane held out the jug and refilled his glass.

'Have you seen the house?' he asked.

'Abel took me over to see it last week. It's coming on well. It is going to be very *big*.'

'Maybe they want a large family?' Solomon looked at her.

'Maybe they do. I must say this house will be too big for me when they've all gone. I shall have to look for something smaller.'

'Oh, what a pity. It's such a lovely house.' Solomon gazed up at the gables, baking in the sun.

'I shall be rattling around in it like a pea.'

'Hasn't it been in the family for a long time?'

Sarah-Jane nodded.

'For a very long time. It was the Yetman family home in the time of Abel's great-grandfather, John. He was the father of the present Lady Woodville.'

'Abel's great-grandfather was Lady Woodville's *father*?' Solomon looked at her incredulously.

'He married for a second time. He was

236

twenty years older than his wife. She died in childbirth by which time, of course, he was nearly an old man. Poor Connie was orphaned at the age of eight. But she didn't do too badly. She was well looked after and, in time, became a very rich woman.' Sarah-Jane paused thoughtfully. 'Though you'd never think it.' She looked across at Solomon. 'Would you, I mean? They live quite frugally. Of course the Woodvilles never had very much money. The men invariably married heiresses, so Carson made it very clear that he wanted Connie for her own sake and not for her riches.' Sarah-Jane paused self-consciously. 'I'm gossiping, I'm afraid.'

'No, I really find it quite fascinating,' Solomon said. 'I mean all the family connections and so on. I come from a small family. I'm an only child and my family is, frankly, suburban. Croydon,' he finished as if that word alone explained everything.

'Croydon? Where is that?'

'It's just outside London. It's a grey, sprawling suburb of the metropolis. My father is an architect with quite a flourishing practice. But he is a man of very limited horizons. Our family is middle-class and rather boring.'

'But you're not boring!'

'It's very nice of you to say so, Mrs Yetman.'

'I don't think you're at *all* boring, and nor do Abel or any members of my family. But why did you come to a place like this? I mean Croydon may be out of the way but Wenham and Blandford...' she finished lamely.

'Are the most *delightful* places!' he concluded for her. 'Here we are really right in the heart of England.'

'Did you just pick a place from the map?'

'Not quite. We used to holiday in Dorset, Weymouth or Bournemouth and my father, being an architect, used to take me on excursions to interesting places, houses or churches of which Dorset has a number. I liked Blandford. Also I had friends in Dorchester who introduced me to Abel. So I stayed.'

'And a good thing you did.' The sun had begun to encroach round the side of the house and Sarah-Jane moved her chair back. 'Abel is very happy with your partnership.'

'And so am I. Nothing could be more delightful.'

'Shall you, do you think, settle here?'

'Oh, undoubtedly. I am in lodgings at the moment, but I am looking for a property round here, if possible. I love Wenham.'

'Well, you may be able to buy Riversmead one of these days. That is, if I decide to sell.'

'I think that would be a great shame but if

it ever is on the market then, yes, I might well be most interested. Although it is a very big house for a single man.'

'I don't suppose that will last long.' Sarah-Jane laughed as she rose and took the tray. 'Any number of young ladies in these parts would be only too glad if you paid attention to them. I can assure you of that. Another drink, Solomon?'

'No thanks, Mrs Yetman. I really must make a start.'

'And I must get on too. The maids have a day off.' She paused to look at him. 'There is no need to call me 'Mrs Yetman', you know. Sarah-Jane's my name.'

'Sarah-Jane, then.' Solomon returned her glance as if a new, unexpected note of familiarity had suddenly been struck between them. 'I feel I've taken up too much of your time.' He began to roll down his shirt-sleeves.

'Not at all. I was glad of your company. You are welcome any time. *Most* welcome.' Her eyes lingered on him for a few seconds and, as she returned to the kitchen, Solomon leaned back and followed her progress through half-closed eyes.

It was difficult to think she was Abel's mother, her appearance was so youthful. She was not beautiful or even pretty and probably never had been. But she was what was known as a good-looking woman who held herself well and had kept her figure. She had short brown hair and blue eyes, an aquiline nose and good cheek-bones, a firm, decisive-looking mouth. She exuded good health and a certain warm sexuality which Solomon found attractive, even exciting.

He wondered why she had remained a widow for so long as, getting up, he retrieved his jacket and followed her into the house.

'Thanks very much for the drink,' he said shrugging into his jacket.

'I enjoyed having you.' She stared at him appraisingly. 'I'm sorry Abel wasn't here.'

'I don't mind at all.' Solomon smiled down at her. 'I enjoyed talking to you.'

'And I to you.'

There was again a pause as if neither was willing to relinquish this moment of new-found intimacy.

'Do tell Abel not to forget we have people coming for dinner.' Sarah-Jane made an effort to suppress this curious, rather worrying feeling of excitement as she saw him to the door by keeping her tone utterly normal, even mundane, her expression polite but vacuous.

She opened the door just as Sophie Turner appeared, walking up the lawn from the river. She stopped, as if surprised to see Solomon standing behind Sarah-Jane.

'Solomon came to see Abel,' Sarah-Jane

explained, but she knew that her cheeks had a high colour.

'Hello, Mr Palmer.' Sophie held out her hand. 'Isn't it *hot*?'

'Very hot,' Solomon replied. 'I was just going.'

'They say there will be thunder.'

'I shouldn't be surprised.' Solomon turned to his hostess. 'Thanks very much for the drink, Sarah-Jane.'

'It was a pleasure.' She bowed her head, rather wishing he hadn't used her Christian name in front of Sophie. 'And don't forget to give Abel my message.'

'I shan't.' Solomon smiled at her once more, then at Sophie and ran down the steps to his car.

The two women stood for a moment watching the car as it disappeared down the drive and through the main gates.

'He's a nice young man,' Sophie said after a while. Then she looked keenly at Sarah-Jane. 'Don't you think?'

'Very.' Sarah-Jane's cheeks still glowed as she led the way inside the house to the cool of the front drawing-room. 'I think it's cooler inside than out, though Solomon and I sat at the back, away from the sun.'

Conscious that this again might seem a compromising statement she added defensively: 'He came to see Abel and I offered him lemonade.' She fanned herself with her hand and slumped into a chair. 'It is *so* hot.'

'I wondered if you'd seen Deborah?' Sophie sat in a chair facing Sarah-Jane, took off her straw sun-hat and placed it on the chair beside her. 'I thought she'd gone for a walk but she hasn't come back. It is a very hot day to go for a walk, even by the river. I'm worried about her.'

'I'm sure there's no need to worry. She's quite able to look after herself. Maybe she's fallen asleep somewhere in the cool. Did you look in the boathouse?'

'Yes.' Sophie folded her hands, anxiously rubbing one against the other. 'I don't know why she has to stray away like this. It seems to have become a habit recently and I can never find her.'

'Well, she's nothing else to do, has she?'

'How do you mean?'

'I mean that for a young woman of her age Deborah is curiously unoccupied. She has no occupation, no interests in the parish. She must be very bored.'

'It hardly becomes *you* to criticise my daughter,' Sophie said tartly. 'It never seems to me that you have very much to do yourself, Sarah-Jane.'

Sarah-Jane looked sharply at the woman to whom she was now allied by marriage. She liked Sophie well enough, there was nothing particularly to dislike about her, but had never felt close to her. She was in many ways a difficult person really to know. Even after living next to her for so many years she felt she was something of an enigma. Somehow one was in awe of her, an older woman, a woman with a past, the rector's wife.

'Thank you, Sophie, but may I remind you that I have brought up three children by myself. I have had a house to maintain and staff to look after, though now that is reduced to two maids and a gardener. I think I can rest on my laurels after all these years.'

'Please don't think I meant to criticise *you*,' Sophie said hastily. 'I chose my words carelessly. The fact is that I do worry about Deborah. It is true she hasn't enough to do. She never felt the call of God that her father and I had and which we might have hoped would have been passed on to our daughters. Neither has she ever been particularly religious.' She looked appealingly across at the woman sitting opposite her. 'I *honestly* didn't mean to criticise you, Sarah-Jane, please don't think that I did. I know you have had a hard life and it was a thoughtless thing for me to say. Maybe we have not given you as much help as we should because we all thought you capable, and then you had the support of Eliza. I am sorry if we have neglected you, or misunderstood you.'

'Oh, I have not felt neglected or misunderstood.' Sarah-Jane gave a shaky laugh. 'I think I gave into the depression and bitterness that followed Laurence's death. I assure you I am beginning to see how much I've missed in life. I'm beginning to come out of my shell.'

Sophie gazed at her thoughtfully, thinking of the tall, handsome but so very much younger man who had stood just behind Sarah-Jane in the doorway giving, even from quite far away, an impression somehow of an intimacy, of a closeness that would not have been expected when one considered the age difference between the two.

Maybe she was reading too much into the situation? On the other hand there was the use of her Christian name that seemed again unusual, when one considered that Solomon was a friend of her son's, and Sarah-Jane a much older woman. In these circumstances the use of a Christian name was, to say the least, unusual.

'Well.' Sophie got up. 'I must be getting back. I have a meeting of my Mothers' Union to prepare for. You wouldn't by any chance be interested in joining the committee, would you, Sarah-Jane? I know you attend the meetings sometimes. We have a desperate need of people to help our good work.'

As she spoke Sophie turned towards the window and, apparently seeing something that interested her outside, went over and peered out as if to make a closer inspection.

'I–' Sarah-Jane began but got no further as Sophie gave an exclamation that made her hurry to her side. Sophie was looking at a car that had stopped by the bridge and at the two people who stood beside it, apparently engaged in earnest conversation, heads close together. Then, as they watched, the heads merged in what was unmistakably a kiss. The man put his hands on the woman's shoulder, drawing her ever closer to him and then, as if afraid of being observed, they sprang apart and the woman started along the path by the river, heading towards the Rectory while the man stood for some time gazing after her.

Deborah Woodville and Bart Sadler. No doubt about it.

Sophie said nothing for a moment while Sarah-Jane remained just behind her. Then she put a hand on Sophie's shoulder and pressed it, as though to comfort her.

'Now you know why she takes so many walks,' she said quietly in Sophie's ear.

'Did you *know* about this?' Sophie's voice was scarcely above a whisper.

'I have seen them before.'

Slowly Sophie turned to face her.

'Don't you think you should have said

245

something to me?'

'Sophie,' Sarah-Jane looked earnestly into her eyes, 'Deborah is a grown woman, twenty-six or -seven I believe. Surely she is allowed to do as she likes? See who she wishes?'

'I suppose it is because Bart is your brother.' Sophie pronounced his name contemptuously. 'You feel you have to defend him.'

'Not at all. You know that I disapproved of Bart as much as anyone. I too thought he had a great deal of responsibility for my husband's death. He mixed in undesirable company...' She paused not wishing to say more for fear of getting too close to the other aspect of Bart's behaviour that concerned her guest. 'But Sophie,' she went on, 'Bart *is* an unattached man. Deborah an unattached woman. They are free to do what they like with their lives.'

'Not if *I* can help it,' Sophie said. 'Apart from his qualities of character, which leave much to be desired, there is a big difference in age, nearly thirty years.' Then, seizing her straw hat, she placed it firmly on her head and hurried out.

Sarah-Jane didn't attempt to stop her but watched, rather helplessly, from the window, as Sophie half-walked, half-ran across the lawn.

Sophie didn't wait for Deborah to answer her knock but threw open the door of her daughter's bedroom and marched in. Deborah was lying on the bed staring at the ceiling, hands behind her head, when her mother seized her roughly by the shoulders and hauled her into an upright position. She then shook her hard before releasing her, almost throwing her back on the bed, and Deborah, entirely bewildered by this turn of events, sat there staring at her mother, wondering if she had suddenly gone out of her mind.

'I *told* you not to see that man again!' Sophie shook her finger violently at her daughter.

'What man?' Deborah stammered.

'You *know* quite well *what* man. I saw you getting out of his car. Sarah-Jane tells me that you meet frequently. How *dare* you, miss, under my very nose?' She raised her hand as though she was going to strike Deborah who, in all her years, had never seen her mother in such a rage.

However, suddenly Sophie seemed to think better of it and, crossing to the dressing table, stared hard at herself in the mirror, as if she could scarcely believe what she had done. She agitatedly pulled down her sleeves, and ran a finger round the neckline of her dress. She then looked through the mirror across the room at

247

Deborah, who sat on the bed, arms folded, staring at the floor.

'Well, say something,' Sophie said, swirling round.

'What can I say?'

'Say that you won't see him again.'

'I can't. I won't.'

At these words of defiance Sophie strode across the room and raised her hand, whereupon Deborah jumped up from the bed and, seizing her mother by the wrist, gripped her arm with her own superior strength.

'You *dare* touch me!' she murmured, 'and the whole town will know of your affair with Bart Sadler, the fact that you had a child by him and that that is the reason you hate him so much and don't want me to see him.'

She paused and, releasing her mother's arm, tossed back her head. 'Anyway,' she went on, a sneer on her face, 'most of them know already. Even the servants know. It is apparently fairly common knowledge that he was your lover, Mother. You used to go openly to his house and when you found you were expecting his child you persuaded poor Father, who had never hurt a soul in his life, to take pity on you and make an honest woman of you because Bart, who by this time despised you for your hypocrisy, would not.'

'That is a *lie!*' Sophie whispered.

'What is a lie? That you had an affair?'

'Your stepfather always wanted to marry me...'

'But he was not Sam's father, was he, Mother? For all these years you, the daughter of a priest and the wife of one, have lied and deceived yourself and others. You are a whited sepulchre, Mother, with your pretend picty, your business with church affairs, your excessive good works. Yet all the time you are a woman who–'

'Stop, stop, stop!' Sophie flung herself on the bed and pressed herself against the pillows in a paroxysm of weeping.

But Deborah felt no pity for her mother. Instead she gazed at her, her lip curled contemptuously.

'Have a good cry, Mother. But please don't threaten me any more. I shall see who I like, when I like, and I like Bart Sadler. He is good to me, kind. He does not treat me like a child as you do, or a fallen woman as everyone else does. He treats me like an adult and I enjoy his company.'

'Even though he was my lover?' her mother said tremulously, looking up at her with eyes swollen by tears.

'That was years ago.'

'It doesn't alter the situation. It is too horrible to contemplate ... it is, why, it is like incest! I don't know how you can do such a thing, knowing what you know.'

'Do *what?*' Deborah asked.

'Well, I must assume, knowing the sort of man he is, and the sort of person, Deborah, that *you* are, that you are lovers.'

She stopped and, sitting up on the bed, wiped both eyes, stuffed her handkerchief up the sleeve of her dress and attempted with both hands to tidy her dishevelled hair. She gazed at Deborah, who was now leaning against the wall still staring at her with that expression of ill-concealed contempt.

'However much I may have sinned,' Sophie hurried on, 'and I confess I *did* sin, I have spent the rest of my life repenting of it. I regard myself as the lowest of the low in the face of the Almighty from whom I never cease to ask pardon. Bart Sadler deceived me all those years ago, as I daresay he will deceive you. He was not worthy of my love, and he is not worthy of yours, if that is how you feel about him.

'On the other hand, Deborah,' Sophie got unsteadily to her feet and walked across the room to the window from the corner of which she could just see the bridge where her daughter had her tryst with Bart, 'maybe it is to be expected from a woman who was capable once of causing me so much pain. You disappeared for six months and in that time I aged a decade. Your poor stepfather could hardly carry out his parish duties he was so bereft. Every time I think of that terrible period I wonder how ever I endured it. Not a word, not a sign you were alive. Anyone capable of *that* is indeed capable of what you are doing to me now. What is more, you have never shown the slightest repentance for all the suffering you caused. Nor do you ever wish to see the son you brought into the world, which is something I can scarcely believe a mother capable of. You leave all that to me and your stepfather, who is a saint, as we know. Meanwhile you lead a life dedicated to yourself, your wishes, your desires. I cannot force you to be religious, but you never even go through the appearances. I can't remember when you last went to church, unlike your sister, who has been a model of everything a mother could wish.

'I never thought I would say this to you, Deborah, but you are one of the most selfish people I have ever known. I love you, for you are my daughter, my first-born. I see, however, that I have no more control over you and, God forgive me saying it, but I fear that from today nothing can ever be the same between us again.'

Later, much later that night, as Sophie lay in bed unable to sleep beside the slumbering form of her husband, she repented yet again for having lost control of herself with her daughter. She should have resisted the

251

temptation to say what she did, to tell Deborah the truth at last about her way of life. She knew she was stung, bitterly wounded, by what Deborah had said, by the open contempt in her daughter's eyes. On the other hand she, Sophie, had said too much, been too frank. Even if what she told her was the truth she should not have said it. Well, not all of it.

Towards the small hours of the morning she thought she heard the sound of a motor car draw up outside the house. She tiptoed out of bed and drew back the curtains and, by the light of the moon she saw the shape of Bart Sadler's big shiny car, and Bart standing by the door, holding it open.

Then she saw Debbie as she hurried along the garden path carrying a suitcase which she gave to Bart who, after kissing her firmly on the lips, ushered her inside the vehicle. Without another glance at the Rectory he drove away as silently as he had come.

Like a thief in the night.

Once more Deborah Woodville had fled; but this time her mother knew where she had gone.

There was some consolation in this, but she knew that she would never, ever attempt to try and find her. She had paid a heavy price for her association with Bart Sadler and so, she was sure, would Deborah.

For did not the Bible say that as you

sowed, so you would reap?

Dawn was greeted by a great clap of thunder signifying that the heatwave which had so afflicted the country was over, and the rains began.

All day the torrent continued and for much of it Sophie stayed in her little sitting room, nose pressed against the windowpane watching the drops of rain which trickled relentlessly down like so many tears, as if the heavens too were weeping yet again for the loss of her once beloved child, Deborah.

Eleven

Carson knocked gently on the cottage door and then pushed it open and peered inside. The sitting room looked much as it must have in the days of his Uncle Ryder, who had lived there for a while before eloping with Aunt Eliza. That event which had brought such scandal to the town happened fifty years ago and, in the meantime, the cottage had had many different tenants all working for the Woodvilles or on the Woodville estate.

Eliza, recalling those happy days, had even looked round it before she went to live with Lally, wondering if it might be suitable as a temporary home for her. But it was much too small: a sitting room, a kitchen with larder, three upstairs bedrooms and an outside privy. There was no bathroom, and washing was done in the kitchen or in a tub in front of the fire, which blazed now in the inglenook. One of these days Carson meant to add a downstairs bathroom, or perhaps turn the third bedroom upstairs into one. Maybe, in view of his new tenant, he would do it sooner rather than later.

The furniture was old but in good

condition. The floor was flagstoned and covered with rugs. There were chintzy curtains at the window, and a large bowl of chrysanthemums from the Pelham's Oak greenhouses stood on the polished table in the middle.

Carson heard a step on the staircase that led upstairs from the sitting room and saw Massie standing looking down at him.

'I'm sorry,' he said, keeping his voice low. 'I hope I didn't make a noise.' Massie shook her head and came down the rest of the stairs to join him.

'How is she today?'

'She had a better night.'

'That's good,' Carson said. Moving Nelly from London to Dorset had been a difficult business, with many stops on the way for rest, even though he had gone to collect her in his comfortable motor car. Reaching Salisbury, Nelly felt unable to continue, a doctor was summoned and they rested in a hotel for two days before completing the journey.

That was not the most minor of his problems, and the last weeks had been fraught, not least because of a deteriorating situation between himself and Connie, who had very much objected to the presence of Nelly at Pelham's Oak, to the extent of threatening to leave and take the children with her. Hence a swift move to Ryder's old cottage.

'Would you like to see her, Sir Carson?'

'Please drop the 'Sir' and call me Carson. I have asked you before, Massie.'

Massie put a hand to her mouth and blushed.

'I forget. It's not that I should, because Nelly always talked so much about you. She always seemed to think she would see you again. She never bore no grudge, even when she saw in the papers you was married.'

'She's a very good soul.' Carson almost choked on his words. 'I hate to see her like this. I wish I'd known before, and I could have done something. Now,' he lowered his voice, 'it may be too late.'

The doctor's prognosis was not good. Maybe six weeks, or six months. A year at the most. It was difficult to tell what the effect on her ravaged lungs would be of a good diet, rest and wholesome country air, also good medical attention which she had lacked. She had neglected her condition for much too long since symptoms first appeared.

'I'll go and tell Nelly you're here. I know she'd like to be seen at her best.' Massie indicated a chair and Carson took his seat, looking broodingly into the fire.

He had done what was right, he knew that, despite Connie's protestations. He could not have lived with himself if he had ignored Massie's pleas, and when he saw the state

256

poor Nelly was in he had no regrets in bringing her to Wenham.

But Connie had been furious. There was no other word for it. And in her defence the whole thing had been a terrible shock. He didn't like to recall too often the day he'd told her about Nelly after his return from London, of their affair twenty years before when he was a young man and how he'd lost her, never to find her again.

Then there was the baby who had been deposited on Lally's doorstep with a note pinned to its shawl commending him to her because she was 'a good woman'.

As Alexander grew older Carson had noticed increasingly a resemblance to Nelly, dark hair, almost black eyes, a child, then a man, from a Renaissance painting; but one who had now grown into a very, very different life style from his beginnings in a house for fallen women in Houndsditch where his mother had given birth to him.

He was only a few days old when she left him on the doorstep of the Martyns' home in Montague Square to which she had once been taken by Carson while his aunt and uncle were away.

And that had been Alexander's life ever since. What now to tell this exquisite, well brought-up, well-educated and well-mannered young man about his origins?

Massie came down the stairs and

beckoned to Carson who went up to the front bedroom, tapping on the door before entering.

Nelly sat up in bed, her hair combed, her eyes shining, though her deathly pallor was as disturbing as it had been the first time he'd seen her.

However, he thought she'd put on a bit of weight due to the nourishing food she'd been eating, the good care that had been taken of her, the rest in comfortable circumstances that she'd been getting.

She held out a hand and he took it, perching beside her on the bed. He always felt immediately at ease in her company.

'How are you, Nelly?'

'I feel much better, Carson, thanks to you.'

'Thanks to Massie.'

'Her too, but if you hadn't come, Carson, I would still be in that awful hole, threatened every day with eviction because we were behind with the rent. I think I would have died very soon if it hadn't been for you.'

'I wish I'd known.' Carson pressed her hand. 'I wish I could have done something sooner. That you'd got in touch with me when you became ill.'

'I didn't know how ill I was until I started coughing blood. The doctor said I'd left it too late.' Nelly looked at him sadly. He

258

pressed her hand again and they sat there for a few moments gazing into each other's eyes, like two star-crossed lovers cruelly separated by fate.

In fact it would have been a misalliance by any standards but, at the time, they were both young and it was a romantic, beautiful affair, perhaps just because it was so doomed. There were so many disparities between them: she a working class girl whose father, a heavy drinker, was a porter in Covent Garden Market, he ... well, in those days she hadn't known he was a gentleman, the heir to a baronetcy, but thought him a farmer's son from Dorset working in the City as a clerk.

Nelly had fantasised about them living in a cottage such as this, spending a lifetime together, raising a family...

How very different reality was.

'Have you told Alexander?' she whispered.

'Not yet.' Carson withdrew his hand, stood up and went over to the window from where he could see his home on the hill about a mile away. Up there were Connie, his three children, his life. And, in a way, Nelly threatened to wreck it, not because she wanted to, but just by being here; first by exposing and then by raking over those old, long buried bones from the past. He turned away from the window and looked down at the fragile woman lying in the bed, this modern Lady of the Camellias taken from the back streets of London, transported to a way of life she had never known.

'It *is* very difficult, Nelly, I must be honest with you.' He sat down on the bed again and once more took her hand. 'You see, Alexander has known no other life than the one he leads now, thanks to you. The Martyns were very wealthy and Alexander has lacked for nothing. I don't know how to say this to you, but—'

'He would be ashamed of me,' Nelly said flatly. 'That's it, Carson, if he knew I was his mother.'

'I'm not saying he would be ashamed. Although he is an elegant young man he is also a person of deep and profound sensibilities. I think he may well admire you and be grateful for what you did for him, even if he might not think too well of me.'

'But *you* couldn't help it.'

'He still might rush to judgement. It would be difficult to explain the exact circumstances of what happened all those years ago. There is also the question of Lally, who adores him. How will she feel? The point is that she doesn't know about you either. The whole thing is going to be a shock, as it already has been to Connie, and we must decide the best way to handle it.'

'Maybe I could see him without him

knowing who I am? That's all I ask, a glance before I die...' Nelly added piteously.

'Nelly, you are *not* going to die.' Carson grasped both her hands and stared at her hard. 'The doctor says you are already making good progress.'

'I feel it in my bones, Carson,' Nelly said mournfully. 'I see it in the blood that I spit up.'

'Not yet, not for a while anyway.' Carson patted her hand, trying his best to stifle the fear, almost the sense of panic, he felt when he thought not only of Nelly's fate, but of a resolution to the situation. 'I will consult with Connie. She is very sound, very practical.'

'But she doesn't *like* me,' Nelly said, folding her hands prosaically across her stomach. 'I know I've caused trouble between you. I didn't mean to. Your wife just wants to see the back of me. Can't say as I blame her. Someone, another woman, coming out of the past, and the mother of your child as well. Can't say as I wouldn't feel the same.'

Connie knew she was being unreasonable and that she was hurting Carson very much. But she was hurt too. Hurt to the quick. It was one thing acknowledging a previous liaison, even the existence of a child you didn't know was yours. It was quite another gathering the woman up, as it were, in your arms and bringing her to your home, expecting your wife to look after her and not to mind.

It was, in fact, outrageous.

Even though it was quite obvious how ill Nelly was it would have been almost too much to expect her not to care, especially as Carson spent so much time in Nelly's company and, despite the ravages of illness, it was easy to see how beautiful Nelly must have been.

It was so like Carson, the universal do-gooder. The Ark to which everyone came in a storm, and if you protested you were accused of lack of feeling, hard-heartedness, not being able to place yourself in the situation of the one who was distressed.

There had been so many and then, when at last she felt she had him and the house to herself, along came Nelly all wrapped up in blankets, spitting blood and needing constant care, plus her friend, although one could perhaps be thankful for her and the fact that one wasn't expected to look after Nelly oneself.

Nelly had stayed several weeks in the house until Connie threatened to leave and take the children with her. She meant it. She would go to Venice, re-open her apartment there and stay while she took stock of things, maybe suing for divorce.

There was not only the question of Nelly's presence, there was the possibility of contagion from such a dreaded disease, the threat to the health of the children.

For, as much as she loved Carson, and she did, she knew he would never change. He was rather like a saint who was married not just to a woman but to mankind in general.

Surely it would have been possible to have provided for Nelly in London? Give her the care she needed there? But no, convinced of the benefit of country air, Carson had to bring her to Pelham's Oak, and a whole lot of trouble arrived with her.

Trouble they had hardly started to face.

She knew that every morning in the course of his ride he went to see Nelly. Today was no exception. She had stood at the window watching him as he entered Ryder's old cottage – it was always known as 'Ryder's Cottage' even though it had once had another other name. Pulver, his horse, was tied up outside for ages, as was usually the case and, as usual, since the arrival of Nelly, Connie had gone about some household tasks, had even breakfasted alone, before Carson returned.

Sometimes she felt that he had fallen in love with Nelly all over again.

'How was Nelly today?' Connie asked with an air of false brightness as Carson, returned from his ride, gloomily lifted the lid of one chafing dish after the other. It then seemed that nothing appealed to him because he returned to the table empty-handed, a most rare and unusual sight in someone who enjoyed his food.

'Nelly is as well as can be expected.' Carson sat staring at the table. 'I don't know what to do about Alexander.'

'What do you *want* to do about Alexander?'

Connie knew there was a waspish tone in her voice, but she couldn't help it. She felt vulnerable. She resented Nelly and the threat she posed to their marriage, their happiness, their way of life. For six years their life had been a dream. She had even been prepared when Nelly first arrived to accept that something that happened long ago was over, past. She could forgive that, overlook it. Carson had been, as he still was, an attractive man, attractive to women, very susceptible to them. But now his obsession with Nelly was making her question the very idea that it was a love that had died.

'I suppose you're *sure* Alexander is your child?' she added, picking apathetically at her piece of toast then dropping it back on its plate. She too was without an appetite.

Carson looked up at her.

'Why should he not be?'

'Well, you only have Nelly's word for it. He doesn't look a bit like you.'

264

'He looks like her.'

'We *know* she's his mother. But we have no proof that you're the father, apart from her word. You just seem to accept it, which is what I can't understand.'

'I think this is a preposterous suggestion,' Carson spluttered, pouring himself coffee, finally deciding to take a piece of toast from its rack.

'I think it is very sensible. You may well be the father, but how do you know that Nelly didn't have other lovers at the same time as you?'

'Because she told me.'

'And you believed her, of course.'

'Why should I not believe her?' His tone was icy cold.

'She was a barmaid, wasn't she? She could have had many lovers.'

'Don't be such a snob, Connie.' Carson was clearly furious.

Connie coloured. 'I apologise. That was uncalled for. What I mean is that merely because she sees your name in the paper...'

'That was six years ago.'

'I don't care how long ago it was. She remembers you, your name, and then when she falls on hard times she contacts you and yes, of course, you being the ... well, I was going to say "sap", Carson, but I expect you'd find that offensive as well.'

'I certainly should.'

'"Kind-hearted person", then,' Connie's voice was heavy with sarcasm, 'that you are, you accept everything she says, take her in, give her a home, money. The devil take your wife and children.'

By now Connie had got herself into such a state that her normally placid, cultured voice was shrill; her gentle, usually happy face contorted with violent emotion.

Carson had never seen her like that and the experience was an unpleasant one. His Connie, his precious, his beloved, was alienating him by her shrewish behaviour, her lack of understanding of poor Nelly's condition, her completely unjustified suspicions about her character. If Nelly said he was the father he believed her.

'I can't understand, you, Connie,' Carson said, after looking at her with incredulous disbelief. 'You're not yourself at all.'

'But you *are* yourself, Carson,' she said, standing up. 'Every inch yourself. In trying to please everyone you end up pleasing no one. What do you think will be the effect on Lally, on Eliza, on the rest of your family, never mind Alexander when this comes out? As if we haven't enough misfortune with Debbie eloping with a monster like Bart Sadler.'

'I never thought he was a monster.'

'No, of course you wouldn't,' Connie, beside herself, shouted at him. 'St Francis of

Assisi, seeing good in everyone, no matter how bad—'

'Oh, Connie, for God's sake shut up!' Carson cried and, flinging his napkin on the table, he got up and stormed out of the room.

For a long time Connie stared at the door behind which he had disappeared. Then she put her face in her hands and dissolved into tears.

Carson and Eliza had always enjoyed a special relationship, a special bond. As a woman whose own life had been unconventional, who had eloped with a man when she was eighteen and lived in sin with him for a long time before they were married, something considered quite shocking at any time but especially in the last years of the reign of Queen Victoria, Eliza had always had a deep understanding of and sympathy with her once wayward nephew Carson.

After his mother died Eliza became Carson's main confidante, but although she knew most things she didn't know everything. She didn't know about Nelly.

Eliza now sat very still, her head on one side as if listening intently as Carson finished his long tale about his meeting with Nelly in the London of 1909 when he had worked at the Martyn-Heering warehouse

267

as a clerk, hating every minute. After work, rather than going back home to the Martyns', with whom he was staying (he particularly didn't get on with his cousin, Roger), he used at night to go to a pub in Blackfriars where Nelly always lent a sympathetic ear and, finally, they had become lovers, sharing an idyll in a room within sight of St Paul's. It was a world away from today, but couldn't you say that about everything, Eliza thought, as the sad tale came to an end with the discovery of Alexander on Lally's doorstep, and Carson's failure to find Nelly?

'I think I might have shocked you, Aunt,' Carson said when he had finished, looking at her grave face. 'I was twenty-two, but Nelly was only twenty. I was a country boy, desperately unhappy. Nelly thought I was a farmer's son. There was no question that she had designs on me.'

'Nothing shocks me, dear.' Reassuringly Eliza reached out and took his hand. 'Especially a story like this. I was, though, quite mystified by the mysterious woman you brought to Pelham's Oak, although I thought it must be something to do with your past. No *wonder* poor Connie is so upset.'

'But I had to do what I did.'

'Of course you did. You couldn't forsake someone who is dying and in need. You did the right thing. The point is, however, what do we do now?'

'Connie threatens to leave me. Aunt Lally will be beside herself, and what do we do about Alexander?'

'I'm quite sure Connie won't leave you.' Eliza looked shocked.

'I tell you she is terribly upset and it is true I do spend a lot of time seeing Nelly.'

'Then perhaps you should spend less.' Eliza set her mouth firmly. 'I mean she has someone to look after her. Go once or twice a week, not every day.'

Carson shook his head. 'I can't do that. Not now. She will think I have forsaken her again. She is bedridden, Aunt. The doctor has given her as little as six weeks to live. If only Connie could *see* this.' He looked appealingly at his aunt. 'Maybe you could talk to her?'

'Certainly I'll do what I can.'

'She talks about Venice and taking the children.'

'Oh no, that's quite silly. But she does deserve consideration, Carson. It is inevitable that she feels insecure, jealous even, of a woman by whom you once had a child.'

'But it is absurd!'

'It is not absurd. Don't forget that you once rejected Connie too. Perhaps she feels rejected again. You bring a stranger to the house, you spend a lot of time with her ...'

269

'But a *dying* woman? Hardly a cause for jealousy?'

Eliza shrugged. 'No matter. It is the bond that is important. Maybe Connie thinks you value Nelly more than her just because of the past. I will see what I can do. Now, meanwhile,' Eliza thoughtfully put a finger to her chin, 'what do we do about Lally and Alexander?'

'You will have to tell Lally and what you decide I will abide by.' Carson leaned down and tenderly kissed his aunt's cheek. 'Once again, dear Aunt Eliza, so much depends on you.'

So much depended on her, not for the first time. On the other hand it was flattering to be called on, nice to be needed and be thought useful. Eliza was sixty-eight, no longer young, far away from that tempestuous young woman of yesteryear, a matron, a grandmother. But she did not feel her age and she knew she did not look it. Only a few streaks of white appeared in that dark, luxurious hair which had always given her a slightly Mediterranean appearance. But there were few lines on her serene olive-skinned face, and the brightness of her tawny-brown eyes was undimmed.

Most of the Woodvilles were fair, including her brother Guy, his children and her own daughter Dora. But Eliza was a curious

270

throwback, perhaps to a Portuguese ancestor of long ago on her mother's side.

After Carson had gone, Eliza remained in her sitting-room for some time trying to decide what to do, how to tell Lally and when. Fortunately, it was term-time and Alexander was away. Eliza rose from her chair and stood for a few seconds looking out of the window. It was a grey, wet, windy day. Not the best time to break the bad news to a beloved friend. Because it *was* bad news and Lally *was* beloved. Eliza alone knew all her secrets: how she had been a dancer when Guy became enraptured by her, and how they had a son, Roger. Only Guy never knew about him either, rather as Carson had never known about Alexander.

Another time, another place ... and yet history had a curious way of repeating itself. There was Deborah's son, Rupert, now almost eight years of age, who would one day have to learn about his mother. And what would he learn?

All that was known about her and Bart Sadler now was that they had married at a civil ceremony in London attended by none of the family and were honeymooning on the Continent. There were those, among them Eliza, who wished they would stay there and never return to the house Bart Sadler had stolen from her.

And then, for how long could she stay

here? She loved being at Forest House. Lally gave her complete freedom and they remained on the best of terms. In fact she knew that Lally would miss her when she went. But where to and, again, when?

She thought tea-time was maybe a good time to choose to drop Carson's bombshell on Lally. By that time Lally would have had her rest, and they always enjoyed a chat over the fire before returning to their rooms where they read or wrote letters before meeting again at seven-thirty in the drawing-room for a drink before dinner.

It was a pleasant, well-regulated life which suited Eliza as much as it suited Lally. How would it change once Lally had heard what she had to tell her? She knew Lally to be a woman of fortitude and wisdom as well as experience; but for so many years she had idolised Alexander to the state of positively believing she was his natural mother.

How could she possibly face the truth?

Eliza spent a restless and unhappy afternoon until tea-time, wondering.

Whatever the occasion Lally always looked perfect. She was a woman of expensive tastes who, from the fortune left by her husband, could afford to indulge them. Consequently, she wore an afternoon dress for tea, different to the one she had worn in the morning, and already her maid would be laying out the more formal dress she would wear for dinner that evening, even for a simple affair between her and Eliza.

Her blonde hair, now enhanced with artificial aids, was beautifully coiffeured, her make-up carefully and tastefully blended to match her complexion, and she looked tranquil and composed as she poured the tea and passed Eliza her cup.

'Did I see Carson's car here today, my dear?'

This remark provided the opportunity needed.

'Yes.' Eliza took her cup and put it on the table beside the plate containing wafer-thin cucumber sandwiches.

'Is he well?'

Lally was nothing if not inquisitive.

Eliza took a deep breath. 'Carson came to me with a problem, Lally dear.'

'Oh, I'm sorry to hear that.' Lally helped herself to a sandwich and then, leaning back, took a sip from her teacup before gently replacing it on its saucer. 'Not too serious, I hope?'

'Lally,' Eliza moved nearer the edge of her chair, 'Carson has a problem. In a way we all have, and it concerns you ... and dearest Alexander.'

'Oh my God!' Lally's hand fluttered to her breast. 'He is not hurt?'

'Oh no, no, dear. He is fine. It is

273

something, my dear, that goes back to before the war.'

And, drawing another deep breath, Eliza launched into the story, almost word for word, that Carson had told her that same morning.

When she came to the end she realised that neither she nor Lally had again touched their tea, which was by now stone cold.

At last Lally, who had remained perfectly composed throughout, spoke.

'I suppose there is no possibility of an error? This woman ... this Nelly, hoping to make something out of the story?'

'She is very near death. She can hardly leave her bed. Surely she wouldn't tell a lie? It is her wish to see Alexander before she dies.'

'But after all these years...'

'Well, she *is* his mother.' Eliza, able to relax at last, took up her cup and looked with dismay at the contents. 'Shall I ring for more tea?'

'Please do.' Lally looked preoccupied. 'Poor woman. One cannot help feeling pity for her and, in giving me Alexander, whatever the circumstances, she greatly enhanced my life. Had I not had him after Roger's death,' at last Lally showed signs of losing her iron self-control and put her handkerchief of the most delicate Brussels lace, to her lips, 'I don't know what I would

274

have done.' Looking at Eliza her large eyes swam with tears and Eliza rose and went immediately to her side. She perched on the arm of her chair and took her richly beringed hand in hers.

'Of course, my dear. Carson regards you as Alexander's real mother and so, I think, does ... Nelly.'

'How can we tell him?' Once again Lally raised eyes, full of anguish, to Eliza. 'It is not only myself I am thinking of. It is him. He is such a good, compassionate boy. He will feel so, well ... it might well cause a nervous collapse.'

'Nelly herself has made a suggestion. When Carson explained the difficulties and dangers of telling Alexander, which she quite understood and appreciates...' Eliza paused, 'I must say she sounds a *very* nice woman. However, she suggested that she might see him even from a distance...' She hesitated and looked at Lally. 'Do you think that is something that between us all we could arrange?'

It was a beautiful December morning and Alexander, home for the vacation, was riding with his uncle Carson in the grounds of Pelham's Oak. The air was crisp, and the sun, low on the horizon, threw its wintry beams across the landscape they both loved so well.

Alexander had driven over in his sports car, a present from his doting mother, and the two men, after selecting a horse for Alexander – a fine roan – set off at about eleven at a brisk canter over the fields.

Carson was proud of Alexander's prowess as a sportsman. Now in his second year at Trinity he had already played cricket and rugger for his college, and excelled on the polo field. He knew he was a rich, privileged young man yet remained curiously unspoilt by it all. As Eliza had said he had a well-developed social conscience and was careful not to parade his wealth. The following year he would be twenty-one and even richer when he would come into the large inheritance his adoptive father had left him, that and a seat on the board of the Martyn-Heering enterprise, now in the hands of the Dutch members of the family, if he wished it.

For a while Alexander and Carson rode side by side chatting about the term, Alexander's progress in his studies and in sports. If Carson felt nervous he didn't show it and Alexander was as self-assured as ever, completely relaxed, a perfect seat on a horse.

'When did Connie go to Venice?' Alexander asked, curious, as he had expected to see her when he arrived at the house.

'A couple of weeks ago.' Carson endeavoured to sound nonchalant.

'And she took the children?'

'Yes. She wants to introduce them to the delights of classical antiquities as early as possible.' Carson chuckled, but Alexander thought his attitude forced, and detected signs of strain. But he was far too polite to question his uncle, whom he so revered.

'You'll be lonely without them?'

'The house seems very quiet.'

'Will you go over for Christmas?'

'That depends.' Carson was looking anxiously at the cottage towards which they were riding, Ryder's cottage nestling in a fold in the valley.

He felt extraordinarily ill at ease and anxious lest this scheme should have unforeseen consequences. Yet Lally, he and Eliza had agreed that Nelly should have the chance to see her son but, for the time being, he should not be told she was his mother.

Carson saw the window of Nelly's room open as they approached the cottage and Massie looked anxiously out and, seeing the men cantering towards her, waved. Carson waved back as Massie abruptly turned back into the room. When Carson looked up again Nelly, aided by Massie, stood at the window, her pale face framed by her dark hair, more than ever like a Renaissance madonna. They were now very near the house and Alexander suddenly raised his head, and saw the open window.

'You have tenants in Uncle Ryder's cottage?'

'A sick woman and her maid.'

'Oh, I'm sorry to hear that.'

'The lady is tubercular and has not long to live.' Carson found himself almost choking on his words.

'How very sad, Uncle Carson.' Alexander drew in his horse and stood looking intently up at the woman standing in the window. She looked down at him and, although he couldn't see it, her eyes filled with tears. Suddenly, impulsively, she raised her hand and waved and Alexander, moved, he didn't know why, by deep emotions, by stirrings of sadness and compassion, raised his hand and waved back.

For a moment Carson took in the tableau: the strange, poignant meeting of mother and son after twenty years. He thought it would remain forever etched in his memory. Then Nelly drew back from the window, Massie appeared at it again and closed it firmly and Alexander, as if brought back to reality, gently prodded his beautiful, patient roan and began to move on. Slowly Carson caught up with him. He was almost too overcome by emotion to speak and was thankful that Alexander was a few paces ahead of him.

'What a very beautiful woman.' Alexander slowed down to let his uncle catch up with him. 'Do you know her history?'

'Oh yes, I am aware of it.' Carson paused. 'One day I'll tell you.'

'You're a very *kind* person, Uncle Carson.' In a spontaneous gesture Alexander put out his hand and touched Carson's sleeve. But Carson drew back, again feeling shabby and ashamed at this act of deception, however well-meant.

He felt there were two victims: Nelly and Alexander, and they deserved better of him.

Twelve

Sarah-Jane Yetman stood back in order to survey the decorations she had just painstakingly put on the large Christmas tree in the hall, with the aid of her two maids, Verity and Blossom. It was a task she always undertook with little enthusiasm since Laurence had chosen to take his life just before Christmas, and thus spoilt it for everyone, not only that year but for many years to come.

As Christmas drew near, a pall inevitably fell on the house as Sarah-Jane retired into semi-mourning and made frequent visits to Wenham church where Laurence was commemorated in a window together with his cousin George. Inevitably, she found Sophie there too, because George had died even closer to Christmas, which thus became, in many ways, a doleful anniversary for both houses, however hard one tried to suppress it and not spoil the festivity for others.

Sacred to the memory
of
George Pelham Woodville, born 1881,

his faithful servant Kirikeu
and their companions, who gave their
lives for Christ in Papua,
New Guinea, December 1907.
Also
in loving memory of his cousin
Laurence Thomas Yetman, born 1882,
who died November 13 1912,
both late of this parish.
This window is erected to their memory
by their family and the generous
donations of the people of Wenham.

Each year between the two anniversaries, a short memorial service was held in the church for the two men. But sometimes Sarah-Jane felt it was time this practice was discontinued, not out of love or lack of respect, but because it made it harder for her to break away from the memory of Laurence to begin life afresh. It seemed in many ways so unfair that he should be commemorated for causing his family so much grief and, as time went on, she felt her attachment to the memory of her dead husband getting more and more remote, but she carried on keeping up appearances for the sake of the family, who expected it.

However, Christmas had to be got through and once it was over she usually felt happier, as though a burden had lifted. Time to move on.

Sarah-Jane dismissed the maids and told them to get on with their household tasks. Then she looked at her watch and saw that it was only eleven o'clock, and she had the rest of the day to get through.

She still had Christmas cards to send and presents to tie up, but this year was different to the ones before because so many sad things had happened in the course of it.

Deborah Woodville had eloped with Sarah-Jane's brother, Bart, which brought new humiliation to her side of the family and grief on the Woodville side. It seemed such an awful, irresponsible way to behave and had caused untold suffering to Sophie. It was also rather deplorable, extremely irresponsible, for Debbie to repay her mother and stepfather in this way for all the kindness they had shown her, though she had never been an easy person to deal with over the years. As for Bart – well everyone had ceased expecting any responsible behaviour from him. He was a law unto himself.

Then there seemed little doubt that Carson and Connie's previously ostensibly happy marriage was on the rocks due to the appearance of a mysterious woman in Carson's life. No one knew anything about her except that she was an invalid. But Connie's objection to her was surely an indication that the appearance of the stranger had some connection with Carson's past, and she resented it.

Connie was a local girl, Wenham through and through, much loved in the small town where she had been born, and her mother and father before her. She had adorned it further in her role as lady of the manor, had participated in all the local activities and given her name to numerous good causes.

The happy family life that had seemed to predominate at Pelham's Oak was a cause for rejoicing on the part of those older members of the community who had been critical of the role of Sir Guy or his foreign wife, Margaret and, although his second wife, Agnes, still lived in the town, she was a virtual recluse. It was whispered abroad that she drank too much in order to drown her sorrows: the defection of her third husband, Owen Wentworth, who had never been traced, so that no one knew whether he was alive or dead, and the alienation of her only child, Elizabeth, which meant that she was denied the company of her many grand-children which might have been a comfort in her old age.

Agnes, who was a sister of Ryder Yetman, was not much older than her sister-in-law, Eliza, yet, in many ways, she had aged prematurely.

It was said that Constance had only gone to Venice for a holiday, but she had been away a long time and showed no signs of coming back. Nor would Carson join her for Christmas. It was a matter he refused to discuss with his family.

Apart from family troubles, the country continued to be depressed in the wake of the war which had ended twelve years before, with over a million and a half people still unemployed, disabled ex-servicemen begging on the streets of large cities, and the Labour Government, which had promised so much, unable to alter the situation. They weren't as affected by the situation in the country as the people in the towns, but it was a gloomy picture whose repercussions were felt throughout the land.

Sarah-Jane shook her head at these sad reflections and wondered what to do with the rest of the day, or how to dispel the melancholy mood that had afflicted her since the appearance of the decorations and the tree and the realisation that Christmas was only a short time away. Felicity would be home but not Martha, and Abel and Ruth would divide their time between Riversmead and the Rectory, but their minds were really on each other and their new home. Not much room there for considering other people.

Sarah-Jane sat down at her bureau and consulted the list of those who were yet to receive cards. She drew a pile towards her and began signing them when there was a tap at the door and Blossom the maid put her head round.

'It's a Mr Palmer to see you, ma'am.'

'Oh!' Glad of the interruption Sarah-Jane pushed the cards to one side and got up. 'Do tell him to come in, Blossom. He will be here to see Mr Yetman. You could also bring in some coffee.'

'Yes, madam.' Blossom exited, only to return a few moments later with Solomon Palmer who, with a pink nose and white lips, looked very cold.

'You look frozen to death.' Sarah-Jane fussed over him and shook hands. 'My goodness, your hands are cold.'

'It is a very cold day, Sarah-Jane.'

'Do warm them by the fire,' she urged, pushing him forward. 'I've asked Blossom to bring us coffee.'

'That's very good of you.' Solomon stood in front of the fire rubbing his hands together. Outside snowflakes had begun to fall.

'Very different from that hot day in August.' Sarah-Jane went and stood beside him. 'Do you remember how hot it was?'

'I do remember indeed.' Solomon looked thoughtfully at her and smiled, and the memory of that day suddenly seemed to re-awaken the mood of intimacy they'd shared then, though neither of them had referred

285

by word or gesture to it again in the half dozen times or so that they had met since, always in the company of other people connected with Abel's business.

Blossom entered and, putting the coffee tray down on a table, hovered as if wondering whether she should pour.

'Leave it, Blossom,' Sarah-Jane instructed, feeling suddenly strangely excited at the close proximity of Solomon. 'I'll see to it.'

'Yes, 'm.' Blossom dropped an awkward half curtsy and left the room. She was new and rather clumsy and, though anxious to please, she found Sarah-Jane a hard task-mistress.

'Servants!' Sarah-Jane shook her head as Blossom shut the door with a sharp bang. 'They're not what they were. But with the country in the state it's in one dare not complain.' She looked across at Solomon. 'Milk and sugar?'

'Please.'

'I suppose you've come to see Abel?' she asked as she passed him his cup. 'He's—'

'Actually,' Solomon began to stir his coffee, 'I've come to see you.'

'Oh!' Confused, Sarah-Jane took her cup and sat down in a chair facing the fire. 'In what way can I help you, Solomon?'

Solomon went on stirring his coffee, the thoughtful expression still on his face. Then he put the cup to his lips, drained it and

286

replaced it on the table.

'More?' Sarah-Jane, as well as this suppressed air of excitement, also began to feel rather nervous.

'No, thank you.' He took the chair opposite her, sat down and leaned forward, joining his hands as if he had something important to say.

'I am very attracted to you, Sarah-Jane. I wondered how you felt about me?'

'Attracted?' Sarah-Jane stammered. 'How do you mean, attracted?'

'You must know what I mean.' More at ease, once he'd put the question, he leaned back and gave a relaxed smile.

'You must know what 'attraction' means. After all you have been married and you have children.'

A blush that started from Sarah-Jane's neck ran swiftly to her cheeks.

'I can scarcely think of anything but you; when I shall see you again.'

'But...'

'I wondered if you felt the same about me? I thought perhaps you did.'

'I *like* you, Solomon, of course I do. But something like that ... why you're ... so much younger than me. You're younger than my son!'

'Is it so preposterous that a man should love an older woman? I find you physically and mentally attractive. Now were you in my place and I in yours, that is *I* were the older one, no one would consider that untoward, would they? You told me that Connie's father was twenty years older than her mother?'

'I really don't know what to say.' As she had felt the blood rush to her face Sarah-Jane now felt it drain away, and she put her head in her hands. Then after a while she said, 'I think you know, Solomon, that what you are saying ... suggesting ... would be very much frowned upon in this small community.'

'Then let us go elsewhere.'

'But that's impossible!'

'Why? We are both free. You said you might want to sell this house. Let's make a fresh start somewhere new, if that would please you.'

'I can't *consider* it.' Sarah-Jane shook her head with great emphasis. 'It is out of the question. I am flattered, of course, and you have done much to restore my self-esteem, but one of my daughters would be far more suitable for you than I. And what *they* and *Abel* would say I cannot begin to think.' She buried her head in her hands again, her mind in turmoil.

She felt a hand on her shoulder, was aware of a face close to hers. Solomon was kneeling beside her and gently he drew her hands away from her face. She looked at

288

him with wonder as he folded her in his arms and then she felt herself melting, dissolving in the warmth of the embrace in a way that, after the death of her husband, she had thought she never would again.

Sophie sat in her usual seat at the base of the window looking, as she so often did, at the image of George kneeling at the foot of the cross. George, forever young, his features unravaged by time. He had only been twenty-six when he died of fever; pure, unsullied, unspoilt, his beautiful soul dedicated entirely to the service of God, for whose sake he had sacrificed his life.

Sophie's eyes filled with tears. She knew some people might accuse her of mawkish sentimentality; but George had been so good and she was sure that, had he lived, he would have continued on the path of goodness. He would have been a wonderful priest, husband and father, returning in time, perhaps, from Papua, New Guinea to be Rector of the Parish of Wenham which had been in the gift of the Woodville family for generations.

If only things had been different she and George would have grown old together and, surely, their two daughters would have been different under the wise and loving guidance of their father? Surely Deborah would not have turned out as she had if

George had been there to correct and instruct her? Oversee her ways? Surely there would have been no illegitimate baby, no elopement with a man so much older, whose child she was now to bear?

The news that Deborah was pregnant with Bart's child had sent Sophie scurrying to the church, as she did in all moments of crisis. Under the gaze of George, carved in glass, she tried desperately to seek consolation, inspiration and, in some mystical way, advice.

It was not that Hubert had been a bad stepfather. On the contrary, he had been a very good one; wise and kind, loving the girls as though they were his own.

But they were not his own and nor was Sam, and it told. Sam was a hot-headed, difficult young man to whose faults it had been easy to shut her eyes because he spent most of his life away at boarding school.

He had never done anything dreadful, never been reported or threatened with expulsion. In fact he was a good scholar and sportsman and his reports were excellent. But when he was at home he was difficult and it was always a relief to see Sam go off again back to school or on some activity arranged during the vacations.

In her heart of hearts Sophie always thought that it had something to do with her attitude towards Sam; the fact that he was only half her child and the other half was the hated Bart. She distanced herself from Sam in a way she never had from the others, whose fathers she had loved. It was sad but it was true and, as a result, Sam was defensive and defiant towards her as if in a futile attempt to command her love.

Her youngest, Timothy, was the complete antithesis of Sam. He was like his father: tubby and cheerful. Unlike his father, however, he was a dunce at lessons, hopeless on the sports field. But he had such a sweet, gentle nature that everyone forgave him his faults.

He and Ruth were their mother's consolation. With Sam and Deborah, much as Sophie loved her eldest child, came tribulations galore.

Christmas had come and gone. The family celebrating as usual with, this year, a forced cheerfulness because of Debbie's absence and the sad fact that Carson and Connie were, temporarily at least, no longer together.

They had seemed such a happy couple, such a loving family. Heaven knew what possessed Carson to give shelter to this strange woman who was dying at Ryder's cottage from consumption. All sorts of rumours abounded, but those who knew the truth, if anyone did, weren't talking; so better not to ask.

Debbie's pregnancy was only a rumour. Mother and daughter had not communicated since Debbie's elopement, but servants were always a good source of information and Polly had it on the best authority – her sister worked as housemaid for Bart Sadler – that Debbie was expecting a baby in the summer.

The tears started to roll afresh down Sophie's cheeks. She looked round to be sure there was no one in the church but, as usual, it was empty.

Outside it was a cold, dank January day, the skies were leaden, overcast, with the threat of snow. All around the landscape was desolate. It was freezing in the church and she hugged her coat more tightly around her. Inside her heart, like her body, was as cold as ice.

Sophie got on to her knees and, head bowed, prayed for the Lord to forgive her this doubt and despair, and to help her. But the more she thought about it the more she knew that, for her daughter and herself to bear children from the same man was not only cruel, it was horribly wrong. Sam would be an uncle to his own half-brother. It went against the laws of nature. How could one live with such a situation, with such shame? And how, how could Deborah have done such a thing?

Sophie got no consolation either from her

prayers or from the pious expression of George whose eyes, raised in perpetuity to the heavens, seemed indifferent to her.

He would pity her and be full of Christian compassion for her situation, but she knew that, in his heart, he would despise her for allowing herself to give into temptation in the first place. She should have said 'no' to Bart Sadler. She had allowed him to break down her virtuous nature, and she was now paying the price.

If it was already known in the town, as Deborah had so cruelly said it was, that Sam was Bart's son, then what would they say when she had his child too? Oh, it was not to be borne. How could one possibly survive such a situation, let alone live with it?

Finally, Sophie rose from her knees and went out into the bleak afternoon. She walked towards her house and then changed her mind and wandered slowly down the path to the river. She reached the boathouse where she now knew that Bart and Deborah had begun to form a relationship. He had found her sitting there, and from that day on she was intrigued, captivated, ensnared by him. She told her mother that Bart was such a sympathetic listener. He listened to her and understood her in a way no one ever had before.

She, Sophie, had failed her daughter. She had failed George. For so many years, while thinking herself to be an example in the parish, people had been sniggering, pitying her behind her back. Hypocrite, they must have thought, saying one thing and doing another.

Hypocrite. Whited sepulchre.

For a long time Sophie stood on the water's edge, brooding on her past mistakes, her mind in a state of turbulence such as she never remembered before in all her fifty-five years. Maybe it was time to end it all, to bring this pretence of goodness and virtue to an end?

She stooped and, carefully searching the ground, picked up a heavy white stone that had once been part of the boathouse and, with difficulty, stuck it in her pocket so that it weighed her down. Then she joined her hands together, eyes tightly shut, and prayed.

Such exquisite happiness Sarah-Jane had never before experienced, she knew, not even with Laurence. Maybe it was because after so many years she had forgotten the rapture of sexual love? Maybe it had been good with Laurence, and she couldn't remember it?

Solomon lay on her, his arms under her body, hers wrapped round his; their limbs engaged as though they had been carved from one solid piece of flesh.

She felt his lips on her face, her cheeks; her mouth opened for him. With such happiness pressing upon her she sometimes felt it would be the right time to die, because it couldn't possibly last and, in time, there would only be regret.

They were reckless, she knew it; they took risks. The maids were often in the house when he arrived and they rushed upstairs to make love. Once they had narrowly missed being caught by Ruth who came round looking for her mother-in-law. She had paused, they knew, outside the bedroom door but hadn't tried the handle to find that it was locked. If she had she would have wondered why.

Solomon eased himself gently from the body of Sarah-Jane and then, lying beside her, drew the bedclothes over them both. 'It's cold,' he said, shivering.

Sophie raised her head and saw that the fire was out. Outside too it was nearly dark. They lay wrapped round each other in the large bed in the room that she'd shared for so long with Laurence, but where she had lain by herself for much much longer.

'It can't last,' she murmured into his shoulder.

'It can. It will. There is no reason for it to end.' She knew that, in the dusk, he was looking past her. 'I want you to marry me, Sarah-Jane. I have known for some time that

I can't live without you.'

'Marry me!' she exclaimed. 'Whatever will people say?'

'Who cares what they say?'

'They'll laugh.'

'Let them. John Yetman was twenty years older than Connie's mother.'

'It's different, you know it is, with a woman.' She swept her hair away from her hot, sticky face. Yes, it was cold in the room, but her body glowed. 'I am forty-nine years old this year. Next year I'll be fifty.'

'Well?'

'There could be no children, Solomon.'

'What about Dora? She just had a baby.'

'She is a few years younger than me. Besides, even if it were possible I don't really think I'd want one. I don't think it would be fair.'

'I'm not very keen on children anyway.'

'No desire to have a son and heir?'

Beside her he shook his head.

'In time you'll change your mind.'

'Your grandchildren will be my children.'

'That makes me sound very old.'

'If we married and you really cared about what people thought – I don't, but I understand your point of view – we can go away. I suggested it before.'

'I thought then you just wanted me to be your mistress.'

'Now I want you to be my wife. We can go

296

away. No one will know your history or mine. No one will care. No tongues will wag. Abel can have Riversmead...'

'What about the house he is building, and your partnership?'

'He can sell the house, or this. The partnership can be broken. That's if that's what you want. Frankly, I am happy to go on living here in a place I like. I don't give a damn what anyone says.'

She thought at last that he meant it. He was serious. She couldn't believe it. Not only was he a youthful, vigorous lover. He was such a nice man; good and kind, thoughtful.

Could it really be that he loved her to the extent of offering marriage?

Solomon kissed her again and got out of bed. He ran across the room and began hurriedly to dress, his teeth chattering.

'You will have to have central heating if we stay on. Here, I've had an idea.' He stopped on the point of getting into his trousers. 'Why don't we have Abel's new home and he can live here? He's always said he loves the place.'

Sarah-Jane held out her hand.

'Solomon, not so fast ... let's think. We are happy as we are. There is no hurry. Let's give ourselves time to think all this over.'

'Very well, darling.' Solomon finished dressing and then went to the window to draw the curtains before putting on the light. He reached up and then stopped looking intently out of the window.

'My God!' he exclaimed, a note of horror in his voice.

'What is it?' Sarah-Jane sat up in bed, clutching the sheet to her naked breasts.

'Someone's jumped in the river!'

'Impossible!'

'I've just seen them. I think it's a woman ... on a day like this she won't survive for more than a few minutes.'

And Solomon grabbed his jacket and ran out of the room.

Sarah-Jane jumped out of bed, ran to the window, saw nothing and, as quickly as she could, got into some warm clothes in order to follow him.

At first Solomon could see nothing. He began to wonder if it was his imagination, but then he saw a ripple under the water close to the boathouse and the top of a head appeared, only to disappear again. He threw off his jacket, kicked off his shoes and, taking a deep breath, dived into the icy waters by the spot where he'd seen the ripple.

Almost immediately he found himself next to something bulky that was undoubtedly a woman's body. He grabbed at it and an arm clutched him with such force that he feared he too would be dragged down. He could feel something very heavy next to him and, searching feverishly with his hand, found an object like a large stone in the drowning woman's coat pocket. Although he felt that his lungs were bursting, with all his might and a supreme effort of will, he managed to extricate it and let it sink into the water. Released from the weight, immediately the body he was clutching, and which was clutching him, shot to the top taking him with it. He heard a gasp, knew that the victim was still alive and struck out hard for the river bank where Sarah-Jane and Blossom were now waiting for him, hands outstretched.

Blossom, who was a large, strong, capable girl, knelt down on the water's edge, and Solomon caught hold of her extended hand, nearly pulling her in. But Sarah-Jane had her arms tightly round Blossom's waist and, feeling the shallow part of the bank now beneath his feet, Solomon clutched at some reeds and dragged the inert body of the woman after him.

Sarah-Jane jumped in the water beside him and, together, they managed to bring the body to the side and haul it slowly up upon the bank. Sarah-Jane immediately got on to her knees and began frantically to administer artificial respiration. At first she thought the woman showed no signs of life.

Solomon knelt beside her and detected a

pulse at her neck, very faint but palpable. Suddenly she coughed and spewed out a stream of water. Blossom burst into tears, but Sarah-Jane, grim-faced, continued the technique she'd been taught in First Aid during the war, how to revive a drowning person. Solomon kept his finger on the victim's neck and gradually the pulse grew stronger. Sarah-Jane had by now peeled aside the heavy coat and, baring her breast, administered vigorous external heart massage.

'She's coming to!' she cried triumphantly, looking at Solomon.

'Oh my God, madam,' Blossom raised her hands to her face in horror, 'if it b'ain't Mrs Turner, the rector's wife.'

Hubert sat, as he had for so many days, beside her bed, sometimes watching, sometimes reading, sometimes praying. Sophie was now sleeping peacefully, but at times she would wake and look very afraid and ask where she was. He would soothe her and tell her she was safe, but the fear wouldn't go away and usually her dreams were troubled.

She had caught pneumonia from the shock and the cold, and it had been feared that this would do what the water failed to accomplish. But she rallied and was now out of danger.

Sometimes she prayed aloud, begging for God's forgiveness, and Hubert would tell her tenderly that God had already forgiven her. He, her husband, was God's minister and in God's name he forgave her.

But why had she done such a thing, such a terrible thing? She, of all people, knew as he did that it was a sin against the Holy Ghost to attempt to kill oneself; the final act of despair, of denial of God's goodness. And there was no doubt that she had intended self-immolation by deliberately putting a large stone in her pocket and jumping.

It was a miracle Solomon had seen her at that instant. Had he not Sophie would almost certainly be dead, and it was doubtful if her body would have been found by now, weighed down as it was. It would have lodged in the mud at the bottom of the river, or perhaps have become snagged by the reeds on the river bed, and it might never have been found because no one would have looked for her there. To all intents and purposes she would have vanished. She would have become another missing person.

The parish rallied round and sent flowers and messages, offers of help. The official story was that it was an accident. The rector's wife had been taking a walk and missed her footing in the dusk on the slippery river bank. Luckily Solomon

301

Palmer had been visiting Riversmead and saved her life. Why had Solomon been visiting when Abel Yetman was known to be away in Scotland with his wife? No one asked.

But Blossom knew it was not an accident and the doctor, speedily summoned, knew it wasn't, and it was doubtful that the truth would remain a secret for very long.

No matter. Hubert put down his book, leaned back his head and closed his eyes. He felt very tired, extraordinarily tired. He had known his wife was depressed, had been for some time, but he wasn't altogether sure why. They were a devoted couple but not much given to confidences. Of course she was not happy about Deborah, but who was? And the split between Carson and Connie was a great source of grief, but they were not immediate family, well, not to Sophie anyway, close as they always felt to the Woodvilles.

Sometimes he wondered if that family was somehow cursed, never to know real happiness, never to enjoy peace and, because Sophie had been the wife of a Woodville and was the mother of two Woodville girls, somehow she was tainted in that way? Certainly she suffered but, especially since Debbie's elopement, she seemed to have suffered more and drawn further into herself.

And then of course the day *It* had happened she had heard from a gossiping servant that Debbie was expecting a baby.

Of all people, Hubert Turner knew that that would scarcely cause her joy.

He opened his eyes to see Sophie gazing at him. A wan smile on her face, she held out her hand, and he took it, clasped it to his lips.

'I'm so sorry, Hubert.' Her eyes filled with tears.

'That's all right,' he leaned over towards her, 'I know you didn't mean it.'

'I did.'

He put a finger on her lips. 'No, don't say it,' but she brushed his hand away.

'I did. I committed the ultimate sin of despair. God will never forgive me now.'

'He has. I am his minister on earth and in His name I have forgiven you. You did not despair.' He put his hand on her brow and began to stroke it. He was not a demonstrative man and she had never known him so tender. 'You temporarily lacked the courage to go on. If you had come to me, my dear, I would have helped you. You must not despair ever again, but have faith in the love of Christ and gather strength from that love.'

'Christ does not love me.' Sophie shook her head. Then she looked again at her husband, a pitiful expression on her face.

'You know why, Hubert?'

'I think I do.'

'It is because of Bart.'

'I know.'

For a moment she looked puzzled. 'But how do you know?'

'I've always known.'

The bewilderment on her face increased. 'That Bart...?'

'That Bart Sadler was Sam's father? Of course.'

'How did you know?'

'Well, in those days people used to talk. They still do, of course. They know that Sam is not my son, so they assume he was Bart's. I think you place more importance on it than they or I do, my dear Sophie. You see,' he leaned very close and looked into her troubled eyes, 'these things matter so little in life's great scheme.'

'You knew all the time it was Bart?'

'I knew all the time, and I said to you when you told me you were carrying a child by a man you did not name that many sins were forgiven you because you had loved much, quoting the words of Our Lord. I say that again. You have always given so much of yourself, Sophie. You have been a wonderful mother and exemplary wife; a loyal servant of the parish and daughter of the church. Yet you go on chastising yourself for one little sin, and the other day you tried to kill

304

yourself. God, in His infinite mercy, will forgive that too as He did the Magdalen.'

'But Bart and Debbie...'

'That is unfortunate, but it is a fact. It is not illegal or sinful. You must put it out of your mind, Sophie, and resume the life of the virtuous woman you really are.'

Clasping her hand to his chest he had tears in his eyes and his voice was thick with emotion. 'My beloved wife. A pearl of great price, a jewel in Heaven.'

Thirteen

Abel opened the door of his cottage next to Riversmead and stood for a while sniffing the air. The crocuses and snowdrops were out at the bases of many of the trees in the garden and the daffodils in bud on the lawn.

Nearly spring again and still the house was not quite ready. He was a perfectionist and so was Solomon. Ruth exceeded them both, so it was all taking longer than expected. But they should be in by Easter.

His wife, however, was extravagant. Budgets went to the board where she was concerned. Her extravagance worried him because he himself was inclined to parsimony, his father having died a bankrupt. Daily he had to dig deeper into his pockets and debts were beginning to mount up, not alarmingly, but more than he liked. He had hoped Ruth would show some degree of frugality as did his mother who had had to scrape to make ends meet, despite the generosity of Aunt Eliza. And then there was her own mother, Aunt Sophie, who was the antithesis of extravagance in all things. Why couldn't Ruth have taken a leaf out of her book?

In a way there was an explanation for Ruth's desire to spend money, possibly an excuse. They were both anxious to have a family, and so far Ruth had shown no signs of pregnancy. Why did some people, Debbie for instance, find it so easy, and for others it was so hard? Sarah-Jane had said, tactfully, that it was early days, but they had been married nearly a year.

Abel paused on his way over to the main house. It would be really quite dreadful, he realised, not to have a family.

Ruth had set off yet again on one of her extensive shopping expeditions, he thought in the company of his mother, and he had returned for some papers he'd left behind.

Maybe he could get a cup of coffee in the kitchen before he went over to the house to hurry up the workmen, the painters, plasterers and craftsmen putting the finishing touches. He pushed open the kitchen door and found Verity standing at the table pummelling dough.

'Any chance of a cup of coffee, Verity?' he asked with his winning smile. 'My wife's not at home.'

'Of course, Mr Abel,' Verity said obligingly, going to the stove and moving the kettle to the hob.

'Gone shopping with my mother.' Abel sat on a chair by the side of the table. 'Costing me a fortune.'

Verity spooned grounds into the coffee pot, poured on boiling water and set it aside to brew. Then she got a cup and saucer from the cupboard, set them on a doily on a tray which she put in front of the young master.

'Your mother hasn't gone shopping with Mrs Ruth,' she said, keeping her eye on the contents of the tray.

'Oh, I thought she had.'

Verity shook her head and, judging the coffee was ready to pour, gave it a brisk stir.

'Is she around then?'

'I think so, sir.'

He failed to detect any nuance in Verity's voice and said: 'I must have a word with her.'

Abel finished his coffee, nearly scalding his mouth, and got up.

'That was very good, Verity, thank you. Any idea where Mrs Yetman is?'

Verity shook her head and turned back to the stove.

Abel pushed open the green baize door that led from the kitchen to the hall and went across to his mother's sitting-room. Empty. He poked his head into the dining-room and found Blossom polishing the table.

'Have you seen Mrs Yetman, Blossom?'

The servant shook her head.

'I thought she'd gone out with my wife and it seems she hasn't?'

'Maybe she's upstairs, sir,' Blossom was careful to avert her eyes, 'in her bedroom.'

'Ah!'

Abel paused for a moment and then, crossing the hall, bounded up the stairs two at a time and reached the corridor outside his mother's room when her door opened and Solomon Palmer emerged, casually adjusting the cufflinks on one of his shirt sleeves.

For a moment the two men stared at each other. Solomon's face seemed to pale and he looked anxiously back into the room.

'What on earth...' Abel began when the door to his mother's bedroom slammed shut and he heard the key turn in the lock.

'For God's sake!' he exclaimed. 'What in the name of heaven is going on? What are you doing in my mother's bedroom?'

'I think we had better go downstairs,' Solomon said gruffly, starting along the corridor. But Abel, instead of following him, knocked sharply on his mother's door.

'Mother, please open the door!'

No sound. No reply. Again he knocked. 'Mother I *insist!*'

Suddenly he heard the sound of the key being turned in the lock and his mother threw open the door, her face also unnaturally pale. She was dressed in her robe and behind her it was apparent that some attempt, unsuccessful, had been made to straighten the bed.

'Mother!' he cried in outrage, staring beyond her at the bed.

'You'd better come in.' Sarah-Jane put out an arm and drew him into the bedroom, closing the door behind her.

'Please *don't* make a scene. The servants will hear.'

'The servants will *hear?*' Abel gave a hoarse laugh. 'You think they don't *know?*'

'Did they tell you I was here?' Sarah-Jane anxiously gnawed at a nail as Abel nodded.

'Damn!'

'Mother, what *has* been going on?' He looked over her shoulder at the bed. 'It seems obvious you're having an affair with Solomon!'

'What point is there denying it?' Sarah-Jane tightened the cord of her dressing gown around her waist.

Abel flung open the door and found Solomon standing outside, as if uncertain as to what to do.

'Come in,' Abel said, standing back, 'and explain yourself.'

'There is nothing to explain.' Sarah-Jane defensively clutched at Solomon.

'There is plenty to explain,' Abel persisted, glaring at them as Solomon responded by putting his arm protectively round Sarah-Jane's waist.

'We love each other,' he said, finally

finding his voice.

'Do you realise what you're saying? My mother is *twenty-five* years your senior.'

Neither replied, and the silence seemed to inflame Abel even more.

'How long has this disgusting state of affairs been going on?'

'What is disgusting about being in love?'

'I find the whole thing disgusting, furtive and disgusting. I presume it has been going on for some time, as the maids seem to know about it? Have you no shame, Mother, no pride?'

'I don't think it's shameful to love someone, and Solomon and I do love each other.'

'I realised you liked my mother.' Abel turned his attention to his business partner. 'You were always hovering by her side, but I was pleased. I never thought for a moment that *sex* came into it.'

'I can understand you're upset.' Letting go of Solomon, Sarah-Jane's tone was placatory. 'I could hardly believe it myself.' She went over to the bed, making a feeble attempt to draw up the covers as though to conceal the evidence of her sin. 'I liked Solomon, and then he told me that he loved me...' She gestured helplessly. 'Things just followed naturally after that.'

'And this was, when?'

'Some time in the winter.' Sarah-Jane

began to falter. 'October I think? Maybe November.'

'And you think copulating in the mornings with the maids busy about housework and probably relaying details to the whole town at large is acceptable behaviour?'

'We don't think of it in that way. We didn't realise they knew.' Sarah-Jane paused. 'Solomon has been here all night. No one saw him come in. He is always discreet.'

'Not discreet enough,' Abel trumpeted. 'I thought you were going shopping with Ruth?'

'I sent a message ... I said I had a head-ache.'

'I want to marry Sarah-Jane,' Solomon said boldly. 'My intentions are, and always have been, honourable.'

'The whole thing is impossible. It is disgusting. You'd better get out of here, Palmer. I'll release you from your partnership and you can disappear. I'll not have you making a mockery of the Yetman name. Ridiculing it. My father is still very much honoured in this community and my mother is besmirching his name. Frankly, Mother, I am ashamed of you cavorting with a man half your age.'

Ruth Yetman sat with flaming cheeks listening to Abel's story.

'How terrible!' she said when he had

finished. 'Your mother will make us a laughing stock. As if my sister hadn't done enough harm, now this. I think we should leave the area and then we shan't have to listen to the tittle-tattle of small-minded people in the town.'

'I think that's a bit extreme.' Abel jingled the loose change in his trouser pockets as if to remind him of her spendthrift ways. He stood by the fire and Ruth sat on the sofa facing him. They had just finished dinner and he waited until they had coffee before telling her the events of the morning. Over dinner he had had to listen to a list of the purchases she had made in the town which had not improved his mood. 'I don't see why we should leave the area when *we* have done nothing wrong. We have a lovely house to go to and our lives in front of us. Why should *we* leave? People will soon forget.'

'Oh, I don't agree. People have long memories. They still remember how Aunt Eliza eloped with Uncle Ryder fifty years ago. When Debbie ran off with Bart Sadler all you heard were odious comparisons with Aunt Eliza and Uncle Ryder. 'Bad blood in the family,' they said and they'll say it again.'

'There is nothing actually immoral in it.' After a thoughtful pause Abel stooped to poke the fire. 'I mean, they are both free.'

'Yes, but they're having an *affair*, aren't they? Do you think *that's* right, that

313

everyone should know? Do you think it reflects well on your mother that she should have a relationship with a man younger than her own son? Personally, I think it's disgusting.'

'I do too.' Abel nodded his head several times. 'Disgusting.'

Abel looked at Ruth and felt remorse for his mother's scandalous behaviour. Ruth was very fragile and inexperienced, a child-woman innocent in the ways of the world despite the fact that she had been a teacher for several years and lived away from home. It was this quality of almost childlike naivete that had appealed to him, a wish to protect her. It also seemed to explain her extravagance as if, like a child, she didn't know the value of money.

He bent to kiss her on the cheek and put a hand on her shoulder. 'Try not to worry too much, darling. I wish now I hadn't told you.'

She wished he hadn't too.

The following morning Ruth stood by the window watching Abel disappear round the corner of the cottage to his car. A hundred yards away was the main house with her mother-in-law inside, and perhaps Solomon too had again spent the night in torrid love-making. Yes, she wished she didn't know. Now she would never be able to feel the same about Sarah-Jane again, but would always associate her with something dirty and underhand.

Ruth was a very proper girl, very correct. At school she was known as a goody-goody. She was liked, but she was never as popular as her sister. She was painfully anxious to please and succeed, to do the right thing.

She was horrified when, at the age of eighteen, her sister ran off with a workman and returned pregnant. To this day she didn't know how she'd lived down the shame. She left Wenham to train as a teacher in Bristol and taught for some years away from the town. Even there she'd led a sheltered life, living as a paying guest with friends of the family. She went to school at eight every weekday morning and returned home at four every day and, apart from that, scarcely ever went out except accompanied by the family friends to a social or whist drive in the church hall.

When her cousin Abel started courting her she knew at once that it would be a very suitable marriage. He was someone like her: upright, God-fearing, hard-working. They were both supporters of the church, regular worshippers.

Yet in her marriage Ruth had yet to experience sexual passion. She didn't think it was very nice. She certainly didn't think it was the sort of thing one talked about, even with one's husband. She wished she'd known a little more about it before she got married. Naturally her mother, being deeply repressed, hadn't said a word.

Ruth decided it was one of those things that had to be endured for the sake of procreation. Only, so far, there were no signs of a baby and she felt nervous and edgy, prone to ups and downs, often not feeling very well.

It would all be better, she was sure, when the house was ready, and so she had flung herself into that wholeheartedly, regardless of how much it cost.

She knew that she disapproved of what Abel had told her about Sarah-Jane because she disapproved of sexual licence, as she also disapproved of her sister and, especially, what her sister had told her about her mother and why she hated Bart Sadler so much.

Her mother, who was always on her knees in church saying her prayers, who was always quoting the Bible and talking about how she and their father had travelled to a far-off country to save the souls of savages, a journey that had cost Father his life.

It was unbelievable. It made the world seem such a wicked, dangerous place.

Agnes Woodville sat looking at Sophie, who was up and dressed, but still not herself. She spent much of the day lying on the sofa in her little room reading devotional books, gazing out of the window on to the wintry landscape or just dozing.

Agnes reached over and took her hand, patting it gently.

'I would have come before, but Hubert told everyone you were to have no visitors. My poor dear, what an ordeal. You should have come and talked to me, dear Sophie. I'm sure I could have helped you.'

Agnes paused as Polly came in with morning coffee which she proceeded to pour, thus momentarily putting an end to the conversation.

Sophie gave a weak smile. She only just felt strong enough to see Agnes. It was true that Agnes was a very experienced woman of the world and probably could have helped her, were it not for the fact that the thought of confiding in Agnes had never occurred to her. If Agnes pitied her she pitied Agnes, who had had a hard life, much of it because of her own behaviour.

Agnes was a Yetman, the daughter of John and half-sister of Connie. She had been married three times, first to an American, then to Guy Woodville, with whom she had had an affair years before and, thirdly, to Owen Wentworth, an adventurer who had given himself a false title and spurious fortune, and eventually made off with all Agnes's jewels.

Once again Carson had been enormously good to his step-mother, even though they had never got on. And Connie had been good too, allowing her to have the house belonging to her guardian which had been left to her. Connie made it over to Agnes for her lifetime and gave her an allowance.

Of course Agnes had not been grateful. She never was. She was grateful to no one and 'thank you' were words that sat strangely on her lips, if ever. She was always so sure she was right, and everyone else was wrong.

She had always been a difficult, imperious, demanding woman who had refused to acknowledge her own daughter even after she'd married the father.

Elizabeth had never forgiven her and never would, and the consequence was that Agnes had retired, a sad and bitter woman, to the house Connie gave her, and she stayed there most of the time seeing few people and scarcely any members of the family.

Thus Sophie had been very surprised when Lady Woodville had been announced (Agnes having reverted to her former name and title when Owen Wentworth disappeared, but as he had never been found she was unable to get a divorce from him).

Polly finished serving coffee and left the room, hopefully leaving the door ajar so that she could hear what was being said. She was in a great flutter of excitement as much was expected from her by the people in the town. She was a prime source of gossip from the Rectory, and if she had received a shilling for every tale she told she believed she would be a rich woman.

But Sophie, who knew Polly's reputation, saw the crack in the door and told her to close it carefully after her. The door clicked shut, and so thick were the Rectory doors that, however hard Polly pressed her ear to them, she was unable to hear a word from the other side.

'It's very *kind* of you, Agnes.' Sophie took a reviving sip from her cup and carefully replaced it on the table beside her. 'Frankly I don't think anyone could have helped me. I was not myself. God could help me, but I didn't listen or place my trust in Him, as I should have.' Her gaze wandered to the book of the meditations of Thomas a Kempis beside her. 'This will be a lesson to me not to place my immortal soul in danger again.'

Agnes, who never went to church despite the fact that she lived next to it, gave a derisory sniff. 'That is all very well, Sophie, but we are talking about the here and now not the hereafter. And if you will forgive me saying so, my dear, and I speak as a friend of many years' standing, you should be careful about becoming too wrapped up in religion. I know you are very religious, and as the daughter and wife of churchmen one would expect nothing else. But your religion did not save you from a foolish act that might have killed you. Well, *would* have killed you had not Solomon Palmer seen you.' Agnes paused. 'How did he see you, by the way?'

'He was visiting Riversmead and happened to glance out of the window.'

'Well, there was an act of God if you like.'

'Indeed.' Sophie smiled again and realised that Agnes was actually making her feel better.

Agnes was a preposterous woman, there was no other word for it. She was utterly confident in her own opinions and beliefs. Over the years Agnes hadn't changed, even if her circumstances had. And her appearance hadn't changed much either. She was a good-looking woman; when younger she had been considered one of the prettiest young girls in the town. She was not tall, inclined now to plumpness and, at nearly seventy years of age, her blonde hair, carefully waved with a little fringe in the front, owed its colour to artifice rather than nature. Her famous blue eyes, flecked with grey, had in her youth been lustrous but, over the years, they had grown steely as her own nature had hardened due to the realities of a difficult life.

Agnes always dressed as though she was going to town. Even to cross the road to the Rectory she wore a hat and gloves. Today, perhaps due to the solemnity of the occasion, she was a symphony of grey. She had a grey woollen dress, grey stockings and high-heeled grey shoes. Her coat, with its fox fur draped around the collar, was also grey. She looked very elegant and distinguished, and it was hard to think of her as a virtual recluse who scarcely ever left her house except for those vital visits to Yeovil to have her hair coloured and given a permanent wave.

Agnes was looking rather defiantly across at Sophie as if trying to divine her thoughts, a cautious expression in those fine eyes.

'You're a tonic to me,' Sophie said at last. 'I need your practical good sense, Agnes. I'd forgotten just how wise you could be.'

Agnes, flattered, lowered her eyes. 'I wish you *would* let me help you more, Sophie. Life is never as bad as you think, you know. And to be so terribly upset about Deborah is foolish. You know I'm very fond of the child and I must confess I hardly know Mr Sadler, but he is a very wealthy man and that counts for a lot. You must try and forgive her in your heart, and remember how bereft you were when she ran away all those years ago.'

'I *do* love her,' Sophie said earnestly, 'but

none of us likes Bart Sadler.'

'You liked him well enough once, I hear.' Agnes put her head knowingly on one side.

'Oh, you know that too?'

'I miss very little that goes on in the town, even though I was not here at the time. My maid, Grace, who has been with me a good many years, keeps her ear closely to the ground. Very little happens in the parish that I don't sooner or later come to know about.

'There is nothing wrong with falling in love, Sophie dear. At the time I understand you were seeing Mr Sadler you were both free, were you not? You a widow and he a bachelor? Nevertheless we all make mistakes and the course of true love never does run smooth.' Agnes gave a brittle laugh. '*And* don't I know it.'

They both paused as there was a tap on the door and, expecting the return of Polly, Sophie called, 'Come in.' The door opened and Ruth stood on the threshold, nonplussed as she saw Agnes.

'Oh, Grandmother, I didn't expect to see you.'

'But it's lovely to see *you*, dear.' Agnes put up a powdered and rouged cheek to be kissed. 'I see far too little of you now that you're a married woman. I hear the new house is looking lovely?'

Sophie noted that as Agnes prattled on

322

Ruth appeared flustered and, finally interrupting her, said: 'Are you all right, Ruth? Has something happened?'

'Well...'

'Have a cup of coffee.' Sophie pointed to the tray. 'I'll ask Polly to bring another cup and a fresh pot.'

'No, really, Mother. I came to see how you were and also...' She glanced across at Agnes as though wondering how much she could say. Agnes, who she used to venerate when she was a child. Grandmother always had a glamour that other members of the family lacked and a rich fund of stories about her exotic past, travels on the Continent and the many years she'd spent in America. Some thought that it was owing to Grandmother's bad example that Debbie had gone astray.

Yes, she decided, Grandmother was close enough to share in the shameful secret.

'My mother-in-law is having a love affair with Solomon Palmer,' Ruth blurted out. 'Don't you think it's *disgusting?* Everyone in the town will know.'

Sophie looked shocked, but Agnes's expression seemed amused.

'Well, well,' she said, 'wonders will never cease. Is that not the young man who is the architect of your house?'

'Yes.'

'I hear he is very talented.'

'He is also younger than Abel, Grandmother. Imagine carrying on with a man young enough to be your son!'

'I have a lot to thank Mr Palmer for,' Sophie said slowly. 'He saved my life...'

'But Mother!'

'I'm afraid I can't think ill of him. I owe him a debt.'

'I don't think ill of him either.' Agnes poured herself more coffee. 'I think, "well done", young man. There is much to be learned from an older woman.' She looked archly about her.

'But what will people say in the town?'

'Who cares what people say in the town?' Agnes chuckled. 'They've had enough to say about me in the past and it has not troubled me one bit, or harmed me at all, as far as I know.' She looked thoughtfully across at Ruth. 'You really must learn to ignore what people say, my dear, and if Mr Palmer and Sarah-Jane are happy with each other I say 'good luck' to them.'

But Ruth still felt a sense of outrage. 'They say they're going to marry. Can you, imagine having a step-father-in-law younger than my own husband? I think the whole thing is dirty and horrible, and I'm frankly shocked that neither of you seem to agree.' Eyes blazing, Ruth turned to her mother. 'You would think as the wife of the Rector of Wenham you would have some standards, Mother, but you don't seem to. You talk about God a lot, yet you ignore His commandments. You set a bad example yourself. No wonder everyone pities you and talks about you behind your back.'

And with that Ruth ran across the room, wrenched open the door and banged it behind her.

For a moment there was a profound silence in the room. Sophie looked suddenly exhausted and leaned against one of the cushions propping her up. Agnes immediately rose and went over to her couch, taking her hand and sitting beside her.

'Don't worry. She is very young.'

Sophie pressed Agnes's hand but still for a while said nothing. Finally, sighing deeply, she murmured: 'I have lost one daughter. Do you think I am going to lose another?'

'No I don't.' Agnes squeezed her hand reassuringly. 'It will blow over. Ruth is still very young. It is not so very terrible. If Sarah-Jane is happy then I'm glad. All right, there will be tongues wagging in the town, but some people will be jealous!' Agnes turned to Sophie with a mischievous smile. 'In their heart of hearts they wouldn't mind a nice young body to keep them warm in bed at night.'

'I think there is more to Ruth's attitude than meets the eye,' Sophie said slowly. 'Something tells me she is not very happy in her own marriage.' She raised anguished eyes to Agnes. 'That all is not exactly as it should be there. Something wrong. I don't quite know what.'

When Agnes got back to the house that had once belonged to Miss Fairchild, and which Connie had made over to her, she removed her hat and coat and went to her neat sitting-room with its view of her pretty garden.

Grace was out shopping and would be doing the usual rounds of the gossip-mongers to report back to Agnes in due course. Well, Agnes could tell *her* something, but perhaps she knew already.

Agnes felt that in many ways the life of the parish was passing her by, that it was peripheral to her existence there. She had become a recluse who scarcely ever went out. She dressed up just to cross the road in an outfit she might have worn in London in the old days, the good old days just after the war.

She sat down and put her feet up on the pouf.

Few people came to see her. Not even her granddaughters, to whom she had once been close, confided in her. Deborah hadn't told her about Bart Sadler, and Ruth only told her about Abel when they were engaged.

She had hurt Ruth by not attending her

wedding, but she couldn't face Elizabeth, a daughter she had once spurned and who now spurned her.

In a way she knew hers was a sad life. Perhaps people pitied her. It didn't do to be maudlin but, really, she had nothing left now except memories.

But what memories! The heady days in America where for nearly twenty years she had run a successful business in New Orleans; two high-class brothels for well-do-do southern gentlemen who were bored with their wives. She had made a lot of money on the stock exchange, tips from grateful clients of her houses. But she had spent a lot too.

When she sold her business and came home she married a baronet, once her lover, and became the woman of title and respectability she had always wanted to be, her past forgotten. Only all this was dashed when, after Guy's death, Carson inherited and treated her with, in her opinion, a mean hand.

On the rebound she had fallen for the charms of Owen Wentworth, who had neither the title nor money he claimed to have. Finally he had fled with all her jewels and left her with nothing, back once more on the charity, the patronage of Carson and Connie.

She was quite pleased they had split up. It

served them right. They were always lecturing her about her extravagances, keeping her on a tight rein. Always so virtuous, and now Carson had another woman and Connie had gone!

Still, on this grey February day her outfit reflected her mood. She felt sad, depressed, despite her attempt to appear cheerful and optimistic with Sophie. But that really was the trouble with her. She was always putting on an act to hide the void inside herself.

Agnes rose from her chair and, taking the bottle of gin from the drinks cabinet, poured a hefty slug into a glass. Then she lifted it, neat, to her lips and drained the lot, feeling immediately better afterwards, more like her old self.

She was nothing if not a survivor.

Fourteen

For once Nelly had slept well, that is relatively well for her, waking only a few times in the course of six or seven hours. She thought it was the sound of birdsong that woke her because during the winter months they had been silent. Now, in late March, there was a veritable dawn chorus as the blackbirds, chaffinches, tits and robins, not to mention magpies and rooks that lived in the surrounding trees, loudly advertised for mates in calls that echoed and re-echoed across the valley.

As usual from her bed facing the window, the first thing she saw was Pelham's Oak about a mile away on the hills: beautiful, grand and timeless. One expected that it would endure forever. The home of the Woodvilles since the seventeenth century. Carson's home.

Soon she would see him leave, a tiny dot on the horizon, as he proceeded down the hill on his dear old horse Pulver. The dot would get larger and larger as he neared the cottage, and she would get more and more excited at the prospect of seeing him again. Day in and day out it was like this. A great love rekindled, passion renewed.

Later she would watch him go up again, and later still the scene would be repeated except that she never saw him return at night. By then she was asleep, Carson watching tenderly over her.

Nelly felt curiously tranquil this particular morning as she lay there listening to the birds, seeing Pelham's Oak on the horizon, knowing that, whatever happened, she was safe. At long last she was safe.

It had been a hard life, the daughter of a Covent Garden porter over-fond of drink and a mother who could match him, glass for glass. It was perhaps natural that she had gone to work in a public house, and her life would never have amounted to anything at all had she not met Carson. In the fullness of time he outlined to her a dream that might one day be theirs: a cottage in the country with wisteria and honeysuckle growing on the walls, and a child or two.

Well, she had the cottage in the country, even though it had come twenty years too late. She had the child, even if he didn't know she was his mother but, above all, she had Carson and the dream had become reality.

Throughout the months of winter Carson was preoccupied with Nelly. One might have called it an obsession. He missed his children but he didn't miss Connie at all. Her behaviour made him see her in a fresh light. He realised things he hadn't before. She was, he thought, basically a selfish woman who had everything compared to poor Nelly who had nothing, who had led a life of self-deprivation and self-sacrifice for the sake of her child, Alexander.

Never very strong, she had spent her years in domestic service until she became too ill to work. She could have called Carson but never did until she was *in extremis,* near the end, and then it was not she who called him but Massie.

Naturally, she had wanted to see her son, and a glimpse of him sufficed as, daily, she drew nearer to death.

Carson felt that his life was wholly absorbed by Nelly and her approaching end. He spent a great part of the day with her. He would return to the house after his morning visit and then go back to her in the late afternoon and sit by her side until she fell asleep. Several times there were crises when she seemed near the end and he slept by her bedside on the floor while Massie kept awake by the fire to ensure it was alight all night. They watched after Nelly with love and devotion, but by the time that the buds began to appear on the trees it was clear poor Nelly would not see the summer.

She and Carson were completely engrossed in each other's company, as if no one else existed. Finally Carson had a bed made up in her room and when her condition caused anxiety hardly ever left her. Life at Pelham's Oak went on but in a curious vacuum, the servants not quite knowing what to do or when to expect their master. His valet, James, brought him down clean clothes, and fresh produce from the farms was delivered to the house: bacon, eggs, butter, meat, fresh vegetables, flowers from the greenhouse, and cream, plenty of cream to try and fatten Nelly up as, daily, her frame grew more skeletal.

How they reminisced! About when they were young, twenty years before, and about the little room in the City of London in the shadow of St Paul's where they had made love. Star-crossed lovers, once separated, they had never met again until Massie wrote to him.

Now he was making up for lost time.

'I worry about your wife, Carson,' Nelly whispered, her hand entwined with his. He had to sit very close to her in order to hear what she said; but he didn't mind. He loved her and he felt he always had. He had been on the verge of telling his parents about his intention to marry Nelly in the year 1910, and then bad luck had intervened.

'You must not worry about Connie,' he said, stroking back her thick dark hair from her forehead. 'She is quite capable of taking care of herself, and she has a grand home in Venice. Connie wants for nothing.'

'But your children? Don't you miss them?'

'Yes!' Carson grew sombre.

'After my death...' she began but he put a finger firmly on her lips.

'Don't *speak* of it.'

He took her in his arms cradling her head on his breast and that was how Massie found them when she came to bring Nelly her broth for lunch.

'Here,' she coaxed, pulling a table to the side of Nelly's bed. 'Drink a little.'

Massie had loved Nelly from the day she met her in the Lady Frances Roper Home where they were both awaiting the births of their babies. For Massie it was quite a regular event and she gave the babies up for adoption without another thought. But Nelly had been different. She had wanted to keep Alexander, and when she knew she couldn't, that he would be forcibly taken away, she and Massie had stolen out at night with the baby well-wrapped in a shawl and left him on the doorstep of Carson's aunt, Lally.

After that they had found various means of employment but had always stayed together. Massie had a number of men and two more children; but Nelly had learned her lesson and never became involved with a man again. Besides, she was never strong.

She would often talk about her son and about Carson, and when she saw his picture in the paper, emerging from the church with his bride on his arm, and read of his war record, Massie urged her to write to him. But she wouldn't, refusing to spoil his happiness; however, she kept the paper as one of her most priceless possessions. She was a simple woman and Carson had been an important event in her life.

Thus it was only much later, when Nelly became so ill and was sacked from employment and unable to work, that they decided on desperate remedies.

Massie knew that Nelly felt guilty. Connie had not taken to her, and the dislike was mutual. Undoubtedly it was based on jealousy; but Nelly knew she had not long to live and, being only human as well as very sick, she was content to seize the moment, luxuriate in the love she had been denied in the knowledge that after her death Carson would return to his wife.

Meanwhile Nelly was happy, and that was all that mattered to Massie.

Carson held Nelly as Massie put the spoon to her mouth but she had only taken a few mouthfuls when she choked, put her hands to her throat as though gasping for air as a stream of bright red blood gushed out and she fell back on her pillow.

Massie quickly put down the soup and got out the bowl kept under the bed for the purpose. But, unlike other times, the blood continued to pour from Nelly's mouth and Carson, gazing at her in horror, desperately tried to staunch it.

'Run to the house, Massie,' he commanded. 'Run all the way. Tell them to telephone Doctor Hardy and ask him to come at once.'

Massie fled from the room and, without changing her shoes or grabbing a cardigan, she ran all the way up to Pelham's Oak to get one of the servants to summon the doctor.

Finally the flow ceased and Nelly, gasping, lay back on the bed, quite unable to speak. Trying to control his panic Carson stroked her brow and when she had recovered a little called Massie who came in, changed her bed, washed her and put a clean nightdress on her while Carson stood gazing out of the window, anxious for sight of the doctor.

When at last he arrived, Carson left him alone with Nelly. He slumped morosely in a chair in the sitting-room while Massie made herself as busy as she could in the kitchen, scarcely able to contain her tears.

Finally Doctor Hardy appeared, shaking his head. He was the latest in a line of doctors from the same family who had looked after the Woodvilles and the parishioners of Wenham for generations. People liked him and trusted him, and he asked no questions. He had looked after Nelly without asking Carson who she was and how she came to be here, even though he had delivered all Carson's children and knew Connie well. Carson respected him for this.

'How long has she got, Philip?' he asked of the doctor who was his contemporary.

'Days,' Philip Hardy murmured. 'Hours maybe.'

'Is there nothing more you can do?'

'I've left some medicine by the side of the bed. I've given her a sedative.' He pressed Carson's arm as he was shown to the door. 'You should notify the undertaker, Carson,' he whispered on the doorstep. 'Her heart is very weak. It will be any moment now.'

When Carson returned to the room Nelly lay asleep. She looked so beautiful with her black hair loose on the pillow. She appeared better than he'd seen her for some time, pink cheeks, lips glowing. But it was the fever that was killing her that, paradoxically, made her look well.

He sat by her side all afternoon and then, just as the sun was going down, she opened her eyes.

'Isn't it beautiful?' she said in a clear, strong voice.

'What, my beloved?' he whispered.

'The sunset.'

'Beautiful,' he replied, looking at her, not out of the window.

'Don't sound so sad, darling.' She looked tenderly at him. 'I feel much better. That medicine the doctor gave me has done me good. Maybe I have a few more weeks, months even. Oh, Carson,' she put her arm around his shoulder, 'wouldn't it be wonderful if...'

'You *are* going to get better,' he insisted. 'We will have a future. We shall tell Alexander we are his parents.'

Suddenly Nelly's mood changed again, one of the symptoms of her illness.

'I know it's a pipe-dream, darling,' she said sadly, 'and it's not fair to your family. You have three young children. You will have to make your peace with Connie after I've gone.'

'*Don't* say that word again,' he commanded sternly. 'I forbid it. But, Nelly, I must ask you one thing. I must be sure.' He gazed earnestly into her eyes. 'Alexander is my son, is he not? There is no question of error? You see, I feel I must know.'

'He *is* your son.' Her voice suddenly sounded weaker. 'After you I never went with another man. Ask Massie. I loved you, Carson, and always have.'

As if even such a brief speech had

exhausted her she sank once more on to the pillow and closed her eyes.

Nelly was never to open them again. Towards midnight, still clasped in Carson's arms, her breathing became stertorous. There was a brief struggle, although she appeared not to wake, and then she sank into a lasting sleep, embarking on that final journey, the one from which no traveller returns.

Carson remained with her until morning, when the birds began to sing again. Then he woke Massie.

'Man that is born of woman hath but a short time to live, and is full of misery. He cometh up and is cut down like a flower; he fleeth, as it were a shadow, and never continueth in one stay.

'In the midst of life we are in death...'

Slowly the coffin was lowered into the grave as the Reverend Turner intoned the words of committal from the burial service. It was watched by only five people: Carson, Lally, Sophie, Eliza and a very tearful Massie, all in deep mourning. It was a day full of sunshine. Spring had arrived in all its glory and the branches of the trees, heavy with buds, seemed to sway in a gentle benediction of farewell as Nelly's coffin sank out of sight.

Hubert took a handful of earth proffered

by the verger and cast it upon the coffin. Then he stood back as the verger offered the same to Carson, who took it in his hand and, for a moment, stood gazing down upon the coffin inscribed with the simple words: *'Nelly Allen, Born 1889, Died 1931.'*

'For as much as it hath pleased Almighty God of his great mercy to take our dear sister here departed, we therefore commit her body to the ground: earth to earth, ashes to ashes, dust to dust; in sure and certain hope of the resurrection to eternal life...'

The four women also each, in turn, cast earth upon the coffin and then stood back as Hubert came to the end of the service.

Carson, taking a rose from the flowers placed near the grave which had covered her bier on the journey from Pelham's Oak, tossed it upon the coffin. He stood, head bowed, grave-faced, for several seconds until, composed, he moved back. He then took Massie by the hand, leading the small procession away from the grave where, after a respectful pause, the grave-diggers began filling it in.

At the church door Carson shook hands with Hubert and thanked him for such a dignified service. Then he turned to Eliza, Lally and Sophie and kissed them each on the cheek.

'Carson, please come back to the Rectory for a drink,' Sophie said, 'and bring Massie too.'

Carson shook his head.

'Thank you, Sophie, but we want to get back. We have so much to do. Thank you all for coming.'

Massie gave an awkward little bob and, still clutching Carson tightly by the hand, returned with him to his car parked outside the churchyard.

The three women stood watching the car drive away then, with one accord, they entered the Rectory where Polly had coffee waiting in the drawing room.

'There seems so little to say.' Eliza wearily sank on to a chair near the fire. 'Except that it's very sad.'

'Forty-two,' Lally murmured. 'No age to go.'

'Carson was very good to her,' Eliza went on. 'He made her last months very peaceful.'

'Yes, but at what cost?' Sophie indicated to Polly, who was loitering in the hope of picking up a smattering of gossip, that she should go and shut the door, and handed Eliza her cup.

'You mean Connie?' Eliza asked, then, glad of the drink, sipped it gratefully.

'Who exactly *was* Nelly Allen?' Sophie asked, taking a seat by the window. 'You must know.' She looked at the two women, who exchanged glances.

'We do know, but I don't know that we're at liberty to tell you.'

'I'm sure Carson wouldn't mind, knowing how discreet Sophie will be.' Lally was standing in front of the fire warming her hands. 'We have kept the secret and,' she glanced severely at Sophie, 'so must you.'

'Of course.'

Eliza, despite the fire, still felt cold and her fingers tightly clasped her cup. Then, slowly and carefully, choosing her words, once again she related the sad sad tale of Carson, Nelly and the baby, Alexander.

When she had finished the profound silence that followed was finally broken by Sophie.

'No wonder Connie went away. I can hardly believe such a story.'

'Carson was always a romantic,' Eliza murmured. 'Unfortunately I think in this instance sentiment got the better of common sense. He could have had Nelly looked after without hurting Connie so much. Naturally she resented this woman from his past, and the attention he paid her, however sick she was. I hope that, now Nelly is dead and Carson has done his duty, he will make an attempt to repair his marriage.'

'And Alexander,' Sophie ventured, 'does he know?'

Lally shook her head. 'We did discuss it, but thought it better not to tell him. We felt it might ruin his life, make him very unhappy. Nelly agreed to this. She only wanted to know he was well when she was dying and, if possible, to see him. That's why she contacted Carson or, rather, her little friend, Massie, wrote on her behalf.

'I imagine she thought that it was unfair, after all this time, to spring on him the truth about his birth. It is also possible that she too was afraid of a meeting with the son she, after all, abandoned. Maybe she felt guilty about it. She did see Alexander when he was riding one day with Carson close to Ryder's cottage. It was done deliberately and she and Alexander waved at each other.' Lally paused on the brink of tears. 'Carson said it was a very touching moment, and later Nelly told him she was content. As far as we know she died happy in knowing what a fine young man he was, how well he had been cared for and what prospects he had. I suppose we did the right thing.'

Lally looked anxiously across at Eliza, who nodded her support. 'I hope so. We shall never know.'

'Has he been told that Carson is his father?'

Eliza shook her head, her brow furrowed. 'What do you think, Sophie? Do you think we did the right thing?'

Sophie gazed for a long time out of the window. She was daily reminded by the sight of the boathouse of her folly, her attempted suicide. It might have been her now lying in the churchyard. How wanton of her to have tried to take her life when that poor woman they had just laid to rest had died prematurely. A woman who had so much to live for, and who had wanted to live. She felt ashamed.

She looked at her friends with a wan smile.

'Who am I to judge?' she said with a deep sigh.

Connie sat back in her deckchair, hands folded in her lap, her eyes on the three children playing in the sand in front of her, carefully watched also by their nursemaid. The waves rolled in from the Adriatic and, although it was not yet warm enough to swim, it was pleasant to play on the beach in front of the villa she had rented on the Venetian Lido for the summer when it would be far too hot for the children in the city.

Next to her, Paolo Colomb-Paravincini sat with his straw hat pulled over his eyes, dozing. Connie looked at her watch. Soon it would be time to go in for lunch.

Very soon it too would be time to make up her mind about something more serious:

Paolo, a valued friend who she had known for many years, wanted to marry her.

He had courted her during the war and after when she lived in Venice, and she had been on the verge of accepting his proposal when she met Carson again.

Did she wish now that she had married Paolo? She flung back her head and closed her eyes.

Her mind went back over the years that, at one time, had seemed so full of hope.

There had been much love, yet there had also been heartache.

Carson had proposed to her when she was young and vulnerable and had gone back on his word. A vulnerable, sensitive child, she had felt unloved and unwanted, cruelly rejected by a man she had adored, and had nearly suffered a complete mental breakdown. Miss Fairchild had taken her away and they had settled in Italy.

Introduced to her by friends, Paolo had helped to restore her confidence in herself. Indeed he had given her that confidence. He was an urbane, distinguished aristocrat, a man of the world, cultured, musical, the possessor of one of the finest palazzi in Venice, with a long family tradition.

He was also wealthy, but wealth didn't worry her because she was wealthy too.

The downside was that Paolo was her senior by seventeen years. He didn't look it and he didn't act it, but he was.

On the other hand Carson was exactly her own age. He was attractive and, moreover, he was a Woodville, a family revered in the small town where she came from. To be Contessa Colomb-Paravacini, whose family had contained two cardinals, several bishops, not a few celebrated warriors and many distinguished men of letters, was quite something. But to a girl born in Wenham, to be Lady Woodville had to it a cachet that any right-minded young woman would covet.

Besides, and more important, she loved the man.

They had had many happy years, but when she learned about Nelly all the stories about Carson's past surfaced to trouble and unsettle her.

In his youth he had had a terrible reputation with women. Farmers had to lock up their daughters. Sir Guy was threatened by angry fathers. Carson's wilful behaviour was supposed to have led to the premature death of his mother.

And then, like some ghost from the past, Nelly appeared, an uneducated woman who had spent her life in domestic service; a woman who had borne him a child.

Carson had called Connie a snob, but she wasn't a snob. It wasn't Nelly's background that mattered, but the child, Alexander.

They all knew and loved him, and Carson was his father, if Nelly was to be believed and Connie thought she probably was. Carson believed it anyway, and Carson still seemed to be in love with Nelly. For what greater, more potent, more nostalgic love was there than past love?

No, despite her wealth and her title, all the insecurity of Connie's former life, coupled with an intense jealousy of Nelly, had come home to roost. It was too much to bear. She snapped and, gathering up the children and their nursemaid, she took a train for London and then the boat train to Venice. And when she arrived in Venice she felt strangely at home, at peace, as if she were on the brink of a new life.

Her reverie was suddenly interrupted.

'Dearest?' The man beside her reached for her hand.

'Yes?'

'What are you thinking of?'

She looked at him and smiled.

'What do you think I ever think of?'

'Carson?'

'And other things. The past. Wenham. Pelham's Oak.'

'And the future?'

'I think of that too.'

'The children are very happy here.'

They were.

Toby was six and Leonard five. Netta four.

The boys missed their father most but, strangely, no one missed him *very* much. Venice was exciting with boats and new people, and trips across the lagoon. The latest thing was a house overlooking the sea and lots of new friends to play with on the beach. No time to miss Daddy.

But how long would Carson put up with this situation? Already there were angry letters demanding answers. She had been away nine months, when she had told him originally that she was going for a visit. He told her Nelly was dead, but he didn't say that he was sorry or that he wanted her back. He did however want his children. In the course of time Toby would inherit Pelham's Oak and the title. Was it fair to bring him up in Italy, far from home?

Paolo was incredibly good to them and with them, but they regarded him rather as a doting grandparent than a father. He had his own two children, now both married and living in Rome, and was a real grandfather to their children.

'Are you going to make up your mind, Constance?' Paolo urged gently. 'I think it is important for the children to be settled. Or...' he paused, 'do you still love Carson?'

But that was a question that, at the moment, she couldn't answer.

Eliza threw back the shutters at Riversmead

347

which had been closed since the winter when Sarah-Jane and Solomon Palmer had decided to go and live in Brighton. The hostility of her children rather than the opprobrium of the town had helped to make up their minds. All of them were outraged at Solomon's presence in the house when they were visiting, and an ultimatum was delivered.

Solomon and Sarah-Jane shook the dust of Wenham from their feet and went off, putting Riversmead on the market.

'What do you think?' Eliza looked at Carson who was thoughtfully wandering around the sitting-room.

'You really want to live here again, Aunt Eliza?'

'Why not?' She removed the dust cover from one of the chairs and sat down. 'I had many happy years here. If I don't live here it will go out of the family. I've taken an option. My children were born here. It was a very happy place for me and could be again.'

'In that case I think you should buy it.' Carson also threw back the sheet covering one of the chairs and sat down, stretching his long legs in front of him. 'I should do it all up, completely. Throw out the furniture, get new carpets and curtains. Make it your own once more.'

'And you, Carson, what will you do?'

348

Eliza looked anxiously at her nephew, always a favourite, a very great favourite. She loved him like a son. 'Pelham's Oak is a very big place for a man on his own.'

'Oh, I've lived there by myself before.' His tone was carefully guarded so as not to betray his real feelings; he was that sort of person.

'*What* about the children, Carson? Is it really all over between you and Connie? Sometimes I can hardly believe it has happened. I grieve about it all the time.'

'It was her decision,' he said defensively. 'She left. She took my children and she left. I hardly had a day's notice. How do you think I feel about that? I feel very bitter, as a matter of fact.'

'But Nelly...'

'Nelly belonged to the past. I was just paying my dues. She came here, a dying woman, and Connie was jealous of her.' Carson rose and started to pace agitatedly around the room. 'I can't understand it. *Imagine* being jealous of someone who was dying? I found it incredibly difficult to understand and I find it hard to forgive even now. You would have expected Connie to want to make Nelly's last days comfortable, not to be jealous.'

'Perhaps she felt insecure?' Eliza suggested.

'Insecure!' Carson banged the table he

happened to be passing. 'How could she be insecure? What did she have to feel insecure about?'

'Alexander. You had a son by Nelly. It must have been a shock.'

'And I had three children by *her!* No, Aunt Eliza, my feeling is that when I needed, really needed, the support of my wife at a very difficult time in my life she failed me, and that has altered very much the way I feel about her.'

'But what about the children? Supposing she stays in Italy and they grow up there?'

'Oh no!' Carson's expression was fierce. 'They certainly won't stay with her. As soon as we start divorce proceedings I shall apply for custody. My lawyer has already written to ask her intentions. They are my children. Toby is my heir, and I want them to be brought up in Wenham, as we were. Wenham, not Venice, is where the Woodvilles belong.'

After Eliza had left Carson stood at the gate of Riversmead for a while and then picked his way across the lawn towards the river.

He thought it was a good thing that Aunt Eliza was returning to her roots. Not to her roots exactly, because she had been born at Pelham's Oak, but for many years she'd lived at Riversmead and it seemed fitting that she should go back. And what of him?

He wandered along the river bank towards the churchyard, conscious of a feeling of isolation, of loneliness. He had been lonely at many times in his life, but not like this.

Nelly had gone, Connie and the children had gone. He was perfectly alone.

Nelly was alone too, in a strange dark place. He stopped and looked up at the cross on top of the church tower. Or maybe there was a heaven and she was there?

He made his way up the hill and, reaching the graveyard, stood for a long time looking down at her grave. There was, as yet, no headstone until the earth had settled.

The boughs of the tree that had bent low over her coffin at her funeral, heavy with buds and the promise of spring, were now shedding their tired leaves, heralding the approach of winter. They fluttered to the ground covering the grave with a soft blanket as though, safe and secure, at peace at last in the bosom of her mother, the earth, Nelly merely slept.

This Large Print Book for the partially sighted, who cannot read normal print, is published under the auspices of

THE ULVERSCROFT FOUNDATION

THE ULVERSCROFT FOUNDATION

... we hope that you have enjoyed this Large Print Book. Please think for a moment about those people who have worse eyesight problems than you ... and are unable to even read or enjoy Large Print, without great difficulty.

You can help them by sending a donation, large or small to:

**The Ulverscroft Foundation,
1, The Green, Bradgate Road,
Anstey, Leicestershire, LE7 7FU,
England.**
or request a copy of our brochure for more details.

The Foundation will use all your help to assist those people who are handicapped by various sight problems and need special attention.

Thank you very much for your help.